SHADOW OF THE LION

An Alex Whitney Historical Romance

Katie MacAlister

PRAISE FOR THE NOVELS OF
KATIE MacALISTER

Memoirs of a Dragon Hunter
"Bursting with the author's trademark zany humor and spicy romance . . . this quick tale will delight paranormal romance fans."—Publishers Weekly

Sparks Fly
"Balanced by a well-organized plot and MacAlister's trademark humor."—Publishers Weekly

It's All Greek to Me
"A fun and sexy read."—The Season for Romance
"A wonderful lighthearted romantic romp as a kick-butt American Amazon and a hunky Greek find love. Filled with humor, fans will laugh with the zaniness of Harry meets Yacky."—Midwest Book Review

Much Ado About Vampires
"A humorous take on the dark and demonic."—USA Today
"Once again this author has done a wonderful job. I was sucked into the world of Dark Ones right from the start and was taken on a fantastic ride. This book is full of witty dialogue and great romance, making it one that should not be missed."—Fresh Fiction

The Unbearable Lightness of Dragons
"Had me laughing out loud. . . . This book is full of humor and romance, keeping the reader entertained all the way through . . . a wondrous story full of magic. . . . I cannot wait to see what happens next in the lives of the dragons."—Fresh Fiction

ALSO BY KATIE MACALISTER

Dark Ones Series
A Girl's Guide to Vampires
Sex and the Single Vampire
Sex, Lies, and Vampires
Even Vampires Get the Blues
Bring Out Your Dead (Novella)
The Last of the Red-Hot Vampires
Crouching Vampire, Hidden Fang
Unleashed (Novella)
In the Company of Vampires
Confessions of a Vampire's Girlfriend
Much Ado About Vampires
A Tale of Two Vampires
The Undead in My Bed (Novella)
The Vampire Always Rises
Enthralled

Dragon Sept Series
You Slay Me
Fire Me Up
Light My Fire
Holy Smokes
Death's Excellent Vacation (short story)
Playing WIth Fire
Up In Smoke
Me and My Shadow
Love in the Time of Dragons
The Unbearable Lightness of Dragons
Sparks Fly
Dragon Fall
Dragon Storm
Dragon Soul
Dragon Unbound
Dragonblight

Dragon Hunter Series
Memoirs of a Dragon Huner
Day of the Dragon

Born Prophecy Series
Fireborn
Starborn
Shadowborn

Time Thief Series
Time Thief
Time Crossed (short story)
The Art of Stealing Time

Matchmaker in Wonderland Series
The Importance of Being Alice
A Midsummer Night's Romp
Daring in a Blue Dress
Perils of Paulie

Papaioannou Series
It's All Greek to Me
Ever Fallen in Love
A Tale of Two Cousins
Acropolis Now

Contemporary Single Titles
Improper English
Bird of Paradise (Novella)
Men in Kilts
The Corset Diaries
A Hard Day's Knight
Blow Me Down
You Auto-Complete Me

Noble Historical Series
Noble Intentions
Noble Destiny
The Trouble With Harry
The Truth About Leo

Paranormal Single Titles
Ain't Myth-Behaving

Mysteries
Ghost of a Chance

Steampunk Romance
Steamed

Alex Whitney Historical Series
Shadow of the Lion

ONE

"Votes for women!" Above the jeering of the crowd, a suffragette waved her banner, her voice piercing the air high over the rumble of motorcars and rattle of carriages. "Support the cause! Votes for women!"

In one of those odd quirks that sometimes occur in a raucous situation, a moment of silence descended, just long enough for the following to be heard with the clarity of a crystal bell: "Bloody, buggery hell!"

Several heads swiveled in my direction. The suffragette nearest me stared, her eyes wide. The steady stream of people passing froze for several seconds; the faces of the men and women headed inside the magnificent building behind me all reflecting the same astonishment.

There was nothing else to do. I turned and glared into the bushes, saying loudly, "Merciful heavens! What *is* the world coming to when people hide in shrubberies and yell out profanities?"

My suffragette neighbor looked suspicious as the people once again moved past us.

"Is there a problem?" she asked when I cleared my throat and shook the chain that was giving me so much grief.

"Problem? Me? Whatever gives you that idea?"

She pursed her lips and gestured to her right. All along the massive, wrought-iron fence that bounded the grounds of Wentworth House, women were arranged with their backs pressed firmly against the cold metal railing, chains holding them in place.

"It's just my chain," I told my neighbor, shaking it at her. "It's defective."

"Your chain is *defective?*" She gave me a look that, by rights, should have been accompanied by a thick clout upside the head. As it was, I took a step back from her, relieved to see that her chain bound her firmly to the fence. "Chains are not defective. Why did you volunteer for this protest if you have no intention of participating fully?"

I ignored the murmurs of a particularly deep-voiced old gentleman as he passed by, giving my chain a firm shake and making another attempt to wind it through the fence. "Do not underestimate my devotion to the cause. I have been to Hel…er…Hades and back again just to stand here, at this moment, with this obstreperous chain."

"Are there problems?" One of the Women's Suffrage Union officers moved down along the line, pausing when she got to me at the end of the fence.

"Yes, there are problems," I muttered, catching my fingers painfully on the shrub that poked through the railing.

"She *claims* her chain is defective," my tattletale neighbor said with irritating smugness.

I gave her a stern look, which she returned with saintly indifference.

"Defective?" the officer asked, looking puzzled. "In what way?"

"It won't go through the fence," I explained. "I think there's something wrong with it."

"Or something wrong with you," my neighbor muttered *sotto voce*, but not nearly *sotto* enough. Beyond her, two other suffragettes giggled.

I glared over her head at them. They quickly averted their gazes and stared out defiantly at the passing crowd.

"Well… do the best you can," the officer said, looking a bit peevish. I knew just how she felt. "We were promised coverage by the press tonight, and it is vital that we present a unified front."

"I think *someone* simply doesn't wish to ruin her fancy gown," my neighbor commented in what I could only call a waspish voice.

"What you want to be wearing something like that to a protest?" the woman beyond her asked, craning her head to look at me.

Irritated, I jerked my coat closed, cursing the fact that I had forgotten to have Annie repair the buttons I'd torn off earlier while I'd practiced chaining myself to a tree in the park. "I really don't see that my choice of garment has anything to do with my devotion to the cause."

"Ignore the crowds, sisters, and stand tall!" the officer cried as she faced the line of women. "Remember, you are fighting for a glorious purpose!"

"It'll all be for naught if we don't show solidarity," the woman next to me said with a glint in her eyes that I felt was most unwarranted.

The heads of women all down the fence turned to look at me.

"I am doing the best I can! But how I am expected to work with a defective chain is beyond me—" A shove at my back had me spinning around to confront my assailant. "Sir!"

"I'd apologize for bumping into you if you were a decent woman, but it's clear you're not." The rotund, top-hatted gentleman who had plowed into me scornfully considered the women on the fence before returning his attention to me. "Simply appalling! Such displays are most unwomanly! Ought to be stopped! Interfering besoms!"

I jerked my coat closed again. "You leave my bosom out of this!"

The man snorted and clutched the arm of a thin, pinched-faced woman, escorting her down the sidewalk to the gate. Because of the crush of carriages and motorcars inside the short drive, many people had opted to disembark from their vehicles down the block and walk the rest of the way to the charity ball. The change from light drizzle to rain had lessened their numbers, but a few brave souls ventured forth bearing large, glistening black umbrellas.

"Oh, this is ridiculous," I snapped, so frustrated I could scream. "I'll just stand here and pretend I'm chained to the fence."

"I knew you'd give up. You're afraid of getting your pretty frock dirty," my neighbor crowed.

"I assure you it would take a lot more than a little rain to disconcert me," I answered with a sniff. "I am a New Woman, and New Women do not frighten easily. We smoke, although I haven't yet started, and we wear trousers, although I have no real occasion to wear them, and of course, we take lovers."

The woman's jaw sagged slightly. I had a horrible feeling that I'd gone a bit too far in my determination to prove how New my Woman self was. "You don't!"

"Well, no, I haven't taken one. As yet," I admitted. "But any day now I'll get around to it. The New Woman takes all those things and more in her stride."

A motorcar hooted its annoyance as part of the steady stream of carriages and automobiles stopped outside the gates to Wentworth House. Shiny dark umbrellas continued to bob by, their everyday appearance in sharp contrast to the finery displayed below them. Although the night was dark and damp, the parade of ladies in brilliant colors, flashing jewels, and exotic perfumes was almost overwhelming to the senses.

Midnight blues, pigeon's blood reds, and greens the color of the sea passed by. By contrast, our group was a somber gathering in browns, blacks, and dark grey...other than my copper-colored evening gown, which made me feel like a flame amongst the shadows.

Unfortunately, I stood out in one other way: each member but me had a swath of white across her bosom, proclaiming *Votes For Women.*

Pride filled me as I read the sashes. At last, at long last, I was taking my place. I had found my people, and I was going to prove to them I was worthy of membership.

"Where's your sash?" my neighbor asked in an acid tone.

"I was a little late, and didn't get one. I don't suppose—"

"No!" my neighbor almost snarled as I turned admittedly covetous eyes to hers.

"Charity begins at home," I reminded her, but to no avail. "Fine. You keep your sash; I'll do my part, regardless."

"You're not even chained," she said with a sniff. "No one will know you're with us. Why don't you go home to your servants?"

I took a deep, calming breath, determined to fully take part despite her bitterness. "If appearances are all that concern you, perhaps I will simply drape the chain over one shoulder…there. This is the best I can do. Will that suffice?" I turned, one cold, damp length of chain hanging over my shoulder and down to the opposite hip, hopefully giving the appearance of binding me to the fence.

It was another voice that answered.

"You should be ashamed of yourself!" The bulky shape of a woman rose before me, her spiteful face thrust into mine. "Don't you have any humility? What would your parents think of you now, Alexandra Whitney? Making a fool of yourself in public!"

I was so shocked to see Eloise McGregor, one of my late mother's oldest friends, that she could grab my arm and drag me down the street a few yards before I pulled to a stop. "Eloise, what a surprise. I'm afraid I'm busy at the moment. Perhaps we can talk later?"

She jerked me down another few yards, puffing obnoxious peppermint-scented breath in my face as she blocked the entire sidewalk in order to chastise me. "What can you be thinking, girl? Have you no shame? No dignity? How can you stand there like a common trollop and make such a spectacle of yourself?"

A hasty glance down the fence confirmed my fear that the demonstration was proceeding without me. My neighbor chanted, "Votes for women!" with an obnoxious vigor, accompanied by frequent triumphant glances sent my way.

My lips tightened as I bit back a few choice oaths.

"It would disgrace your parents to see you here, as would all your family," Eloise continued, snatching my chain off my shoulder and throwing it to the ground before taking my arm again. I winced at the strength of her grip. "Such folly! Such insolence! I shall be sure to inform your sister of your unwomanly conduct when she returns."

I struggled to free myself from her grip, my temper—always prone to get me into trouble—rising with the frustration of the last few minutes. "Damnation! You're bruising me!"

"Profanity! Blasphemer!" Eloise's voice carried extremely well over the noise of the crowd. Several heads turned our way in what appeared to be hopeful interest. "Your presence here just goes to show how low into depravity you have sunk."

Eloise was not a small woman, causing a small clutch of people to be bottlenecked behind her. As she berated me, a tall man with a pale woman on his arm scowled and tried to get Eloise's attention, asking to pass. Dismay filled his companion's face as she glanced at the stream of muddy water that flowed down the nearest edge of the pavement. Although the rain had slowed again, the gutters gurgled with the recent downfall.

Eloise ignored the man and continued to harangue me. "You always were a headstrong, obstinate girl. No wonder your father kept you confined where you could not distress others!"

I glanced down the fence to where my sisters in suffrage attracted considerable attention, including that of the beat constable who was pleading with them to release themselves. A crowd made up of working folk also gathered and shouted suggestions to the constable, many of them offering in unpleasant terms to help "take care of the troublemakers."

A deep male voice rumbled, "Madam, would you allow us to pass?"

"…goading your poor father into extreme actions in order to control you…" Eloise's words were almost painfully shrill above the general cacophony.

"People wish to pass." I tried to get my arm away from her again, but she held on like a limpet. One filled with iron determination.

The man behind her spoke louder. "You are blocking the pavement, madam. Please allow us by."

"You may think nothing of such a disgusting show of your true character, but I will not allow you to taint your parents' memory in this manner." She pulled hard on my arm, jerking me forward.

Mortified by the scene she had dragged me into, I hissed, "Stop it, please! I have a duty to perform, and by God, I will do it."

Another policeman arrived, his whistle piercing the discord.

"Madam, please let us by!" The deep voice roared over the growing clamor. The man behind Eloise tried once again to move her aside, but she simply tightened her fingers on my arm, her nails digging painfully into my flesh.

"I will save you from the depths of degradation with which you are so intent upon besmirching yourself!" Eloise all but spat at me.

"Votes for women! Votes for women!" chanted the suffragettes.

Desperation gave me the strength to clutch the fence, annoyance making my voice harsh as I attempted to join the demonstration. "Votes for…dammit, Eloise!"

More constables arrived, their whistles so loud I could almost taste the shrillness. The noise was borderline deafening, an assault on the ears and the mind.

"We wish to pass, blast you!" the man bellowed.

A second man joined the first. "This is a public street, madam. I insist you move!"

Swearing to myself in aggravation, I used both hands to grip the fence.

"…always thinking of yourself and never of your sainted father…" Eloise snarled, the chaos around us taking half her words.

The bystanders were frenzied now, keyed up by the arrival of several policemen on horseback. To the left, a small cluster of partygoers was still blocked by Eloise, loudly expressing their desire to move by us. To the right, the demonstrators, all successfully chained to the fence, chanted and sang in unison, while beyond them, constables and citizens alike yelled abuse.

"My father was a monster, a demon placed on earth, and I did not survive his torments to allow you to ruin everything. This is my chance to belong!" Goaded past all bounds of sanity, I shouted over the noise to Eloise just as she heaved her ample bulk and pried me off the fence. At the same moment, the man she blocked gave her a shove, which sent me hurtling forward.

The force of my not-insubstantial weight thrown off balance had me careening onto him. We crashed to the pavement in an awkward display of petticoats, umbrellas, chain, and limbs. I lay stunned for a moment, staring stupidly down into the diamond studs in the shirt beneath me. Before I could think to move, hands lifted me to my feet.

"Good heavens," I gasped as soon as I could gather my breath. "I do apologize! Eloise—my late mother's friend—was much stronger than I imagined. Are you injured?"

The man swore into his chest as he bent down to assess the damage. He was muddied and wet down the left side, and, I feared, extremely damp on the back. His top hat was ruined, and his white gloves were black with mud. Although my coat was without buttons, its heavy material and the fact that I fell on top of the gentleman left me relatively unaffected by the mishap.

"Just you wait and see, Alexandra Whitney!" Eloise screeched as the momentum of the crowd carried her forward, thankfully beyond reach of me. "You'll come to a bad end!"

Two ladies and a short, bald gentleman had stopped near us, inquiring anxiously as to the muddied man's state. One woman handed me a jeweled comb that had flown from my hair.

"Please forgive me," I stammered as the man I'd been flung onto continued to examine his sodden garments. I dabbed at a dark spot of wetness with my handkerchief. "I am mortified. Let me help clean you off. I don't think it's too horrible—"

I patted a spot of dirt, but pulled away my handkerchief only to find I had left a long, diagonal smear across the snowy white expanse of his shirtfront.

The man looked first at his chest, then at me, his jaw tight, and his eyes glittering in a manner that made me feel as if my belly was filled with cold, wet gruel. Without thinking, I took a step back, my palms suddenly damp.

"Young woman, you have done quite enough damage for the night with your savage excuse for manners." A balding man spoke in a voice that sounded like he was gargling acid. He was clearly in the company of the mud-splattered man, a suspicion that was confirmed when the former added, "Kindly stand away from my brother and allow us to pass."

A sudden swelling of noise washed over us, the suffragettes' collective enthusiasm rising over the bass rumble of the gathering crowd. I half turned to them, feeling I should make amends to the unintended victim of Eloise's attack upon me, but also sick at heart at the thought that the demonstration was proceeding without me.

Once again, I was being left behind, isolated and excluded from the things I cared about.

The short man's eyes widened at the vocal output of the protesters. He sputtered a few times, barking, "Why aren't the police arresting those anarchists? What has this country come to when such displays are tolerated? Those harlots should be horsewhipped!"

I took three steps forward intending on rejoining the suffragettes, now disappearing from view as with each passing minute more bystanders came to harass them, but guilt nagged me into turning back to offer another apology to the man who was now trying to wipe mud off his leg.

"I can't begin to apologize enough. Or rather, I could, but it would take quite some time, and I suspect you'd find that almost as embarrassing as I would," I murmured, flinching a little when he straightened up and the long smear of mud across the white of his shirtfront was still visible.

"Why would I find your apology embarrassing?" he looked up to ask. He had amber eyes, clear and warm, and highly disconcerting eyes.

So disconcerting that I spoke without thinking. "Because I would be effusive, and not at all coolly dismissive, as I should. I am a New Woman, you see. Falling on men is nothing to us. In fact, I am shortly to—" I bit back the information about my intention to engage a lover, feeling that there was a time and place for that detail. "—learn how to smoke cigarettes, and have a pair of trousers made."

His lips twitched. I stared at his mouth, my breath caught in my throat. For some reason I was unable to understand, the instinctive fear that had arisen in the face of his anger melted away.

"At the same time?" he asked.

"Hmm?" I liked his lips. I liked his mouth. His eyes gave me a moment of unease, since they seemed to see right down to my soul, but even that wasn't a wholly unpleasant sensation.

My overactive sense of self-preservation rose, however, and recalled me to the moment. I might not fear the man, but it didn't mean I could stand and ogle him. "Of course not. For one, I am a very poor seamstress, and for another , it would be awkward, and quite possibly a fire hazard.

Although it *might* be possible. I shall have to think about that."

His lips twitched again, delighting me. I had a shocking urge to run my thumb over his lower lip. "You do that. Are you all right?"

A shout arose to my right. I glanced over, my fear returned, but this time it was due to my failure to remain focused on my goal.

I nodded absently even as a thin, unpleasantly sharp woman in a dress that was a bilious shade of green brushed the man and said, "Come, Griffin, we're late. You can repair the damage this creature did to you once you are inside." She paused to toss a hateful stare at me before taking the arm of the sputtering bald man, the pair of them moving down the sidewalk with stately arrogance.

Griffin. What an interesting name. I eyed him, thinking that it suited him. No man with eyes like his, and such an expressive mouth, should be saddled with a common name. Another shout at the suffragettes had me lecturing myself. I must stay focused! I would not allow myself to be sidetracked, not when I was so close to achieving my heart's goal.

The crowd was too large to allow me to get through to where my sisters in suffrage were bound. As I turned to move out into the street in order to get in from another angle, I noticed that the man named Griffin spoke a few words to the other woman with him, who cast me a curious glance before she followed the others.

"I apologize again," I said as I hurried past Griffin, attempting to squeeze my way in through the now densely packed mob. "I hope I haven't ruined your evening. I wish I could make Eloise apologize as well, but as you may have noticed, she's quite deranged."

He gazed at me for a moment, then unexpectedly tipped his head back and laughed. "As it happens, I didn't particularly wish to attend this ball." He handed me the bag and umbrella that was knocked from my hands earlier. Looking at it rather curiously, he picked up the chain in his ungloved hand. As I reached out to take it, a fawn-colored motorcar pulled up alongside him. The driver leaped out and opened the door.

"Will you be going inside?" Griffin nodded toward the ball. "Or can I offer you a ride somewhere else?"

I looked at the street children, passing citizens, party-goers, and now a sizable number of constables surrounded the women protestors. The noise was almost deafening. My heart sank at the knowledge that I had failed even so simple a task as joining the suffragettes. "Actually, I am with them. At least, I was supposed to be with them. My chain is defective, though."

"I see. If it's defective, then you won't be wanting it back." He held up the chain, making no move to return it to me, his gaze making me feel suddenly overly warm.

I fought the urge to fan myself. "Not particularly. I'll admit that at this moment, I feel nothing but animosity for the beastly thing." Why was his mouth holding such fascination for me? Was he married? And did he like tall women of overly abundant upper quarters and red hair?

"A just feeling, I suspect." A frown creased his forehead as he considered me, his gaze bold as he considered me just as I was eyeing him. "Why would you want to be part of such a spectacle?"

"Hmm?" He had very broad shoulders, the sort of shoulders that made me, a tall woman who despite deprivations remained on the substantial size, feel almost petite in comparison. They were shoulders that shooed away the gloopy gruel sensation in the pit of my stomach, filling it instead with a pleasant glow of warmth.

"You appear distracted," he said.

A somewhat shocking thought crawled across my mind, and refused to vacate it. Men who were built such as he was—with nice shoulders, and a chest that made one feel downright diminutive, and sensitive, pleasing hands—those sorts of men usually had quite muscular derrieres. I wondered what Griffin's looked like.

My fingers flexed in response.

"Are you?" he asked.

"Distracting," I murmured, my gaze now on the length of his legs. They, too, looked sturdy. Manly. I particularly liked the way the material stretched across his thighs.

"What is it, exactly, that you find so distracting?" he asked, the conversational tone of voice at odds with the discord to my right.

I wrested my thoughts away from the mental image of just what his thighs would look like without his trousers, and blinked twice. It is a bad habit, but one that I find hard to break. "Your thighs, mostly, although I will admit that your shoulders and derriere were also in consideration."

He stared at me for a few seconds before his lips twitched a third time.

My own curled into a smile that I feared made it all too clear just how charming I found him.

Until one word that had been rattling around in my mind finally came into focus.

Spectacle.

"You are a very forward-speaking woman," he mused in a fat voice, even as my outrage grew.

Spectacle!

"I find that refreshing. Most women say only what they think will please a man—"

"That's because most women are trodden upon by the men in their life until they cease to have any identity themselves," I snapped. "I am not such a woman, despite a man's best attempts to make me one. And I object to *spectacle*."

His eyes widened for a moment, then narrowed on me. "And yet it *à propos* to the situation. Surely you should be inside waltzing with a suitor rather than chaining yourself to a fence in a manner that does nothing but amuse the general population."

Those fascinating amber eyes flashed in the night, but they were no match for mine. My temper was the only thing that kept me alive, and I unleashed it now. "You are very opinionated on the subject for someone whose rights have never been denied. Also, you don't know what it's like to be a woman."

Surprise flickered in his eyes. "What the hell does that have to do with anything?"

"You are a man," I pointed out, waving toward his groin. I had the worst urge to walk around behind him to see if his wet trousers were plastered to his rear parts, but managed to squelch that desire and focus on what was important. "You do not understand at all what it is to be subjugated."

"I assure you, madam, one does not need to be a woman to think," he retorted.

"No, but it helps. As for your accusation, I don't consider the pursuit of emancipation a spectacle. Quite the contrary; by chaining myself to the fence I can strike a blow for the rights of women everywhere. And I would do so if I wasn't cursed with a chain that was clearly forged in hell."

He eyed my low décolletage speculatively. "You certainly are dressed for the event."

"Why is everyone obsessed with my gown? I had a dinner engagement! I could hardly dress in something suitable for political demonstrations, could I?" I clutched my coat tight across my bosom.

He crossed his arms, speculation dancing across his face. "Dinner with one of your trouser-wearing female friends?"

"I don't have any trousers yet, nor do my friends, not that it's any of your business. My dinner engagement was with a man I was considering for the position of...well, what I was considering him for doesn't matter because he dribbled soup, and I draw the line at a man who dribbles soup."

He glanced at my breasts, now hidden beneath my coat. "Given the amount of cleavage you were showing, I'm surprised soup is all he dribbled."

"My dress is the very latest fashion!" I snapped. "And the amount of bosom I display isn't any concern of yours."

"Unless I find said bosom on top of me while lying in

the mud," he said quickly, a slow, heated smile curling his delectable lips.

My legs felt wobbly under the influence of that smile. I stiffened them. "I have apologized for the unfortunate accident. If you aren't gracious enough to accept that apology, perhaps you will allow me to get on with my business."

"By all means. Would you like me to round up a few men so you might consider them for the position of, I assume, your swain?"

"I don't need your help to find a man!" Although the noise from the crowd still drowned out most other sounds, the heads of those nearest us swiveled in unison to look at me.

Griffin leaned back against his car. "Temper, Alexandra Whitney. First swearing and now bellowing like a stevedore—you wouldn't want people to think your disposition is as fiery as your hair."

Momentarily confused by his use of my name, I remembered Eloise's mean, and regrettably public, comments earlier. "Alex," I said without realizing it.

"Pardon?"

"Only my father—and Eloise—calls me Alexandra. I prefer Alex." I was in the middle of formulating an exceedingly clever and biting retort when a great cheer from the crowd distracted me. Several police vans had arrived with reinforcements. Numerous constables emerged and swarmed along the protest line, shoving aside bystanders, and arguing with the bound women before trying to forcibly remove the chains. "Bloody hell!"

"I *beg* your pardon?"

I glared at the irritating man opposite me. He was laughing at me, the rotter. Tears burned behind my eyes, tears of frustration and anger and fear. "My first demonstration for the rights of women, and I've missed it all."

"Is that so great a tragedy?"

For a moment, I wanted nothing more than to sit down on the wet pavement and sob out my troubles. "You don't understand."

"No, I don't. But I have a feeling that a New Woman like yourself will inform me just how I—who, as you so rightly point out, am not a woman—am wrong."

An ache in my throat built as helplessness washed over me, and for a moment, I was once again a prisoner of my own emotions. I couldn't answer the irritating man, so I simply shook my head, my internal struggle to absorb all my energy.

To my surprise, he did not continue to goad me, he simply gave me a little bow and said, "As you like," before getting into the waiting motorcar.

Shame made me want to run. To have failed something I had wanted so badly was one thing, but to have that failure witnessed by another—and a man who viewed the cause as foolishness—was almost unbearable.

I wiped away wetness on my heated cheeks, but before I could dwell further on my failure, screams, jeers, yells, and a variety of expletives washed out into the damp night when several newly arrived constables rushed past me, roughly jostling the crowd in order to yank at the nearby protesters, and forcibly dragging my sisters in suffrage from their positions.

"Stop it," I whispered to myself, hating the weakness that even now, some five months after my father's death, still clung to me. I wrapped my arms around myself, trying desperately to force reason back into my mind. "Stop it, stop it, stop it."

Feminine screams punctuated the rude cries from the onlookers.

"Stop it," I yelled at last, and using my elbows, pushed my way in to strike the nearest constable on the head with my umbrella as he struggled with my unpleasant neighbor.

Without looking, he shoved me back into the crowd, which closed tightly around me. Crushed by the mass of people surrounding me, I could not move forward as the constable tried to squeeze the suffragette out of the chains that bound her.

"No, you don't understand. I'm with them! Please allow me forward. I am one of them! I am part of this!" Struggling, I tried to force my way forward again, but they impeded me just as the crowd swelled backwards. I was flung up against a man behind me, to whom I apologized as I righted myself.

"No harm done, miss." A gold tooth winked as he gave me an amiable smile. Then he touched his bowler and melted into the crowd.

A horrible noise rent the air. The crowd's mood had changed abruptly from that content with simple jeers and verbal abuses to an active participation in removing the women from their chains. Horror crawled up my spine as two constables held my recent neighbor while a third man cut off the chains with a heavy bolt cutter. As they freed the woman, the constables seized her and dragged her off to the Black Mariah, much to the delight of the crowd. Cheers rose as, one by one, the constables swarmed the struggling women, cutting them from the fence.

"No!" I said, the word rife with the despair and defeat that bit into my heart with dagger-like claws. "I'm with them. I'm part of this."

My chain lay glinting dully in the sodium lights, cast there by the annoying but extremely handsome Griffin, as abandoned and ignored as I was. A familiar sense of failure wrapped itself around me when I watched the last of the protesters bundled into the Black Marias.

The police quickly disbanded the crowd of bystanders, waved off the urchins, and broke up the groups of onlookers. In a short amount of time, there were no other protesters left.

I stood alone, disheveled, and damp on a wet, empty pavement. A sudden gust of wind caused an object to flutter across my feet. I reached down to pick up a torn *Votes For Women* sash and stared at it.

Echoes of the past dripped down upon me as the rain started again, and before me, the image of my father rose, his face as hard as flint. *You failed your cause, failed the others, and failed yourself. What man would want a woman so inept she couldn't complete a simple task?*

I flinched at the words, my shoulders slumping as I adopted the familiar submissive pose, the one I donned whenever I was too tired to fight.

Your actions this evening were contemptible, and open to ridicule from my friends and family. You are worse than I ever thought you were. You are nothing.

It was that last oft-repeated phrase that drove me out of the very downtrodden state I had decried to Griffin. "No," I said, squaring my shoulders, and glaring defiantly into the night. I would not allow the specter of my father torment me. Not any longer. I snatched up the wet chain and shook it at the memory of him. "I am free of you, and I have chosen my path. Think about that while you roast in hell for an eternity."

There was no answer on the wind, but a sudden chill that left me shivering. I looked about for a hansom cab, but none were in sight. With a mental sigh, I gathered up my accessories, chain included, and made my way home feeling stripped of pride, confidence, and purpose.

TWO

"Several women were arrested last evening for causing an obstruction outside Wentworth House in Holland Park, where their Royal Highnesses, the Prince and Princess of Wales, attended the annual charity Hospital Ball," Freddie read aloud from a fainting couch, his booted feet resting carelessly on several lovely tapestry pillows. The mauve shawl draped across one end would no doubt be irrevocably stained with his hair oil. "Good Lord, Alex, don't tell me you were mixed up with that crowd?"

"Freddie, read to yourself. Aunt Caroline isn't interested." I turned back to my aunt and accepted the cup she held out. "I hope you don't mind Emma joining us. She's been such a dear friend to me, and I don't think she knows a great many people in town."

"I am delighted that you brought her," my aunt replied in her usual dulcet tones, although a slight frown wrinkled her brow. "However, I feel I owe it to your dear mama to mention… well, you know."

I frowned over the cup of tea. "No, I don't know."

"It says here that they fined several women half a guinea for assaulting police officers," Freddie continued.

My aunt and I ignored him.

"It is so difficult to explain," Caroline said faintly, glancing toward the door. Emma, my oldest friend, had excused herself to use the water closet. "You know, of course, that she has… leanings."

"Leanings? What do you mean?"

She glanced toward Freddie, who was watching us over the top of the newspaper. He choked and quickly hid behind it.

"Leanings," Caroline repeated, her hand making a vague gesture that confused me even more. She appeared to think for a moment before saying, "You have heard of Sappho, have you not?"

I searched the rather dusty hallways of my memory. "A poet? A woman poet? Greek, I think."

"Yes, she was, amongst other things, a poet." Caroline smiled gently at me. "Your friend is a follower, I believe."

"Oh, I have no doubt about that," I said, sitting back. At last it had dawned on me what Caroline was so carefully alluding to. "You need not fear that I am offended by that."

"You're not?" Her eyebrows rose a smidgen.

"No, not in the least."

"You're not… like her, are you?" Freddie asked, still peering over the newspaper.

"You know full well I'm not," I answered.

His eyes widened, and I could swear he blushed as he stammered a protestation to our aunt. "I know nothing of the sort!"

"Yes, you do. I've never been to university, while Emma spent several years there. Frankly, given Father's opinion on education for women, I'm lucky I can read and write. I will never be the eminent scholar she is."

"Who is an eminent scholar?" the woman in question asked as she reentered the room and accepted a cup of tea.

"You are," I answered.

Emma Debenham, whom I had known for some twenty years, looked surprised by the word, but made no comment.

"I explained that you are my oldest friend," I added.

"It has been many a year since I saw the little redheaded girl peeping out at me from behind the hedgerow. I used to see Alex when I walked to the village," she told my aunt.

"Emma was the only one who defied Father's order that no one speaks to me," I said, a lump in my throat when I thought of all she'd gone through to befriend me. "I believed that earned her more than one whipping from her father."

She shrugged. "I was forever getting into trouble because of one interest or another. I wasn't about to let your despotic father rule my life as well. Besides,"—she touched my hair with a gentle hand—"I've always had a weakness for redheads. There's no way I could resist you."

Freddie choked on the sip of tea he'd taken.

"I just wish I could convince you to stay with me while you're in London," I told her.

"You know how much I appreciate that offer, but I am quite comfortable in my rooms, I assure you. Besides, having me with you would infringe upon your New Woman freedom."

"New Woman?" my aunt asked, her gentleness reminding me of the few memories I had of my mother.

I held her gaze while I spoke, wanting her approval. "Following the long overdue death of my father, I have become a New Woman."

"Indeed. Although I am not sure it is kind to refer to your father's death as overdue, I would agree that I would have been much easier in my mind about you had Henry and I been able to persuade him to let us have you. But what, exactly, is new about you?"

"The term New Woman doesn't apply just to me, but to all women who act with independent spirits," I said, taking pleasure in being able to share my newfound philosophy with those I loved. "She controls her own mind, her own life. She is not bound by outdated and misogynistic rules. She lives her life to the standards that *she* holds dear, regardless of the view of others."

"In short, she is a nightmare," Freddie murmured, then glanced at his pocket watch and excused himself, saying he had to make a telephone call.

"Freddie is in fine form today," I told my aunt, my gaze on the door. "I don't know how you can stand having him abuse your hospitality as he does."

"He is family," Aunt Caroline said with what I felt was a gentle chide. "And your uncle feels that for your sake, we should keep his mood sweet."

"My sake?" I asked, startled. "What does Freddie and his mood have to do with me?"

"Your father named him your guardian." She shook her head. "I told him that Henry would be happy to serve that role, but you know how your father was."

I bit back a rude retort. Emma had to feign a coughing fit to hide her laughter. "But Father named Freddie as a guardian when I was a girl. I'm no longer a child and have full control of my own estate and life."

"Yes, of course you do, but Freddie can be a little...difficult...if he feels he is being thwarted, so we've found that it's easier to keep him in a happier state of mind if we allow him to live with us."

I wanted to protest that she had every right to boot him out on his own, since he had inherited enough money from his father to live on, but in deference to her decision, kept my opinion to myself.

"Returning to the subject of my new life model, some men may not approve of New Women, but that is because women who are not subservient threaten them," I told my aunt just as Freddie returned from his call.

"Ah," she said, sipping her tea. "Yes, I believe I understand."

"And of course, there is the matter of the New Woman's attitude toward men." I cleared my throat and sat up straighter.

Emma smiled into her cup.

"And that is?" Aunt Caroline asked.

"I will, at some point in my life, probably twenty or thirty years from now, marry. Until then…" I took another deep breath. "I shall take a lover."

Silence filled the overstuffed, overheated room.

"Dearest, might I offer myself—" Freddie started to say.

"No," I said quickly, keeping my eyes on my aunt. To my surprise, she didn't look shocked or scandalized, or even unduly impressed. She merely hummed a little song to herself and sipped her tea.

"You're not angry with me, are you?" I couldn't help but ask, suddenly worried that I hadn't prepared her well enough for the new me.

"Not in the least. I've never thought first cousins should marry. Naturally, I exclude the queen from that statement."

"No, not about Freddie—about the…er…lover situation." I bit my lower lip, watching her carefully.

She smiled a gentle smile that made me feel as if I was bathed in early morning sunshine. "Why would I be angry? Alex, my dear, you are thirty years old."

"Twenty-nine!" I said quickly. "Only twenty-nine!"

"That is certainly old enough to know what you want. If you wish to flaunt convention, then far be it from me to stop you."

"Oh." I glanced at Emma. She winked. "I see. Well… good. I am much relieved. I was concerned that my lifestyle might give you pause."

"No," she said, lifting the teapot. "None at all."

"Good." I felt deflated for some absurd reason.

"And this organization you have joined? Are they, also, New People?"

"New Women, and yes, mostly, I believe. The Women's Suffrage Union is working to gain the vote for women. It certainly is nothing scandalous, as Freddie would no doubt wish for you to believe."

"And yet, I believe there is always violence connected to their…demonstrations," he answered quickly.

I tched. "There has been violence only because people fear what the Union represents."

Freddie waved at his newspaper with an almond biscuit. "Suffragettes, that's what they're calling you, dearest one. You simply must urge your group to come up with a less amusing label."

Caroline frowned at Freddie before asking me, "But demonstrating in public, my dear, is it prudent?"

"You don't mind at all the fact that I intend to take a lover, but you object to me taking part in a support parade?" I asked with a little laugh.

"One can be discreet with a lover," she said, shocking me to the very tips of my toes. She and my uncle Henry had always seemed so devoted that I couldn't help but wonder if she was speaking from experience. "The same cannot be said of marching about with signs and chaining yourself to a railing."

"I don't believe Alex is looking for attention, if that concerns you," Emma said in my defense. "She told me that last night she'd chosen a spot farthest from those who organized the event, no doubt out of respect for the finer feelings of her relatives."

That, or I was simply late from my dinner out with the soup dribbler. I cleared my throat and nodded, trying to look considerate of my family's finer feelings.

Freddie opened his mouth to speak, but was stopped when Hargreaves, Caroline's butler, opened the sitting room door to announce visitors.

"They're here early," I murmured to Emma as Caroline went forward to greet her guests.

"Who's expected today, do you know?" Emma asked in a whisper, looking vaguely worried.

I patted her hand. She was a naturally shy person, quite timid around men she didn't know. "A very tame group, just a countess whose husband had become an important political acquaintance of Uncle Henry's, and an opera singer who will make her debut next week in Covent Garden."

"Ah. That is tame."

Emma stood beside me a short while later as we greeted the opera singer just as Hargreaves announced the entrance of the countess, Lady Sherringham.

"Do women in Spain have the vote yet, Señora Montañeros?" I inquired as I glanced over to the door and promptly froze.

The countess was none other than the thin-faced woman in bilious green from the past evening, and she had brought with her the pale, shy-looking girl I had last seen on the infuriatingly attractive Griffin's arm...who was himself three paces behind, his amber eyes immediately seeking mine, his gaze just as disconcerting as I remembered it.

"Bloody hell," I swore.

This would not be the boring afternoon I'd envisioned.

"Which one of them?" Emma whispered.

I fought down the panicked urge to run, to hide away from someone who had witnessed me in the moment of my shame, and turned to squint at Emma. "What?"

"Which one of them is bloody hell?" she asked, watching with interest as the countess and the young woman greeted my aunt.

"Er..." My gaze went to Griffin despite wishing I would never see him again. No, my inner self corrected, that wasn't true. I wanted badly to see him, all of him, especially his derriere and thighs and possibly chest.

"Ah. I see. He is very handsome," Emma said, giving my arm a gentle pinch before she moved forward to be introduced.

I looked about for an escape, and was looking with longing at the door when my aunt's light, piping voice reached me. "Alex, dear, I'd like you to meet Lady Sherringham."

"I am not a coward," I said under my breath as I forced a smile on my lips. Griffin's expression turned concerned at the sight of it, and I had a horrible feeling the smile had come out all wrong. "I've been through infinitely worse things than facing the man who saw me at my lowest. I can do this."

"Alex?" My aunt was waiting, but it was the three pairs of eyes that bore into me that had me walking forward like a marionette operated by an armless baboon.

"Lady Sherringham, may I introduce my niece, Alex Whitney? My dear, this is Lady Helena St. John, the earl's sister."

The countess's hand felt cold, even through her gloves. Lady Helena, the tall, willowy young woman with hair the color of burnished gold, smiled a genuine smile, and greeted me with obvious pleasure. I liked her at once and pitied her for having such a cold sister-in-law.

"And this is the Honorable Griffin St. John, the earl's younger brother."

Shame at the memory of the night before warmed my cheeks, and my stomach flipped over, the cold gruel back with a vengeance. I dreaded looking up into those beautiful amber eyes, knowing what I would see there. Dismissal. Acknowledgement of my weakness.

Contempt.

"Miss Whitney, it is a pleasure."

Raising my gaze to his, I steeled myself and offered him my hand. He took it gravely and bowed over it with only the slightest hint of a smile on his lips.

I used the opportunity to examine his face. He was not handsome by conventional standards, but I decided his features were pleasing overall. The tanned cheeks bespoke time outdoors, while the firm set of his chin and his direct gaze gave him an unmistakable air of a man who was comfortable with himself.

His eyes, those glittering amber eyes, held an intense regard that challenged, however, and I recognized he was a man who wasn't used to having his authority questioned. For a moment, my own gaze wavered, a lifetime of experience warning how men of his ilk would react. But then I quelled my inner gruel, and lifted my chin in response, an action that in the past would have had the direst of consequences.

The corners of his lips curled, and the gruel in my belly seemed to turn to flame for a few seconds. He shook my hand firmly, then let it drop, and I couldn't help but notice the way the corners of his eyes crinkled when he smiled. I glanced again at him, wondering why he wasn't gloating over the fact that he had seen me fail, but there was nothing in his face or body language that said he was laying a trap for me.

Could it be that he wasn't going to lambaste me for my failure?

"You are in town long, Miss Whitney?" The glacial tones of his sister-in-law ended such enjoyable thoughts.

"I am. I have lived my life in the country and thought a change would be pleasant."

"Indeed," she said with frosty grandeur, accepting a cup of tea from Caroline.

At a look from my aunt, I gestured to the couch. "Lady Helena, please sit down."

I perched myself on a yellow and white striped chair next to her, thankful when Emma drifted over, and seated herself on the couch next to Helena. "And have you been in London long?" Emma asked.

Helena's expression brightened. "Oh yes, for some time. I live with my brothers. I would like to travel with Griffin, but he always refuses to take me, so I have to content myself with reading about his journeys instead."

We chatted for a little while about commonplace subjects until Emma left to help my aunt with the volatile Señora.

"Tell me, do you enjoy novels, Miss Whitney?" Helena asked, leaning forward.

"The more lurid, the better," I said with candor. "I feel it is part of my duty as a New Woman to read a wide range of topics, but I admit that novels are my favorite. What about you?

"Alas, Letitia doesn't feel it is suitable for me to read anything but improving books. I do read Griffin's, though."

"Your brother writes?" I felt vaguely surprised by that. I wanted badly to look at him, still half-believing I would encounter the scorn of men like him always felt for others, but he was behind me, and it was impossible to turn without being noticeable. "What sort of books?"

"He records the adventures he has around the world. They are most exciting, and he has received a great deal of acclaim," she said with obvious pride.

"St. John," I said slowly. "Hmm. The only book by a St. John that I am aware of is a horrible little volume pontificating the superiority of men over women explorers—something about the Englishmen abroad…"

I stopped as an appalling thought crossed my mind.

"*The Englishman's Role Abroad* is the title," she said, her smile obviously intended to soothe, but it just added to my discomfort. "It is a very popular book, although I don't agree with all Griffin says in it."

I stammered an apology for my rude comments. Helena waved it away and continued. "He has written other books as well, ones I'm certain you would enjoy."

"I shall certainly look for them. I have always wanted to travel, but have had to stay at home with my father in the country."

"I would be happy to lend you my copies if you would really like to read them. He's written seven books—the last is my favorite. It's a journal of his travels in Africa last year."

Her voice faltered as she looked over my shoulder. Then she leaned forward conspiratorially. "Miss Whitney, might I ask you a personal question?"

The cold gruel threatened to strangle me. Had her brother told her about my failure last night? My voice was weak when I answered, "Yes, certainly."

"Last night you were—*demonstrating* with a group of women."

I nodded, bracing myself for the worst.

"Can you tell me—" She threw another worried glance toward Lady Sherringham, then hurried ahead in a rushed whisper. "Would you be kind enough to tell me about the suffrage movement? I am so interested, but my brother will not let the subject be spoken of, and I rarely have the opportunity to talk about such things."

I sagged back against the chair, my stomach settling again. "I would be delighted to tell you about it. The goal of the Women's Suffrage Union is to obtain the right for women to vote."

"Yes," she said intently, "but *why* do you want to vote? Women don't have the experience that men have in politics. I don't wish to be rude, but I don't see what there is to gain by being able to vote."

"There are many reasons, but the most important are that men refuse to allow women the right to serve on a county council, stand for Member of Parliament, or to vote about imperial matters."

"The issue is moot—women *are* allowed to vote, but on matters they are familiar with, such as health, education, and welfare." Griffin had moved behind me without me knowing it. He loomed over us now.

I half expected fear to grip me, but to my surprise—and no little delight—his words irritated my sense of justice and fairness.

Accordingly, my temper rose, driving before it all else. "If women are incapable of making lucid decisions regarding anything outside the home, then why aren't we allowed the same education as our male counterparts so that we might be better informed?"

He scoffed at that, and my Inner Alex—the part of my mind that was obsessed with his naked derriere—greatly enjoyed the fire in his eyes. "Women are free to attend Cambridge and Oxford. What more do you want?"

"Free to attend, yes, but not free to acquire a degree. My dearest friend Emma is a noted scholar in Greek works. Yet why should she not be recognized for her detailed and meticulous research into the works of the poet Sappho, while men may do so?"

Griffin's amber eyes glittered with a light that both heated me, and left me with a desire to push him further. "I have seen much of the world, Miss Whitney, and can tell you one result of educating women and releasing them upon the unwitting public: hordes of *educated* British women trample every spot dear to man, clutching their cups of tea and shoving their idea of civility down the throats of the indigenous people."

Emma appeared at my side, a cautioning hand on my arm as I got to my feet, turning to face Griffin fully. My temper was fully engaged now, and heedless of my experience with my father, I gave tongue to my thoughts. "Why are men allowed to force their political ideas, mores, and culture upon citizens of other countries, but when women try to bring education and welfare to those who need the aid, we are damned for meddling in affairs of which we known nothing?"

"Alex, perhaps you should moderate your voice," Emma murmured.

"The only reason the average Englishwoman wants to travel is to show the world that she is capable of doing so." Griffin faced me across a small occasional table. "She cares nothing about attending to the education and welfare of anyone, let alone natives. All she cares about is ticking off items on her Baedeker's list of sights to see."

Helena made a squeak of distress and rose to stand beside him, twisting her gloves. "Griffin, there is no need to speak so harshly—"

"I am delighted to know you are such an expert on women's feelings and thoughts," I said warily, still half expecting him to lash out in a personal attack. That he was confining his argument to subjects open to debate left me feeling unbalanced...and intrigued. "Perhaps you will write a book about *that* as well!"

The retort made him tighten his lips.

"Perhaps I will." He looked down his nose at me in the most annoying fashion. "I've found it doesn't take much to understand the minds of women."

"You are the most insulting, insufferable, misinformed man I have ever met!" I pounded the table in front of me, Inner Alex shocked at such an action and warning me to step back, lest Griffin should lash out at my audacity.

"Alex!" Emma grabbed my arm squeezed it hard. Behind her, Caroline stared at me in stark horror.

"You are the most obstinate, stubborn, *emotional* woman I have met, and I've met several of your kind!" Griffin growled back at me.

"Merciful heavens!" Helena's face was as shocked as my aunt's. "Griffin, you must not say such things."

Emma's tone was level, but the restraining hand she placed on my arm gripped firmly. "My dear, I urge you to moderate your voice. I understand your wish to educate, but there is no need to yell at Mr. St. John." She turned to him and offered one of her gentle smiles. "I'm sure you will forgive my friend her passion. It has afforded her little opportunity to express it before now."

Griffin stepped back as well, making a stilted bow. "As a matter of fact, I believe passion is an admirable quality in a woman. However, I am to blame for causing the argument. My apologies."

I stared at him with my mouth making a little O before I realized what I was doing. He moved off, leaving me in befuddlement, trying to work through the emotions and strange thoughts that danced through my head.

"I must also apologize," Helena said softly, giving my hand a fleeting little dab. "I fear I started the argument—"

"Helena!" A shrill voice cut through her comments. "You will stop your discussion with Miss Whitney this instant. We are leaving."

I felt wholly ashamed of myself. Caroline had particularly asked that Freddie and I be pleasant to the countess for our uncle's sake, and what must I do but enter into a screaming match with his infuriating, arousing brother. No doubt I ruined any chance of the earl's offering to sponsor to the bill Uncle Henry supported.

"I meant what I said, you know. Passion is something we should nurture rather than stifle." The voice that spoke behind me was intended for my ears alone.

I lifted my gaze, unsure of what I would see in his face. His expression was somber, and in the depths of those incredible eyes, I beheld mingled exasperation and anger that made another flush wash up from my chest. But as I held his gaze and refused to look away, the anger faded and he gave me a long, questioning look.

"But not, perhaps, as cherished as restraint?" I heard myself ask. The quirky part of my mind fainted dead away at such boldness.

He bowed slightly and left the room.

With one hand on my burning cheek, I shut my eyes as my aunt passed by me, asking softly, "What were you thinking, Alex?"

THREE

"Do I strike you as a pink fairy sort of person?"

My maid Annie giggled. "No, miss."

"Hmm." I eyed the pair of pink fairy dancing slippers I had pulled from my wardrobe and handed the objects to her. "I must have been deranged or intoxicated when I bought them. Add them to the stack for the unfortunate governesses."

"Perhaps it was a whimsical desire?" Annie asked, but duly deposited them on the collection of garments I was gathering for donation to a worthy charity.

"I think it more likely that it directly resulted from freedom upon the death of my...good God, what was I thinking buying mustard-colored stockings? Governess them! What is it, Mullin?"

My sister's butler, a stately if rotund man, looked horrified at the clothing strewn with wanton disregard around the room. "Lady Helena St. John to see you, Miss."

A brief spurt of anticipation warmed me at the thought that the intriguing Griffin might have accompanied his sister, although the second that thought hit the sane part of my brain, it pointed out that in two meetings with him, I'd embarrassed myself both times.

I ignored what I was sure was a blush heating my cheeks to say, "Really? How curious. You know what I don't wear,

Annie—separate those things out and pack them up for donation."

I brushed off my knees and hurried down to the drawing room, worry accompanying the anticipation I had of seeing Griffin again. Would he continue to think me an addlepated woman? Did he find me as interesting as I found him? Would he argue with me as he had done on both previous occasions?

Did he like redheads?

Sadly, none of those questions were answered because Helena, seated on a slippery horsehair loveseat, was alone. She was clad in a lovely peach-colored watered silk day dress cut in the latest fashion that left me envious at the sight of it.

As I entered the room, she twisted matching peach-colored gloves, too distracted to notice the destruction she inflicted, jumping up when she saw me.

"Lady Helena, how delightful to see you again. Is Lady Sherringham with you?"

"Oh no," she gasped, horrified. "Letitia thinks I'm at a fitting. She would not be—that is, she would not approve—" She stopped, blushed, and started again. "Forgive me for visiting this way, Miss Whitney, but I simply must speak with you."

I waved her back to the couch, partly relieved that I wouldn't have to see her brother again. I paid no mind when Inner Alex laughed at that falsehood. "In what way may I help you?"

"It is I who wish to help," she declared dramatically, one hand to her bosom, the other outstretched. "Miss Whitney, I would very much like to join the Women's Suffrage Union and to fight for the rights of women everywhere. You were so eloquent yesterday. I wonder… would it be possible—would you take me to one of their meetings? I would like to join their cause, but I would be afraid to go on my own. If I could attend with you, I would feel much more comfortable about participating."

I admit I was surprised, but hesitant. It was true that a pleasurable picture arose in my mind of the two of us, side-by-side, marching in sisterhood for women's rights, waving our banners and breaking down the wall of male domination, but there was a blot in such a heartwarming image.

Her family.

"There is a meeting tonight at the home of one of the officers, Mrs. Knox," I mused out loud. "Although not strictly a membership meeting, I don't see what objections they could have to your attending it. My concern, however, regards your family. Surely they will pose objections? I am afraid that I have not made the… er… very best of impressions with your brothers."

"Your introduction may have been slightly unorthodox, but you have made quite an impression with Griffin, at least." She paused. "And while he does not support women's rights, I don't believe he would have any objections to me attending meetings in your company."

I gawked at her until I realized what I was doing and then arranged my expression into one more befitting a New Woman. "I find that difficult to believe. Mr. St. John seems rather…" Annoying, but filled with a sort of magnetism that has kept me from striking him completely off my Potential Lover List. "…vocal, about both the idea of suffrage, and of me in particular. You might be in for more dissension than you allow."

"I'm not afraid of dissension." She bit her lip and hesitated a moment. "There is one thing I should tell you, Miss Whitney. It is about my brother, my older brother. He has very different opinions than ours, as you might have noticed."

I remembered with clarity the earl's rude comments outside of the Hospital Ball.

"He has…there's no other way than to just say it…he has taken a stand against suffrage in the House of Lords and is one of the leading opponents of our noble cause."

"We certainly have our work cut out for us, do we not?" I asked, swallowing my concern.

She clasped her hands together, her face alight. "I look forward to joining the Women's Union tonight and declaring myself in the war against men."

"It's not quite a war," I cautioned, not wanting her to believe that violence was a part of Union work. "The meeting starts at seven."

"We are to go to dinner at a distant cousin's tonight, but I am sure I can get out of it." She looked up at me with sudden humor. "I believe I shall have a headache and retire early to my bed."

I hesitated, the sane part of my mind warning that to facilitate her entrance into the suffrage movement against the wishes of her family might do her a disservice, but I have never liked having others decide for me, and I wasn't about to condemn another to that state. "If you are sure this is what you want, despite your family's objection, then you can come here first and we will drive to Mrs. Knox's house."

"I'm sure, I'm very sure," she said, her smile lighting up the room.

The day passed quickly, and I was still dressing for the meeting when Helena arrived. As Annie buttoned me into a cream-colored linen skirt with thin blue stripes and matching pale-blue shirtwaist, I hunted for my small leather notebook. "Have you seen it, Annie?"

A short, stout woman with charming dimples, Annie was the one person I was happy to bring with me from my old home. Despite having a hard upbringing, she normally maintained a sunny disposition and never failed to cheer me up. "I thought it was in your stocking drawer."

"Why would I put it…well, for heaven's sake, so it is. I won't be home until late, Annie, so you may have the evening off."

"Thank you, miss."

I eyed her before I left the room. Annie was a favorite with my sister Mabel's household, but tonight she seemed moody and distracted, although she denied any ailment or personal problems. "Is anything wrong?"

"No, miss. I'm fine, thank you."

Hmm. She didn't look fine. Still, I hated to pry. I told her to enjoy herself and hurried down to Helena.

She was wearing a stunning pale pink dress—a sheer tunic covered the dark silk underskirt, very narrow and elegant, with a matching coat. A pink hat decorated with feathers and dried flowers completed her fanciful ensemble.

"Good heavens, Lady Helena," I said in stark admiration. "That dress is absolutely mouthwatering. It's like spun sugar."

She waved her hand depreciatingly and asked, "Please call me Helena. I don't use the title, and even though we've known each other only a short while, I feel as if you are an old and dear friend. Is your friend Miss Debenham not joining us?"

"Emma? No, she's not at all interested in the cause," I answered, sending Theodore the footman in search of a cab. "Well, I should correct that—she is interested, but she has her studies to attend to. Her insights are very much in demand at Sappho's Circle."

"Is that a literary salon?" Helena asked.

"I believe it's some sort of club for Greek scholars. She mentioned something about occasionally staying overnight when she was engaged in late-night study sessions."

Helena, no more a scholar than I was, murmured something noncommittal.

"Did you manage your headache with success?" I asked, wondering just how duplicitous she could be.

"Oh, yes." She sucked in her lower lip for a few seconds. "Well, I think I did."

"Oh?" There was much I wanted to ask about her tantalizing brother, but I decided that just because he danced in and out of my thoughts didn't mean I had to press her for details.

"I'm afraid Griffin suspects something. He told me, just as he and my brother and sister-in-law were leaving, to please be careful with whatever it was I was planning."

"Oh, dear. That does sound rather ominous." I chewed over this tidbit as we entered the cab. "I'm surprised he let you stay home alone. He doesn't seem to have a very high opinion of our gender."

"You are mistaken about Griffin, truly you are. You must give him credit for having suffered a broken heart."

"A broken heart? Mr. St. John?" I asked, both incredulous at the idea, and more intrigued that I knew I should be. His private life was *not* my concern.

Inner Alex rolled her eyes at that thought. I ignored her, feeling such behavior was not something I wanted to encourage.

Helena turned slightly to face me, her expression eager. "It happened a long time ago, when I was a girl, but I know Griffin still feels it a great deal."

I said nothing, but looked at her inquiringly.

"When Griffin was eighteen, he fell madly in love with Grace Perry, the cousin of my sister-in-law, Letitia. I was living with Harold and Letitia then, my parents having died some years earlier, and Griffin had just returned from his Grand Tour. Grace was staying with us, and Griffin—well, you know how these things can happen."

I nodded, feeling strongly that the fine quality of his derriere had a role in the situation.

"Grace was a very outspoken woman, rather rough and common, I think now, although she impressed me at the time. She was a little older than Griffin and had done a lot of traveling by herself. Although she was fond of him, I don't believe she ever loved him in return."

"Were they engaged? Or…er…lovers?" slipped out before I could stop it.

Helena, to my relief, didn't look scandalized by my bold question. "No, not formally engaged, although I believe he had been pressing her. As for the other…" She gave me a smile that was mischievous to the extreme. "I was just a child, so I couldn't say."

"Ah." Disappointment mingled with an odd sense of relief.

"There was a big scene one night in particular that I remember," she continued, her lips curling slightly. "My sister-in-law was having a dinner and Griffin tried to press Grace into a commitment so they could announce their engagement that night. I was supposed to be upstairs since I was too young to attend the dinner, but I had hidden in the library and was reading a book of fairy tales. Griffin and Grace did not know I was curled up on a chair when they had an argument about their future."

"Ah. So the lady jilted your brother?" This was delicious gossip, and as ashamed as I was for participating in it, I reveled in every moment.

"Yes. She told Griffin that she had no intention of marrying him, that he was not the type of man any sane woman would spend the rest of her life with, and she did not intend to waste the best years of her life adapting her lifestyle to his."

My eyebrows rose. I drew them back into a more seemly position and tried to look sympathetic. "That was blunt of her."

"Grace made rather a common scene and stormed out of the room. She refused to appear at dinner and left shortly thereafter. Griffin would not speak of her, but I knew she hurt him."

I suspected that a good part of the hurt was due to wounded pride, but did not voice that opinion.

"That is why, dear Alex, you must make allowance for Griffin's attitude towards outspoken women. Should the right woman come along,"—she dropped her gaze to her hands—"she might find that she could heal his wounded heart."

"More likely she would have her head snapped off for trying," I said dryly and spent the remainder of the ride in contemplation of him nonetheless.

Mrs. Knox lived in a small, white stone building on the quiet side of Russell Square. Climbing the steps to the house, I cautioned Helena about detailing her relationship with Lord Sherringham. "It isn't that they would refuse you admittance into the Union, but they might feel hesitant to discuss sensitive topics, such as the plans for our next demonstration and protests, before they know you well."

She nodded, but had no time to say anything before they admitted us. The women welcomed her, and with little delay, the meeting commenced. Each member contributed many ideas and opinions as to the Union's planned activism, so many that although I wrote quickly, I was hard put to keep up with the ideas that flowed forth. Petitions were organized, deputations were planned, marches plotted, demonstrations ordered, and processions detailed. I tucked a list of volunteers assigned to each event into my notebook to be typed up later.

"I can't see what good these plans will be when we won't be taken seriously by the press and the public until they see we are committed body and soul to the cause," a petite Irish woman named Maggie interrupted the speaker as she reviewed the final list of activities for the next month.

"We do not condone violent acts—" one of the other Union officials started to say.

"I say we strike and strike hard!" Maggie cried, rising to her feet. Several other members nodded. "You talk about marches and protests and petitions—we have tried them all, and they have failed. This is the time for action, and without it, our cause is doomed."

"You are out of order," Mrs. Heywood, the head of the Union, tapped on the table for order.

Maggie bristled. "I have a voice just as does any other member in the Union!"

"A voice, yes, but the National Women's Union has never condoned violence, and we will not start now. *We will not start now*," Mrs. Heywood repeated over the grumbling of a handful of women who favored such extreme forms of protest.

I held my breath, worried that the militant faction would continue to press the issue, but although they demanded a vote to determine the type of future actions, a clear majority outvoted them. I breathed a sigh of relief and a short time later, Helena and I took our leave with several of the other ladies. I tucked my notebook into my coat pocket, checked my bag to make sure I hadn't left anything behind, and walked down the steps to the street.

"We can take you home, if you don't mind being crowded," one woman offered, indicating her motor.

"Thank you, but the evening is fine, and I need a pleasant walk. But perhaps Miss St. John…"

"I'll walk with you," she said quickly, with a bright smile.

"You are welcome to take a cab home," I said as we set off. "I really don't mind walking by myself." I stopped to allow her to catch up to me.

"I never thought of the problems of walking any distance when I bought this terrible gown," she said, vexed.

I surveyed the narrow skirt with some skepticism. "Why men want to hobble women in the name of fashion is beyond me."

"It *is* pretty."

"Very." I took her arm and slowed my steps to hers. "And we have a nice evening for a leisurely stroll. Since we are closer to my house, I suggest we head there first, and my sister's coachman drive you home."

As we walked, we chatted about the meeting, with Helena siding with the more militant ladies.

Just as I was about to warn her about the follies of violence, a sharp blow to the middle of my back sent me sprawling into a nearby lamppost. I slumped against it, dazed. Shaking my head to clear it, I attempted to stand up. On the third try I was successful and looked around for my attacker.

"Next time ye'll think twice afore ye go meddlin' in matters that don't concern ye," a thick voice growled from the shadows of the building. A dark shape moved, clearly retreating down a darkened alley. I rubbed my head and limped over to the street.

Helena was dumped unceremoniously about thirty feet away, directly into a large mound of horse droppings. "Alex, I can't… and it's all over… It's oozing on my leg!" she wailed as she tried to get up.

I helped her to her feet and surveyed the result, her lovely pink coat now covered in muck.

"What am I going to do?" Helena held her arms out stiffly and promptly burst into tears.

"Are you hurt?" I asked, looking for signs of injury.

She shook her head.

"Thank heavens for that. Take off your coat. Let me give you my handkerchief. You are certainly a mess. Damnation! My bag has been stolen."

She shivered in her thin gown.

"Here." I removed my coat and handed it to her. "Wrap this around you. You'll have to clean your coat before you can wear it again."

She protested, but I was in no mood to argue. I buttoned her into my coat and picked up her soiled garment with two fingers.

"This is covered in filth. Luckily, it's long enough to prevent most of your skirt from coming in contact with the refuse." I set the coat down again and considered our situation. "We are less than a mile from my home, further from yours. I suppose we could walk back to Mrs. Knox's and beg for assistance."

"No!" Helena wailed. "I couldn't face that. I just couldn't!"

"Then we won't go there," I said soothingly. Muck was smeared up to the ankles of her lovely boots, her hemline was soiled, and her face was tear-stained and grubby. Her chin quivered ominously, and her eyes shined with tears on the verge of falling again. I gave a mental shrug and looked around for a cab. "Do you still have your bag?"

She nodded.

"Do you have any money?"

"A little. Not much, though." Tears coursed down her cheeks again as she peered forlornly into her bag. She handed me a few coins.

"Ah. There." A hansom cab loitered far down the street at an intersection. Indicating it, I grabbed the spoiled coat in one hand, Helena's arm in another, and pulled her towards it.

Her tears had stopped by the time we were settled in the cab. "Did you see the thug who attacked us?" I asked.

"It was so quick. I didn't notice him at all."

"I didn't, either. I was too busy seeing stars from my collision with the lamppost. All I saw was his shadow."

"Oh, Alex." She gasped, turning to me with concern. "Were you injured?"

"Just my pride," I said, my voice as grim as my spirits.

Helena was quiet during the ride to her brother's house, and a quick peek at her strained, white face told me she was nervous about her reception.

"Your family will still be out, won't they?" I asked. "Not that it's my place to interfere, because I believe every woman has the right to make choices for herself, but I do worry about your reception."

She gave me the faintest ghost of a smile, and her icy fingers tightened briefly on mine. "You are a good friend to care so much about what happens to me."

I hesitated for a few seconds before answering. "I know what it is like to be reliant upon relations who do not have your best interests at heart. If there is anything I can do to help you, please know I would do so."

She blinked rapidly and dabbed at her eyes with the handkerchief I had given her. "You are beyond kind, Alex. But I—"

I was doomed to not find out what her objection was because at that moment, the cab stopped at Lord Sherringham's house in Balmour Street.

"There are lights on," I pointed out, telling the cabby to wait.

"I have a key," she answered, and pulled out a latchkey. I snatched up her repulsive coat and entered the house when she gestured for me to follow.

"Let me take the coat directly to Mariah," she whispered. "That way, no one will—"

Her face froze. The transformation was so quick, her expression so awful that I looked over my shoulder to see what grisly sight had such a terrible effect on her.

Lady Sherringham came out of a nearby door. Swift on her heels was the stout, bald man I remembered from the scene outside of the Hospital Ball. Across the hall, another door opened and the tall figure that had taken to haunting my thoughts emerged.

I closed my mouth, and with a swift move, scooped up the coat from where it had fallen and turned to stand in front of Helena. She gripped my arm from behind, her hand shaking as she moved to my side.

"Helena, my dear sister. How is it you come to be here and not in your bed?" her sister-in-law inquired in an acid tone, looking not at Helena, but at me. "We rushed home to tend to you, and now we find you are not in bed, but instead are sneaking into our home in the company of this… *this woman!*"

Before I could think up a reasonable explanation, the earl spoke directly to me.

"Who are you, madam, that you feel it appropriate to wrench my sister out of the safety and security of her family at this time of night? Have you no feelings of decency? What are your morals that you would secretly spirit away a young girl from those who are responsible for her welfare?"

Lady Sherringham saved me the effort of answering the question.

"Surely you recognize her, Harold," she crowed. "This is Alex Whitney, Sir Henry Benson's niece. She is the woman we saw outside of the Hospital Ball—the one who threw herself upon Griffin in that repulsive attempt to attract our notice."

"I did no such thing," I retorted, finding my voice at last. "It was an unfortunate accident. I had no intention of throwing myself on anyone, least of all Mr. St. John. And as for your sister, I did not wrench her from your house—"

"Isn't it clear?" The countess's voice had a barbed quality that made me flinch. "She has taken our dear Helena to one of those anarchistic suffrage gatherings! I knew this would happen—I could tell at once what sort of person she was. This comes from allowing women of her low morals to mingle with decent people. Helena, dear, are you hurt in any way? Those women are so rough. There is no telling what they might have done to you. Come, child, let me look at you."

Griffin stood outside the circle of light with his arms folded across his chest, a shadow on his face leaving his expression unreadable. He watched us, saying nothing, until Helena turned to him with her hands held wide in a gesture of distress. Walking forward, he put one arm around her shoulders and pulled her toward him. He faced his brother and sister-in-law, the symbolism of his stance clear—he would support Helena against any further attack. Relieved and warmed at the example of brotherly love, I felt it was an opportune time for my withdrawal. Excusing myself in a low voice, I turned to leave.

"Young woman," a voice trumpeted across the hallway, stopping me mid-step.

I turned slowly at the earl's harsh voice. His face was red with fury, my stomach turning at the sight. It took everything I had to stand there, but bile rose in my throat, and I struggled to keep my hands from shaking.

I'd learned early that to show visible signs of fear gave my father pleasure, and I suspect the earl was cut from the same cloth.

He swaggered forward, and I had to stiffen my knees, praying I would not shame myself a third time before Griffin. "Let there be no misunderstanding whatsoever concerning my feelings in this matter. I forbid you to see Helena again. I forbid you to meet her. I forbid you to have any further contact with her. She is young and innocent, and I will not have you dragging her down to the level your type inhabits. Women such as you ought to be flogged and placed in prison with the whores, where you belong."

My throat was tight and sore, and I couldn't swallow back the fear that filled my mouth with an acid taste.

Griffin stood and comforted his sister, his head bent close to hers as she clung to him, sobbing quietly into his chest.

For a moment, I wanted to cry out at the injustice of the world, that fate should force me to survive on my own, when others had no such burden, but immediately, I was ashamed of myself. I was strong. I had survived hell on earth. I would not allow this blustering, obnoxious man to shake me from my goal.

"I have no qualms in consulting with the police about your behavior. It is shameless and godless, and if I had my way—"

A low growl broke in. "That's enough, Sherry."

"I have a great deal more to say, and I'll thank you for staying out of this, Griffin." Lord Sherringham's voice cut through me like a knife. "You may not be aware, madam, but I am currently very much taken up with the topic of suffrage at the House of Lords. Your behavior is proof of just how dangerous is the idea of giving women the vote. I assure you I will remember your actions when discussing the issue with my fellow peers."

"I see no reason you should," I said softly, my stomach churning with fear. I knew it was the sheerest folly to speak, but I had sworn upon my release from hell to never again be voiceless. "It is apparent that you have already made up your mind against women's suffrage."

"Of course I have," he snapped. "It is a ridiculous subject, one no decent man would even consider."

"Stop it!" Griffin roared.

The volume and tone of his voice were surprising in their intensity, and caused me to step back, but I realized almost immediately that his ire was directed at his brother.

He turned to me, his voice brittle with anger, "My apologies for my brother's rudeness, Miss Whitney. Thank you for accompanying Helena home."

Silence filled the hall as I turned towards the door, the familiar numbness that I associated with the aftermath of one of my father's rages leaving me silent as I left the house. I gave the cabby my address automatically and rode in an unthinking state all the way home.

I was still numb an hour later when I hung up the telephone. Mullins, who had periodically popped into the hall, no doubt intrigued because I was using the machine so late at night, hovered when I slumped against the back of the small seat attached to the telephone table.

"Trouble, miss?" he asked.

"The police are idiots," I said, wondering at the fact that, although I was annoyed that no one seemed to mind that Helena and I were accosted, I wasn't at all surprised.

"Indeed." He continued hovering, obviously hopeful I would share details.

"You can lock up now, Mullins. I will retire for the night." I got to my feet, feeling as if I was a hundred years old.

"Yes, miss. Is there anything I can do to help with the police situation?" he asked, his curiosity clearly getting the better of him.

"No. My bag was stolen on the walk home, that's all. No one was hurt, as the police repeatedly pointed out. Good night."

"Good night, Miss Alex," he said as I dragged my leaden legs up the stairs to my bedroom.

There was only so much I could do, I told myself. If the police didn't see a problem, then I would simply dismiss the incident from my mind. After all, they were correct that we hadn't been harmed. No doubt it was just a random bag theft, and nothing personal.

That thought gave me little comfort, but it wasn't the attack that kept circling in my mind.

It was the image of Griffin, so strong, so secure.

So very intriguing.

FOUR

A restless night dawned into an equally restless morning. Exhausted, I lay in bed and watched the sky lighten from indigo to a soft blue-grey as I considered the matter that consumed my thoughts.

"Let us look at it from a strictly analytical point of view," I told my hollow eyed reflection when I sat down at the vanity.

My reflection didn't look very impressed with that idea, but I didn't let that stop me from continuing.

"One, I was brought up unusually sheltered."

Inner Alex made a face at that.

"Yes, I agree it's just one facet of the hell we survived, but still, it can't be denied that I have not had contacts with many men who were not in my family. Thus, it's entirely reasonable that this attraction I feel for Griffin is natural. As a New Woman, I refuse to be ashamed of my desire to view his derriere."

One of my eyebrows twitched. I knew full well my inner self wanted to cock it at me, but I am nothing if not the mistress of my own eyebrows. It held firm, and with my mind easier about the fact that I couldn't stop thinking about Griffin, I attended to matters at hand, eventually settling down with my typewriting machine to transcribe my notes from the prior evening. I looked around the desk, but couldn't find my notebook. Frowning, I tried to remember what I'd done with it, and when Annie came in to tidy my room, I asked, "Have you seen my notebook? The one with the brown leather cover?"

"No, miss, I haven't. Would it be in your bag?"

I pulled my head out from where I'd been peering under the bed and sat back on my heels. "It was stolen last night, and no, fortunately the notebook is too big for that. I thought it might have fallen out of my skirt, but I can't find it. You didn't take it out of my pocket, by any chance?"

"No, I haven't."

"Hmmm." I chewed my lip again in thought. "It must be in my coat. Have you seen…oh, good lord!"

The sudden, horrible thought came to me I was no longer in possession of my coat—I had given it to Helena the night before when her own had been ruined. I raced downstairs to locate the coat I brought home. I had a vague memory of throwing it into the corner of the hall because of its stench.

My sister's household staff is most efficient. No coat lay anywhere in the hall, so I went through the green baize door, hoping someone would know of its whereabouts. "Mullin, did you find a coat I left in the hall last night?"

He looked up from polishing a particularly ugly silver fish knife. "Yes, miss, I did. It seemed to be soiled, so I sent it to Smith. I hope I've not acted expeditiously."

"No, not at all," I said over my shoulder as I flew down the stairs to the basement. Smith was the laundress who came in three days a week to do our laundry. Luckily, today wasn't one of her days. With a muted groan, I lifted Helena's pink coat from the pile of garments.

"Oh—damn!" I swore out loud as I surveyed the offensive item, checking to be sure the notebook hadn't magically appeared in its pockets.

Every moment the notebook resided in Lord Sherringham's house, the more opportunity he would have to stumble across it and read the notes I'd so thoroughly taken. Sick at the thought of him becoming privy to the Union's plans, I hurried upstairs to consider the problem. I'd just settled down to write a note to Helena when I was summoned to the telephone.

A light baritone voice was audible through the crackling connection. "Alex, my dearest, I was hoping you would be home, so I might call on you around tea time. I have an important subject to discuss with you."

"Your important subject wouldn't be one of a matrimonial nature?" I asked my cousin, suddenly feeling all the hours I'd lain awake. My shoulders slumped for the second time in twelve hours, and once again, I leaned against the wall of the telephone cupboard.

"My dear, your suspicious mind! Can I not visit without being expected to propose?"

"I should hope so, but unfortunately, I am engaged this afternoon. What, if it wasn't marriage, did you wish to discuss?"

"Your happiness, dearest cousin." He sighed dramatically.

"Freddie—"

"You know how devoted I am to you. It is not my own passionate feelings that I consider. No, it is your welfare that is uppermost in my mind. I want to save you from the grief your life as a spinster must give—unloved, unwanted, living with relations in the fruitless quest for a home..."

"In other words, you want to save me from a life like yours," I wanting to laugh, but was too tired and too inured to his charm to muster up anything but mild amusement. "Thank you for the tenth proposal. Consider it denied."

"My dearest, my own, think of what I offer! Position, a husband who worships you, protection—"

I wondered if I'd told the cook to have chicken for dinner.

"Protection," he repeated, his voice silky, "from all sorts of evils. With myself at your side, you would never need to worry about your personal safety."

"I don't worry about my personal safety."

"But you should, Alex. If you continue your connection with the suffragists, you must surely expose yourself to many violent elements, and I know how you abhor violence."

"Freddie—" I protested, slightly uncomfortable with the turn the conversation had taken. Beside Emma, Freddie was the only other person who knew what extreme lengths my father's fury had often taken, and how I was subjected to fits of his madness.

"Fairest one, I do not wish to cause you pain by reminding you of the unpleasantness of the past, or the sad state of your father's mind. Indeed, it is my intention to shield you from ever having to experience such atrocities again, and pray you never go down the path of lunacy that your father trod."

"Freddie! I am not going mad—" I started to protest, but he interrupted.

"You must see, however, if you continue to pursue your work with the suffragists, you risk becoming involved in unwholesome situations."

"Unwholesome? Now you're exaggerating." I dismissed my uneasiness. Freddie was simply being his nosy self. He was never happier than when he had received family gossip.

"Alex, I have seen you beaten and bruised time after time, and could not do anything about it. I will not allow you to put yourself in such a position again."

It was on the tip of my tongue to point out that I had no choice in the matter of my father's abuse, but I knew he hadn't really meant to imply I *allowed* myself to be mistreated. "Your concern is appreciated, but I am using the utmost caution and have every intention of continuing to do so. Now, if there is nothing else, I really must go."

"Cousin—"

"Goodbye, Freddie," I said firmly, and rang off.

It was noon when I sat down again to write Helena. I was not altogether sure if the note would reach its intended recipient, since Lady Sherringham seemed the type of person who would feel no qualms about interfering with Helena's mail. I was in my bedroom, chewing on the end of a pen and staring at a blank sheet of writing paper when visitors were announced.

"I will never get this blasted note finished at this rate. Who is it now—"

Theodore the footman gave me a card, and I leaped up with joy. I almost trampled the poor lad so quick was I to run down the stairs, flinging open the door to the drawing room and saying, "Helena! I am so glad you brought my coat; I was about to write to you to request it. You will never guess—"

Griffin stood by the window. My heart jumped unreasonably, and suddenly there was no air in my lungs. He turned and looked at me curiously.

Helena held out her hands as she approached, kissing my cheek as she said, "Please forgive us, dear Alex, for calling without notice. I hope we haven't disturbed you."

I looked at her elegant tweed walking suit with cream satin waistcoat, then down at my new dark green day dress with black corded piping, and sighed to myself. No matter how new my clothes are , Helena always put me to shame.

"Not at all." I offered my hand to Griffin; he took it, but looked at it as if it were something faintly unsavory before he released it and turned away.

Irritation mingled with fascination, and a smidgen of residual embarrassment from our past encounter. Despite that, I wondered what it was about him that had caught my fancy. Once I had thought him pleasant in appearance, but nothing more. But now I looked at his features—his nose a shade too pronounced, his jaw set with a firmness that belied obstinacy, his eyes too penetrating for comfort—and my heart beat with a rhythm it had never adopted for anyone else.

I was considering how he might react to a proposition of a carnal relationship when it struck me that Helena was giving me an expectant look.

"Where are my manners? Please, sit down." I urged her over to the non-horsehair sofa, but she refused to budge.

Her jaw was set in a manner that brooked no dissent. "I must first unburden myself and beg your forgiveness."

"Beg my forgiveness?" I asked with confusion, amused by her dramatic air. "What have you done to me that you need to be forgiven?"

Her eyes filled with tears, and she seemed to have a hard time speaking. I looked at Griffin helplessly. He stood with his hands clasped behind his back, sunlight from a nearby window casting a halo over his hair. His face was inscrutable as he watched his sister.

"Helena?" I asked her gently. "Whatever is the matter?"

Two tears spilled over her lashes as she clutched my arm and sobbed onto my shoulder, weeping as if I broke her heart.

"I am no stranger to tears, but you are the weepingest woman I know," I told her, prying her off my shoulder and steering her over to the sofa. "Now please wipe your eyes and tell me what the problem is."

Griffin, with a twitch of one side of his mouth, responded to my gesture and took a chair next to her. His left hand was heavily bandaged, although the bandage appeared ragged, as if he'd been worrying it.

Helena sniffled loudly. "I'm so sorry, Alex. I would never have asked you to take me with you last night if I had known Letitia would return home early. Can you ever forgive me for exposing you to such abuse?"

"Since you weren't the one to abuse me, there's nothing to forgive." I looked over at her brother, who was being unusually—and to my mind, suspiciously—quiet.

"That is understanding of you." She sniffled again, this time confining it to her handkerchief. "Harold and Letitia have been particularly… unhappy since Rosewood burned down."

"Rosewood?" I asked.

Griffin spoke. "Rosewood was our family home in Devonshire. The house burned down a few years ago."

"I'm sorry to hear that."

Gripping my hand, Helena gave me a strange, impassioned look. "I can't tell you how I cherish your friendship. It means a great deal to me, and I wouldn't want anything to destroy it. You are so good, so kind—"

"Hardly either." I interrupted, uncomfortable with her fervent gaze. Intense people could easily become fanatics. "Your brother did no harm to me other than a little damage to my pride, and that will repair itself in no time. I admit I was concerned about what sort of reception you would meet after I left."

"I'm not afraid of Harold when Griffin is home," she answered, casting a look of devotion to her brother.

Griffin fidgeted, tugging on his collar in order to rub at his neck beneath it. "My sister has told me of the evening's activities."

"Did she?" I glanced at Helena, surprised she would mention the exact details of our outing.

With an air of martyrdom, he continued, although he averted his gaze from mine, and spoke quickly, "I attach no blame to her or you for the events that transpired. I was glad she had you as a companion." I remained silent, although I badly wanted to ask what had changed his mind, until I decided that devotion to Helena must drive him. "This is not easy for me to say. You… er… know my feelings about the subject of women's suffrage."

I started to make a face, then remembered he was a guest in my home and nodded instead, adopting the expression of one who is solely interested in elevating subjects such as suffrage, and not at all the base desire to know what he looked like unclothed.

Inner Alex rejoiced when I threw some energy into that mental picture.

Griffin glanced at his sister. "My feelings haven't changed about the appropriateness of women's participation in politics. However, I have discussed the issue with Helena and have agreed to allow her to attend meetings as long as she is in your presence. I would prefer it if you took a footman with you, given the situation last night. If you do not have one, I would be happy to provide one for your safety."

"My sister employs a footman, but I don't believe that's necessary," I said, remembering my phone call with the night before. "I contacted the police to report the theft, and they assured me that since the thief did not harm us in any way other than the loss of my bag, and the damage to Helena's coat, we were in no grave danger."

"Nonetheless, I believe it would be wise to have someone else with you. Or at the very least, forego walks at night, and instead take a carriage. I can put mine or my motor at your disposal—"

"Thank you," I said firmly. "I appreciate you are concerned about our safety, but I assure you I do not wish to be harmed, let alone put Helena at risk. I had already planned to use my sister's carriage for any further nighttime events."

"Ah. Good." He looked somewhat disgruntled, as if he had been hoping for an argument.

Helena leaned slightly to the left and prodded at him.

He turned a brief frown on her before giving a little cough. "What? Oh. Erm...despite my better feelings, I have also agreed to let her become a member of that women's club you belong to."

"The Women's Suffrage Union." I spoke absently, suddenly wondering about his bandaged hand.

As his words sank in, I looked up in surprise. Given the feelings the earl had so vehemently expressed the night before, I had no doubt that Helena's foray into political activism would be swiftly and irrevocably nipped in the bud.

"However," he said loudly and with some force, "that does not mean I authorize her to take part in any demonstrations or public displays. I cannot control *your* actions..."

My eyebrows—in blatant defiance of my standards of behavior—rose at the very idea.

"But I would recommend you stop your campaigning as well. I've heard from Sherry that the new head of Scotland Yard is proceeding with a strict policy of non-tolerance against suffrage demonstrators. If you don't want to be arrested, I'd advise you to stay clear of any further public scenes."

His speech over, he sat back down, a belligerent set to his jaw as if he expected me to make a defense. I wondered briefly if he had an ulterior motive in allowing Helena to join in the union, but could not think of any benefit her participation would have for him or his brother.

I surprised both of us by saying simply, "I agree with you. It would be unwise for Helena to expose herself to any danger by becoming involved in a suffrage protest. I am sure she will agree."

Helena gaped at me, her mouth an O. "I don't agree at all!" she cried. "How can you say that—you who feel so strongly and know how strongly I feel about the cause?"

I spread my hands in a placatory gesture. "There is no reason to risk your personal safety."

"I see no such thing. I *will* be at the rally tomorrow!"

"Rally tomorrow?" Griffin repeated, his amber eyes narrowing on her. He turned the gaze to me, which I felt as if he was rubbing my naked self with velvet. "What rally tomorrow?"

It took me a couple of tries before I could dismiss the image of him stroking my bare flesh with a velvet cloth. "It's a small rally in Hyde Park, a minor gathering, no demonstrations, no protests, just an attempt to raise funds and public awareness for the Union."

"Helena will not be attending the rally, Miss Whitney." He toyed with the bandage on his hand as he spoke. "And I strongly urge you to reconsider your attendance at such a public spectacle."

"Mr. St. John, I took umbrage with you when you used that specific word before, and I take umbrage at it now. How you can interpret a peaceful, organized rally at Speaker's Corner as a *spectacle* is beyond me."

"You may consider your cause one that is peaceful and organized," he answered, his voice a rich, deep tone that sent a little sensual shiver down my spine, "but I would wager that the public doesn't see it that way. Helena will not attend."

"No!" We both turned to look at Helena, who had risen and was standing with fists clenched. "If I choose to take part in a peaceful rally in Hyde Park with my dear friend Alex, then I shall do so."

I gave her a mental pat on the back for standing up for her beliefs and glanced at her brother, worried he might get angry. Although Griffin seemed much different from his brother, I was wary. *All men get angry eventually*, whispered Inner Alex.

A dull red color flooded his face as he started to answer, but I interrupted, wanting to deflect his attention from Helena. "What did you do to your hand?"

"Eh? Oh, my hand. I had an accident—some damned fool knocked me down with his motor car."

I stared at him. "How very odd. You were lucky to escape with only a minor injury."

"Lucky?" he snorted, tearing off a shred of bandage and placing it absentmindedly in his pocket. "I would be a good deal luckier if people would learn to handle their motors before they took to the public streets with them."

Helena, reminded of her brother's recent accident, lost her belligerent look. I could see a glimmer in her eyes, and hoped we wouldn't have a repeat of her tears. "You are having too many accidents since you've been home, Griffin. First, there was the ruffian in Limehouse—"

"A common navvy under the influence of a local opium den. It wasn't a personal attack against me," Griffin interrupted.

"And then there was the incident a few weeks ago when you fell down the back stairs—"

"A loose carpet rod."

"And just last week you had that terrible bilious attack that Doctor Treadway called suspicious."

Griffin he glanced at me, obviously embarrassed by his sister's candor. "I doubt if Miss Whitney wants to hear about my internal complaints, Helena. We are boring her. And I'm not through discussing this rally tomorrow—"

"You're not boring me at all. In fact, Helena, your brother's recent escapades strike me as the melodramatic stuff that makes up popular novels. The type with a dark, brooding character who possesses disgustingly horrible secrets, forcing someone to kill him to effect long-deserved justice."

Griffin muttered a rude comment under his breath, just loud enough for me to hear. "About that rally you plan to go to tomorrow..." he said, then fell silent as the butler stepped into the room.

"Miss Debenham."

"Emma! You will remember Mr. and Miss St. John." I rose to greet my old friend.

"Of course. It's a pleasure to see you both again. Alex, I'm sorry to interrupt. I did not know you had visitors. I can come back another time—"

"Don't be silly; I'm always happy to see you. Mullin, we'll have tea now." I escorted Emma to a chair and sat beside her, giving her hand a little pat of support. Despite our success the other day at my aunt's tea, I knew Emma still felt awkward in the company of anyone but her oldest friends.

Griffin looked with much speculation, first at Emma, then at my hand on hers, then at me.

"You look flushed, Alex. Are you feeling well?" Emma asked as silence descended in the room.

"Quite well. I had a busy morning. Helena—"

The slight young woman jumped as I spoke her name. Emma and I looked in surprise at her reaction.

"What's the matter?" I asked.

"I'm sorry. It's just..." Helena wrung her hands. "You mentioned... you don't think... oh, surely it can't be true! Griffin, say it isn't true!"

"It's not true," he said.

"What's not true?" Emma asked me.

"I have no idea. Mr. St. John?"

He shrugged. "Helena has a vivid imagination. No doubt that is giving her grief right now."

"Helena, what—" I started to ask, but she gripped my hands then, her fingers digging into mine with unexpected strength.

"Griffin," she whispered hoarsely, her face a bloodless mask. "Do you really think someone is… someone wants to… someone plans to do away with him?"

FIVE

We all looked at Griffin—Helena full of concern for a beloved brother, Emma with thoughtful surprise, and me with more than a little amusement.

Griffin rolled his eyes at Helena's question. "No one is trying to kill me. That suggestion was a figment of Miss Whitney's mind, which she herself just admitted is overheated with the inane ramblings of women's novels."

"I admitted nothing of the kind," I protested. "I can think of several reasons someone might wish to murder your brother. Certainly there must be a vast number of women travelers who would be delighted to see him in the hereafter, but I must admit his recent accidents seem more a result of his own clumsiness than a planned assault by an unknown person." I thought for a moment. "Or persons, perhaps even an organized group with an international membership—"

"Blast you, woman, I am the mildest of men!" Griffin, eyes alight and nostrils flaring, glared at me in a magnificent example of a righteously enraged man.

And for the first time in my life, I wasn't afraid. I stood with one hand on the back of Emma's chair, poking at the emotions that twisted around inside me. Where there was once the feeling of cold gruel in my stomach, now there was interest, and a warmth that I took to be sexual, and even a tiny little spark that glowed in the blackness of my soul—hope.

Helena bleated at him in a distressed manner, while Emma choked on what I suspected was a bubble of laughter.

"I have no enemies other than the ever-increasing hordes of women who insist on interfering in situations where they cause more harm than good," he continued.

Even the wariness of a few minutes ago was banished, and all because Griffin had shown himself different from his brother, different from my father, different from other men. He didn't stop Helena, he supported her. He didn't talk down to me, or verbally abuse me, or even dismiss my arguments.

"Surely such attitudes are not confined solely to women?" Emma inquired.

No, he didn't attack. His bark was all bluster, and with that realization, I relaxed for what felt like the first time in my life.

"Of course not. Men are just as bad, if not worse," he answered, making a grand wave of his hand. "I include them in that statement."

I wanted badly to tease him, but since I'd never teased anyone in my life, I wasn't sure how to go about it. Instead, I lifted the tea pot that Mullin brought into the room, and said with a banality that was at odds to the charged thoughts in my brain, "Tea, Helena? Emma, you must try the seed cake. The cook does it particularly well."

"Alex, I must know—do you really feel Griffin is in any danger?" Helena asked.

I looked up from pouring tea. "Unfortunately for the future of women travelers, no, I don't feel he is in danger. I think he is just clumsy—or accident-prone."

"Typical female attitude," he muttered as he accepted a cup of tea and a plate of cake. "If you women weren't so determined to meddle in a man's affairs... And speaking of that, this rally tomorrow—"

Wishing to avoid another argument, I asked, "Emma, did you know Mr. St. John was recently in Arabia?"

"Really?" Interest lit her dark eyes. "Did you enjoy yourself?"

"Yes," he said indistinctly around half of a piece of seed cake.

Unable to keep from learning more about him, I asked, "Why don't you tell us about the trip? When exactly did you return home?"

"Three weeks ago." There was a decide glint in his cat-like amber eyes.

"Arabia… it sounds so exotic," I mused. "Minarets."

"Camels," Helena said, a faraway look in her eyes.

"Rugs and tiny cups of very strong coffee," I added.

"Harems," Emma said, her voice breathy with pleasure.

Griffin snorted. "There is a lot more to the country than rugs, camels, and harems."

"Tell us about it," I invited.

He gave me a long look, then, grudgingly at first, told us about his latest journey. As he spoke, animation crept over his face, passion for a topic near to his heart softening his features and giving him a vitality that took him beyond merely handsome to breathtakingly gorgeous.

My admiration grew as he spoke. Here was a man who wasn't content to live in a settled, safe life. Not for him, the routine, the humdrum; instead, he walked a path that few Englishmen had walked before. Brave, heroic, adventurous, he faced life and death daily and relished every minute.

"How I wish I could have such adventures!" I cried, envious and rapt with admiration at the same time. "Oh, Emma, don't you wish we could do the same?"

She raised her eyebrows, nibbling on a lemon tart. "It sounds very exotic, but I believe I prefer familiar surroundings to those of a more daring nature."

"I would love to have adventures," Helena declared, sitting forward on the chair. "Life here is so tame."

Griffin shot her a look, but continued his narrative. Although he was a fascinating orator and told his spine-chilling tales well, I found my concentration waning.

Instead of thrilling to his adventure with a camel thief in Baghdad, I gazed appreciatively at his broad shoulders. He told of a narrow escape through a bazaar while I admired the way his hair curled back from his brow, my fingers itching to touch the silky curls. When he took off his coat and rolled up his sleeve to show us a tattoo received at the hands of a Zulu warrior, I noticed the way the fine, golden-brown hairs grew on his arms. The ease with which he moved wove a spell of captivation about me. His deep, resonant voice rolled around the small room, sweeping me up in its warmth and making me tingle in places I'd never known to tingle before.

This is no soup dribbler, I told myself. *He is prime lover material, a virile man who thinks nothing of staring fear in the face.*

And I was determined to have him.

My mind wandered pathways that involved his bare flesh under my hands, my breasts growing heavy at the overwhelming desire to be pressed up against him. I desperately drew forth to my memory the recollection of every Greek statue I'd ever seen and wondered how he would compare.

Would his fig leaf bulge in as enticing a manner as the statue of Apollo I'd once observed?

With a start, I realized he'd stopped speaking. Both Emma and Helena watched me with evident concern.

"Fig leaf," I said, then realized my mouth had spoken without my thinking and cleared my throat. I picked up the cold teapot. "More tea, anyone?"

Helena and Griffin took their leave not long after that. As I was seeing them out, Helena stopped suddenly in the hallway.

"I've forgotten!" She darted forward and snatched up a package. "Your coat. Griffin returned it to me this morning. I had foolishly left it in the hall."

She smiled warmly as our eyes met, and I doubted if it had occurred to her to look in the pockets.

"Thank you for thinking of it," I said in a voice that wavered a little, relief easing the tension in my shoulders.

She gave me a shy smile and turned to leave. As she did, Griffin leaned towards me and withdrew a familiar leather notebook from his coat and murmured. "In the future, I would advise you to keep such information safe and not make it available to people who could use it to your detriment."

"Thank you," I said in a small voice, too horrified by the thoughts running through my head to congratulate myself on keeping the topic of tomorrow's rally from discussion. I watched silently as they entered their motorcar, then ran back to the sanctuary of the library, my heart pounding loudly in my ears.

"They seem like pleasant people," Emma commented as I stood panting at the door. "Without the odious sister-in-law. I like Helena very much. I think she'll be a good friend for you. Her brother is—what on Earth is the matter with you?"

I caught my breath and staggered into the room, collapsing on the sofa next to her. Quickly, I explained about the events of the previous evening. "The question is, will he tell his brother? Familial duty would require it, but would he betray Helena and me in such a manner?"

"I don't know," Emma said thoughtfully. "Men are such curious creatures. So unpredictable."

"Was that why he warned me against any further demonstrations? Was he trying to tell me the Union's secrets were no longer safe? Can I trust him, or not?"

"I'm afraid I don't know any of those answers. Alex..." Emma gave me a curious look.

"Hmm?"

"You like him, don't you?"

"Griffin? Er... Mr. St. John?"

She laughed. "I can see you do."

I set down the notebook and did my best to look like a worldly New Woman. "I'm considering him for the position of lover, yes."

"Considering him for—" She came to an abrupt stop, her lips pressed together tightly for a few seconds. "Have you told him of this opportunity?"

"No, I thought it best to wait until I had made a final decision," I said, idly rubbing a spot on the knee of my gown. "I won't mention anything until I've narrowed down the candidates to just him."

"That would seem eminently wise," she said with a tremor in her voice. "Would you think me rude if I asked about the other candidates?"

"Well, there's the dribbler."

She looked somewhat startled. "Who?"

"Soup dribbler." I named the man, an acquaintance of my uncle. "I could never have carnal relations with a man who dribbled soup. Griffin doesn't look like he'd dribble, does he?"

"Not soup, no," she said.

I narrowed my gaze at her. She seemed to be developing some sort of facial tic.

"Any other candidates?" she asked.

"Not really, no. I know so few men, it's rather difficult. There's Theodore the footman, but I caught him picking his ear." I shuddered.

She made a face. "Definitely not. I would say that Mr. St. John stands a fair chance of being suitable for the position."

I beamed at her, pleased with her approval of my choice. We chatted for a few minutes about her latest events—her literary circle was having some sort of reenactment of a historical event, and she wanted to get her costume just right—but my mind was consumed with worry, and I fear she noticed.

"The interpretive dance sounds lovely, Emma, although I don't quite understand why you need to apply oil to the dancers. Does it have some historical importance?" I asked.

"You could say that. You have something on your mind, don't you?"

I sighed. "I'm sorry, I haven't been a good friend at all."

"You've been the truest friend I have, but you know that. Tell me what's bothering you. Is it the business with this notebook?"

"Yes." Tracing idly around the notebook's leather cover, I let my mind play with suppositions.

"All right." She set down my sister's orange cat Marmalade, who seemed to prefer the library to any other room of the house. "Let's take this in an orderly fashion. You believe Mr. St. John has read the notebook and might have told his brother about it. What if Lord Sherringham saw the information? What potential damage could he do with it? It isn't as if he could use it to stop the campaign."

Marmalade wandered over and begged a piece of seed cake from me before settling down on my lap. I stroked him absently as I thought. "I'm not so sure about that, Emma. There's the arrest of the ten women protesting at the Hospital Ball. If the police are not tolerant of suffrage protests, the information from my notebook might allow them to halt the demonstrations before they began."

"That does sound rather ominous. What are you going to do?"

I worried my lower lip with my teeth. "I don't know. I will, of course, tell Mrs. Heywood about the mishap with the notebook. She will certainly see the potential for damage and may censure me. As for the other matter, I can see no way to find out whether Griffin has revealed the information to his brother without Lord Sherringham becoming suspicious."

"Have you thought of simply asking Mr. St. John about it?"

I stared at her, then gave her a little tap on the leg. "I couldn't do that!"

"Why not?"

"He's a potential lover. The question would be tantamount to accusing him, and I couldn't possibly treat a lover in such a cavalier manner."

Her facial tic returned. "As I see it, you don't have many options open to you. I suppose you considered asking his sister for help?"

"Yes, and dismissed her for similar reasons as her brother, although without the carnal implications, naturally."

"Naturally."

I could have sworn I heard laughter in her voice, but when I glanced at her, her expression was somber. "It is a difficult situation, to be true, but I feel sure that whatever course you choose will be the appropriate one."

Shortly after that, Emma exclaimed at the time and dashed off for her historical reenactment costume fitting. I retired to my typewriting machine and transcribed my notes, my heart heavy, my spirits dulled, and my libido glum despite the potential of Griffin and his captivating mind and body.

SIX

"I'm glad we're alone. I don't think I could cope with any more of Freddie's proposals," I said, a few hours later, accepting the cup of tea my aunt poured. "I have had a very trying day, and I much need a few moments of respite."

"Trying how?" Aunt Caroline asked.

I thought of my mental excursions into the land of a naked Griffin and felt a blush creep up from my chest. "It's… it's a rather delicate situation."

"Really?" Aunt Caroline looked at me with undisguised interest. "That sounds most intriguing. I hope it's something scandalous, or at the very least, mildly shocking."

I couldn't help but laugh. "It is both, I assure you."

She leaned back and sipped her tea. "Ah. Then it must concern—"

"Ah, good tea time!" Freddie popped into the room, rubbing his hands.

"Hellfire and damnation!" I swore, setting down my cup in a manner that led to splashing, which I then had to mop up all the while glaring at the intruder.

Freddie clasped his hand over his heart in a fashion that would be perfectly at home on the music hall stage. "Dearest cousin, beloved Alex. I knew you could not refuse me for long." He perched himself on the arm of my chair and attempted to catch one of my hands in his. "You see, Aunt—she has come to her senses at last and has decided to accept me. Happy day!"

"You are the most annoying man I have ever met," I said, giving in to the emotions that had been swirling around inside of me all day, and pushed him off the chair. "What are you doing here?"

"I was at my club, but it's too tedious for words, so I thought I would return home. Since Aunt and Uncle have asked me to stay here, I think it only polite to be available when my presence might be wanted or needed." He seated himself next to my aunt and leered at me in a suggestive manner.

I was a little taken aback by the wolfish smile and looked at my aunt. She was busy with the teapot, however, and obviously missed it.

"You really are beyond the limit, Freddie. I wish to have a private talk with Aunt Caroline, so please take yourself elsewhere."

"Have some good gossip, eh?" He looked interested.

"If you don't go now," I warned, sending him a look brimming with portent, "I will tell Uncle Henry what you did your last year at Cambridge."

Freddie's eyelids dropped to shield his gaze, but not before I could see the irritation in them.

"Naturally, I will not intrude when I am not wanted." To my relief, he made a stiff bow and left the room.

"I can't tell you how grateful I am that blackmail always works on those of weak character," I said as the door closed behind him.

Aunt Caroline asked curiously, "What *did* Freddie do at Cambridge?"

"I'll tell you another time. It's something that Emma's oldest brother, who was in the same year as Freddie, told her, and she told me."

"It sounds delightfully scandalous. But tell me about your problem with Mr. St. John."

My jaw dropped a little as I stared at her. "How on earth did you know my dilemma concerns him?"

She smiled and ignored the question. "I like him very much. And his sister, of course."

"Sometimes I think you're a witch. The problem does concern the St. Johns, but not in the manner you think."

"I wasn't thinking of him in any manner," she said gently as she poured me another cup of tea. "Were you?"

"I...he's..." The blush that had started earlier warmed up. "He's...er...on my list of candidates."

"Candidates? Oh, for a lover?" She considered that idea for a moment before shaking her head. "No, I think not. He wouldn't be suitable in the least."

"He wouldn't?" My voice came out a squeak. I cleared my throat and asked in what I hoped was a nonchalant tone, "Why do you say that?"

"He isn't the lover type of man," Aunt Caro said, fussing now with a plate of tiny biscuits. "Some men are; those men may appear interested in one, and quite devoted, but after a certain length of time, their interest wanes. That is the type of man you should have for a lover, not Mr. St. John."

"I see." I slumped back in the chair and had to fight the urge to kick at the nearest table.

"Mr. St. John is the sort of man who, once his affections have been engaged, will be steadfast. His interest will not wane. You would find yourself with a permanent partner, not a lover with whom you will eventually grow tired and replace."

It was on the tip of my tongue to say that the thought of having Griffin as a permanent lover didn't sound at all unappealing. Quite the opposite.

"There is that, of course," I said slowly. "But I've always had admiration for constancy in a man. Uncle Henry, for instance, is most devoted to you."

"Yes, Henry is the same sort of man as Mr. St. John," she said, smoothing out the lace at her wrists. "He is the ideal husband, but as a lover... no. He would not have done."

I made a little face as I thought over what she said, feeling as if someone had pulled the rug from beneath me. Griffin seemed so ideal for the role of lover. What if, knowing I wished to remain unmarried for many years, he refused me? Would I ever be able to suffer the mortification of that? "Thank you for your opinion," I finally said, my mind full of miserable speculation.

"You are quite welcome. Before I forget, are you engaged tomorrow night? If not, Henry and I would like you to attend the opening of that new opera tomorrow. What is the name of it—the one where everyone dresses as peasants and drinks wine and the woman dies? Henry has taken a box for the season, and we both would like for you to use it."

I thanked her and accepted, nursing a general sense of self-pity. I stayed a few minutes more, then took my leave, emerging into the hall to find Freddie holding my russet wool coat.

"What are you doing?" I asked, wincing at the edge to my voice.

Freddie whirled around, one of his broad smiles easing my suspicion. "I was just going to help you on with your coat, of course."

"How thoughtful." A little ripple of unease tickled my awareness. There seemed to be a strange dichotomy about Freddie of late—normally he was a warm, charming man, if overly affectionate. But for the first time, I imagined something other than unwavering affection in his eyes.

"Might I take this opportunity, dearest—"

"Thank you, I would prefer you not," I said, allowing him to help me into my coat.

He sighed and placed a hand over his chest before making an exaggerated bow. "My poor heart will never heal at this rate."

I studied his face for a moment, wondering if I was letting my temper see things in his manner that weren't really there. He looked as banal as ever, and I decided I was being overly critical. Freddie had been nothing but supportive; to imagine otherwise clearly showed how tangled my emotions were. "I have every confidence your heart will make a miraculous recovery just as soon as you meet a woman with a larger fortune than mine," I said, but added a smile to take away the sting.

"Cousin, you wound me!" he said, a flash of emotion in his eyes that had me hesitating for a second before I left, directing my sister's coachman to Mrs. Heywood's house in Islington. When I arrived, I was shown into a small study on the ground floor. I paced the room, biting my lip as I tried to formulate an explanation regarding the notebook.

Loud voices interrupted my pacing. I would have ignored them had one not caught my interest. The Irish brogue strongly resembled that of Maggie Greene. Curiosity sent me to the door, where I opened it enough to hear.

"...take it to a vote of the full membership. I'm sure the members won't consider any such actions, Maggie. They are dangerous, unnecessary, and deliberately inflammatory. Such a plan would alienate us from the very people we strive to reach."

That had to be Mrs. Heywood. I eased the door open a smidgen more, and was rewarded immediately.

"Unnecessary, is it? Inflammatory, is it? Shame on you, Lenore Heywood, for turning your back on danger! Where our glorious cause is concerned, the end is worth any means. No action is too extreme, no sacrifice too great. We must strike now, while the House of Lords is still debating, to show them we will not go quietly!"

"Definitely the troublesome Maggie," I murmured under my breath, and peeped out to see what was happening.

Maggie stood very close to Mrs. Heywood, saying, "I warn you, Lenore, there are many women both in the Union and outside who are behind me on this. The time is coming when you will find your precious non-violent Union disabled and ineffective. You have one last chance to achieve success. Will you take it?"

"I have told you we will not adopt a militant policy—"

Maggie spat out an invective as she strode to the front door, pausing to point her finger dramatically. "If necessary, we will bring the Union to its knees to attain our goal. We could survive such a division—could you?"

She turned and stalked through the doorway before Mrs. Heywood could answer.

More than a little shocked, I hurriedly returned to my chair. A half minute later, Mrs. Heywood entered the room and greeted me. "Miss Whitney, what a pleasant surprise. What can I do for you?"

"This is just like taking medicine," I told her. "Best done as quickly as possible."

"How alarming," she said, but despite her gentle tone, her shoulders tensed. With words that seemed to tumble over each other, I explained the situation with the notebook.

"And so the *brother* of Lord Sherringham returned the notebook to you?" she asked when I was finished.

"Yes." The cold gruel was back in my stomach when I thought of the consequences of my carelessness.

"I see." She contemplated the typed notes that I had given her. "You are aware of Lord Sherringham's position in the House of Lords, aren't you?"

"I am. I can't tell you how sorry I feel about this terrible, terrible calamity—" I halted myself. I was beginning to sound like Helena.

She was silent for a moment, then said, "You have no sign that the information was disseminated, although I believe it would be prudent to change the dates and locations of those demonstrations to be held a few weeks hence. We cannot do anything about the events in the next few days, but we will trust that there is too little time for action to be taken against us."

"The rally tomorrow?" I asked, miserable.

"That is public knowledge, so we have no fear for the integrity of that gathering." Mrs. Heywood rose and headed for the door.

Obediently, I followed, feeling duly chastised even if she had been nothing but kind. I glanced at the footman who was standing at attention next to the front door in preparation for my departure. I moved closer to Mrs. Heywood and dropped my voice. "I couldn't help but overhear Maggie Greene earlier and admit that I am concerned Maggie is trying to divide the membership. Is there anything I can do to help?"

She gave me the ghost of a smile. "Nothing now, although there may be a time when you are called upon to stand behind the Union. As for Maggie…well, time will tell. Good night, Miss Whitney, and thank you for bringing the situation with your notebook to my attention."

I couldn't ignore that gentle but pointed hint, and so departed for home. When we arrived at my sister's house, Jackson silently handed me down and prepared to return the horses to the stable behind the house.

"I'd will probably need you later—good lord!"

I turned to look at the man who swayed into me as he walked past. He smelled of powerful spirits and I would have thought nothing more about it except I saw a glint of gold when he begged my pardon. He moved off down the street in rather a serpentine fashion, pausing now and again as if lost in thought.

"Yes, miss?"

I dragged my attention back to Jackson. "Have you ever seen that man before?"

"No, miss."

"Hmm." With another look down the street at the disappearing man, I shook off my suspicions and entered the house.

The next morning arrived with a wire announcing my sister's imminent return. I avoided thinking about Mabel's reaction to my New Womanhood, and my support of women's rights, by borrowing my aunt's horse Marianne for a solitary ride in Rotten Row.

The Row was busy that Saturday, with couples and families out riding in the unusual spell of warm late spring weather. I saw one or two acquaintances as I rode, but kept my conversations short.

A sudden bellowed, "Good morning, Miss Whitney," from immediately behind startled me into a precarious lurch, forcing me to jerk back on the reins to keep my seat. Marianne stopped abruptly, directly in the path of the horse behind, which responded to the sudden obstacle by giving her a sharp nip on the rump. She bucked in protest at the assault, and I slid out of the saddle and onto the ground with a solid thump.

I looked up from where I was sprawled in the dirt and commented, "I should have known it was you. What other man would find it necessary to knock a woman to the ground in order to greet her?"

Griffin may have been able to keep from laughing outright, but the laugh lines around his eyes deepened even as he leaped down to help me to my feet.

"On the contrary, experience has shown that you are just as likely as I am to be the catalyst for such a greeting."

Brushing myself off, I went to retrieve my horse. I checked the bite; it was minor and did not require attention.

"Help me up," was my only comment as I tried unsuccessfully to remount.

"Certainly," he replied cheerfully. "Always glad to be of service. Put your foot here." He made a step with his hands. Placing one hand on his shoulder—and ignoring Inner Alex's happiness at the feel of it—I stepped onto his hands. He heaved me up and almost over the other side of the horse.

Clutching the sidesaddle and arranging my skirt as best I could, I gathered the reins and reached for the offered riding crop. My hand closed on his, and I looked down at him for a moment.

"Are you riding alone?" I asked, flooded with the by-now-familiar conflicting emotions and various tingling body parts that seemed to accompany his presence.

"I am." He mounted his horse and walked over to me. "May I join you?"

"It would certainly be better to have you where I can keep an eye out for you, in case your horse takes another bite out of Marianne." I tapped at the mare with my heel, and we set off at a brisk trot.

Griffin eyed my tenuous riding posture with some concern. "Are you sure you're not going to fall off again?"

"I would never have fallen off if your horse hadn't savaged mine."

He grinned, and my heart melted into a puddle. "Winston wouldn't attack a lady unless provoked. He's as gentle as a baby."

"Oh really?" I questioned, noting the firm hand he used to control the gray stallion. "Then I am sure you wouldn't have any qualms about letting me try him."

"No."

"But if he's so gentle—"

"No!"

"He is lovely." I reached over to pat the stallion's neck. "I don't suppose you'd be willing to part with him?"

"I'd sooner cut off my left... er... No, I am not selling him."

"I notice your hand is better," I said conversationally, my brain sadly unable to draw forth any form of intelligent conversation. It was too busy thinking all sorts of illicit things about him.

"Yes."

"It is curious, you having so many accidents since your return home. You don't think—"

"No!" he snapped.

I glanced at him out of the corner of my eye. He seemed to be somewhat moody now, yet he made no move to part company. Deciding any further comments about his accidents would be poorly received, I broached a subject about which I was curious.

"Tell me about Rosewood."

He looked startled by my request. "Rosewood? Why do you want to know about Rosewood?"

"It burned down. That's odd. Was it an accident, or something more nefarious?"

He gave me a considering look, then sent Winston into an easy canter. Marianne followed suit without my urging.

"Well?" I asked, unable to keep from admiring the breadth of his shoulders. He made me feel positively petite, and given that I was taller than many men, that was no small feat.

He shot me an unreadable amber-eyed look. "Why do you want to know?"

"It's part of my theory of why someone would want to do away with you."

He frowned in response to my smile. "You've been reading too many novels. There's nothing suspicious about my run of bad luck lately, and as for the fire at Rosewood, Sherry decided a faulty gas pipe caused the fire."

"Ah. So there isn't a tribe in Africa that has condemned you to death for the sacrilegious act you committed upon the chief's eldest daughter?"

"Not his *eldest* daughter." He smiled again, sending my heart soaring, and my inner New Woman parts tingling for all they were worth. "No, no angry African tribe. You'll have to look closer to home for your murderous theories."

"So, you admit it is more than one person," I teased him gently, wanting for some insane reason to laugh with joy.

"What about you?" he asked, his amusement fading.

"Me? I'm not the one who is having suspicious accidents."

He pulled the horse up, his voice now as flinty as his expression. "Your recent incident indicates otherwise."

"We've discussed that." I waved a hand, thinking of the man with the gold tooth. "The police assured me—and I have no reason not to agree with them—that it was a thief who decided two women were suitable targets. Nothing happened other than the loss of a bag and a few shillings. You haven't finished telling me about Rose-wood."

He didn't bat an eyelash at the change in topic. "I wasn't aware I had *begun* telling you about it."

I stopped Marianne. He rode on a few paces, staring ahead until he noticed I was not at his side. He turned back when I spoke. "Tell me, Mr. St. John, is it women in general you dislike, or is there something specific about my person who you find repugnant?"

He watched me with those intriguing eyes for a few seconds, then his lips twitched, just as I knew they would, and curled into a slow smile that did a great number of things to my insides.

All the tingly New Woman parts cheered when he walked Winston over to me. "What do you want to know about Rosewood?"

Caught once again in the snare of his presence, I stifled the sudden clamoring of Inner Alex as she urged me to throw myself into his arms, and instead tried to remember what we had been discussing. "Why did it burn down?"

"I told you—a gas pipe."

His fingers were white with strain. Without thinking, I placed my hand on his, saying, "I'm sorry. It must have been horrible for your family to lose your home in such a manner."

He looked down at my hand for a moment, then met my gaze. I flushed with his nearness, with the sudden flare of heat in his eyes as he leaned towards me. I was well aware we were alone on a shaded bend of the Row, just the two of us, a man and a woman, and he was about to kiss me.

His saddle creaked as his lips brushed mine, heat from the contact setting fire deep inside me. *Ask him now*, Inner Alex demanded. *Tell him the position is his if he wants it.*

"Why are you doing this to me?" he asked, his breath fanning across my mouth, his eyes burning into mine.

"I don't seem to be able to stop," I admitted, filled with conflicting emotions. Every sensation seemed to be *right* with Griffin, yet I knew better than to give him my trust.

"Good," he answered, just before his lips fully claimed mine. The kiss was hard at first, hard and aggressive and demanding. Then his lips softened. I gasped with surprise at such a marvelous feeling, moaning when he surged into my mouth. It was sinful. It was wrong. It was shameful… It was heaven, and I didn't want it to stop.

He pulled his mouth from mine as a group of people cantered around the bend, turning his horse. I pressed my heels against Marianne, and we walked on without speaking.

"You're sure you wouldn't consider selling Winston?" I broke the silence a few minutes later.

"What? No, I wouldn't." He seemed distracted and looked at me curiously, as if appraising me. I licked my lips, hoping he wouldn't think I was a brazen hussy. His gaze shot to my mouth.

My whole body was tingling now, but I firmly gave my inner self the order to cease so I could focus on what was important, like asking him if he'd like to fill the duties of a lover. "What will you do with him when you go on your next trip?"

"It depends."

"When do you plan to leave?"

He frowned briefly. "I'm not sure. Do you desire me gone?"

"Not at all," I said brightly, trying desperately to rein in an unreasonably giddy feeling. Without my permission, my breasts tightened as I wondered if he would try to kiss me again.

He didn't, but his face lightened at my words.

"I asked because—" I paused as he stared at my mouth. He was thinking about that kiss. I was sure he was. *Now is the time*, Inner Alex urged. *Ask him!*

I opened my mouth to speak, suddenly nervous. What if he refused me? "I simply wanted to know—"

"Yes?" he asked quickly, turning in his saddle to look me full in the face.

"I wondered if you would be interested… That is, if you would like to… er…"

"What is it you're trying to say, Alex?"

I stared at him in frustration and desire, mingled together in a confusion of emotion. "I wanted to know if…" I took a deep breath, telling my jangled nerves to just say the words. *Be my lover*, my brain coached me. *I want to know if you'd like to be my lover.*

"Well?"

The words came out in a rush. Unfortunately, they weren't the ones either of us was. expecting. "I wondered if you might let me borrow Winston when you are gone. I am sure the exercise would be good for him, and—" I halted in faux surprise at his roar of anger. "Is there something wrong?"

He seemed choked for words and had difficulty speaking.

"Women!" he sputtered at last.

SEVEN

"A package for you, miss," Theodore said when I arrived back home. "I left it in the library."

"It must be the gown I'm waiting for," I said, peeling off my gloves before hurrying in to my favorite room in my sister's house. The package didn't contain a garment, but a collection of books.

I lifted the top one off the stack and was surprised to see *From Sultan to Sahara* by G. H. M. St. John. An inscription inside read: *To Alex Whitney, May you wander the paths you seek.*

"That is very thoughtful of him," I said, stroking the leather cover of the book before laughing under my breath. He hadn't included the volume in which he tiraded against women travelers.

"Wisdom, thy name is Griffin…at least now and again," I said aloud as I marched upstairs to don a blue serge suit with braid trim that made me think of a military uniform.

"Er…Annie," I said a few minutes later, noticing a problem with the suit. "You haven't removed trimming."

"Oh. I… er… It must have slipped my mind." She looked guilty at my observation.

"This isn't like you. Are you unwell? Is something bothering you? Have you been crying?"

She avoided my eyes and looked down at the garment. "No, miss. I'm sorry about the skirt. I'll unpick it later, if you like."

"Annie…" I pulled her to a chair, concerned now by her attitude. She looked flushed and close to tears. "If you have a problem, you know I am happy to help. Would you like some time off? Is your mother ailing again?"

She gave a choked half-sob. "No, thank you, my mother is well. There's nothing wrong, I promise."

I wanted badly to press her when it was clear that all was not well in her world, but I knew well what it was to have no autonomy over one's own life, and I would not force her to speak if she was unwilling.

We'd been together through hard times, the two of us, and I knew when she was ready to tell me what bothered her, she would.

The sun hid behind several ominous-looking dark clouds, making me glad of my wool dress as I met Helena near the entrance to Hyde Park.

"You're here early," I told her as we strolled into the park.

"For a reason," she answered, linking her arm through mine. "You give me such support—I would never dare arrive without you!"

Her warmth oddly touched me. "There's nothing to be ashamed about attending a rally for women's rights. There will be no demonstrations, no protests, only speeches. What objection could anyone have to you simply listening to speeches?"

"Harold forbade me to attend." She looked at me from the corner of her eye as she spoke. "Griffin asked me if I was going to attend the rally with you."

"Did he?" I asked brightly, remembering the fires he had started with his kiss. The man's lips should be branded as flammable. "I take it he successfully voiced the objections he began yesterday?"

"Can you doubt that? But I am being unfair. Griffin didn't voice an objection. He just asked me if I was attending."

We passed one of the many groundskeepers' sheds as I mused over this strange behavior. "Hmmm. That's odd. I wonder—"

My only excuse for what followed is that I focused my thoughts on Griffin, not on our surroundings. Thus, when a dark shadow loomed up from a nearby shrub, it didn't register until after I found myself in his foul embrace. A musty black cloth was jammed over my head and torso, effectively pinning my arms to my sides. With no warning, our assailant picked me up and carried a short distance, panic immediately flooding me.

My breath caught in my throat, my heart pounded, and my limbs trembled even though I willed myself to remain calm. *Stay quiet. He likes it when you struggle. Stay still and quiet, no matter what he does—*

With a thump, I was deposited on a wooden floor. Tears burned at the back of my eyes as the nightmare came to life again. *No! No, I left this behind!* my inner self sobbed, and for a moment, I was back in my father's study, cowering before him.

The sound of a second thump and the feminine squawk of protest yanked me back to the present. I struggled to a sitting position, my breath ragged in the confines of the bag.

"It's a simple job, picking off ladies what go out without the protection of a man," an odious voice crowed as the door slammed.

"Helena?" I cried, trying to make my escape from the damnable black cloth. My voice cracked even as I bit back a sob of fear and frustration.

"Alex?" came the answering wail.

"Thank heavens you're not hurt." Desperate to control myself, I rose to my knees and got out of the black bag before turning to the figure that lay struggling next to me. "Here, let me help you get that off. You're just tangling yourself up more."

Once freed, we sat on the floor, flustered, appalled, and in my case, fighting the need to scream.

Screaming did no good. I'd learned that long ago.

"Where are we?" Helena asked, her voice rising to a dangerous note.

I knew if I didn't take charge of the situation, she'd go into a full-fledged panic. It took me a minute, but at last I felt like I had my wits gathered and glanced around. A sagging basket chair, filthy windows, and gardening implements surrounded us. "This appears to be a gardener's shed, judging by the tools."

"What…what happened?" Her voice still quavered, but obviously my calm demeanor did much to bolster her spirits.

If only she knew how my insides quaked at the old fear that had risen so easily.

I pushed aside the fact that even now, my father had the power to affect me, and rose, moving over to the door. Logic was what was needed here, logic and focus. "We have been abducted for some reason I can't explain."

"But why should we be abducted?"

"I have no idea," I replied, bending down to look through the keyhole. No key was in evidence.

"Alex, what are we going to do?" Helena's voice rose again.

I picked up my boater hat from where it had been knocked onto the floor. "Never fear, Helena—we shall make our escape."

She got slowly to her feet, watching as I tidied up my tangled hair as best I could before pulling a couple of hatpins from my boater and bent over the lock.

"What are you doing?" she asked, peering over my shoulder.

"Rory, the blacksmith in the village where I lived, showed me this trick when I was a girl. My father had a tendency to lock me in the coal room when he was away from home."

Helena made a horrified noise.

"Later it was the linen closet, and sometimes, when he was furious, a trunk he kept stored in the stables. I haven't had to do this in some time, but I believe…ah, there it goes." Joy swelled briefly within me when the lock clicked and the door opened. I stepped through it, glancing back to ask, "Shall we go on to the rally, or would you prefer to go home and recover from this experience?"

Helena stood open-mouthed, staring at me with astonishment. The inner part of me hungry for praise relished her look of admiration when she ran over and hugged me fiercely. "You're amazing!"

"On the contrary, it was an extraordinarily simple lock—a child could have made his way out of the shed. Besides," I said with honesty, uncomfortable with her effusive praise, "a groundskeeper was soon to arrive. They are always busy about the area and make, I have noticed, frequent visits to the sheds. I'm sure we were in no danger at all."

Helena murmured something to the contrary, but we walked quickly across the green, discussing the likely reasons someone might want to abduct us in such a manner.

"It must surely have been a prank," I said hesitantly. "What sane abductor would choose such a public place to enact a nefarious plot? No, I feel confident it was a simple prank. That or—"

I paused as an insidious thought struck me.

Helena caught my arm, her face pale and distressed. "What?"

"It could be…" I dropped my voice and whispered my suspicion.

"White slavery?" Helena repeated, a look of disbelief crossing her face.

"If not a prank, that's really the only other explanation that makes sense. You are lovely, and I don't make people retch when they see me, so what other reason would someone have to abduct us? No doubt the kidnappers left us to fetch a carriage by which they would take us to their headquarters."

"But—*white slavery?*" she asked again.

"Can you think of any other reasonable explanation given the words the villain flung at us as he left?"

"Well... no." Helena fell silent, but I suspected I hadn't convinced her.

Fortunately, we neared Speaker's Corner, and I forgot our abduction in the moment's excitement.

"I have been considering what you said." I waited patiently for the other members to gather.

"What is that?"

"Perhaps it is nothing, but doesn't it seem strange to you that your brother was so calm about your attending the rally today? He was angry about it yesterday, and I can't imagine what has made him so unconcerned now, unless he plans to keep an eye on you himself."

"You mean he would follow me?" She looked around nervously.

"I doubt if he would follow you, and surely if he did, he would have seen us detained by the white slavers. No, it seems to me more likely that, as he knows exactly where and when the rally is, he will simply show up."

"He wouldn't!" We both cast suspicious glances about us.

There was a sizable gathering of Union members present, but as yet only a handful of onlookers. While a few women set up a large *Votes For Women* banner, others were donning their sashes. Two women in suffragette suits were passing through the crowd with a basket, accepting donations for the cause. Mrs. Heywood was present, as was the fiery Maggie Greene, the latter holding court with a dozen women from the militant clique. I pointed them out to Helena. She seemed fascinated with their plans.

"Honestly, Helena, you don't want to involve yourself with them," I cautioned, remembering my surprise and dismay at her enthusiasm for the militant's brutal tactics. "Surely, you don't wish to become involved with setting fire to post boxes and throwing stones at officials?"

"No, of course not," Helena said slowly, watching them enviously. "But I do admire their spirit. They seem… so alive! Not content to just sit and let things happen, they *make* things happen. Doesn't that stir you?"

"All it stirs is a feeling of unease and dread," I replied grimly, watching her eager expression with a profound sense of dismay. "I know the result of violence, Helena. It ends in fear and subjugation and hatred. Their radical policy will do us more harm than good."

I brought our argument to an end when, glancing around casually, my attention was caught by a large, bulky shape half-hidden behind a nearby tree.

"My cup runneth over," I said with a sigh, but nonetheless, my pulse quickened.

"In what way?"

I smiled at Helena. "Nothing. I am just pleased to be proven right."

We devoted the next quarter of an hour to handing out pamphlets advocating the Union's stand on suffrage while several speakers addressed the small crowd of about forty people. When Maggie Greene took the makeshift podium, there was considerable agitation in the officials' ranks.

"I wager they were not expecting her to speak," I whispered to Helena, who shushed me so she could listen with a rapt expression. I had to admit the little Irishwoman was an excellent speaker, electrifying the crowd and drawing cheers of support from the public, but I soon found my attention wandering from her rhetoric.

In the excitement of the invigorating speeches, I had forgotten about the shape seen lurking behind a nearby tree. When I turned to Helena, about to suggest we leave, I saw Griffin striding our way in a determined manner. It was at that point the crowd attacked.

Perhaps the word *attacked* is too harsh for the situation. Looking back over the event, I can pinpoint the change in the crowd's mood to the time of Maggie's speech. Regardless of whether the attackers came prepared to wreak havoc (and given their ammunition, there can be no doubt they did), or whether Maggie incited the less controlled members of the audience, the fact remains that suddenly Union members were subjected to a volley of ripe tomatoes.

"Alex!" Helena shrieked as an offensive tomato sailed past my head and struck a woman standing beside me.

"Damnation!" I shouted, infuriated. "How dare they throw tomatoes at us? We are peaceably gathered. Take cover, Helena!"

The situation degenerated into a free-for-all as audience members threw themselves into the fray. Fights broke out around us, men fighting men, women fighting women, and, in a few cases, suffragettes fighting one or two of the men armed with a seemingly never-ending supply of tomatoes.

"Stay back," I shouted to Helena over my shoulder as I hefted a slimy, but intact, tomato. "Run to your brother. He will take care of you."

As I turned my head back toward the attackers, a wet, stinging object struck me on the cheek.

"Oh!" I cried, fury filling me. A roar echoed behind me I assumed was Griffin protecting Helena in the resulting melee. I weighed the tomato in my hand as I considered the best target, took careful aim, and let the tomato fly.

It hit one man in the eye, and I had the satisfaction of seeing him go to the ground before a powerful arm grabbed me roughly around the waist and jerked me back.

"Ooof!" The arm squeezed the breath out of me, so tightly bound around me it left me unable to draw another. My hat slid down over my left eye in a rakish manner as I was lifted from my feet and carried outside the fringe of the confrontation before being set down. Police whistles blew, people screamed, and hoarse voices shouted unmentionable observations while I struggled against the arm, desperate to catch my breath.

"Show me a riot and I know who's in the bloody middle of it," a familiar voice grumbled from above.

I stood clutching my sides, gasping for air. As soon as my vision cleared, it landed on the sight of a furious Griffin. He was arguing with Helena, ordering her to leave, but she refused to go until I could walk.

He turned back to me with a look that almost made me flinch. "Of all the foolish… Have you no brain in that pretty head?"

I blinked at him as I held my ribs, still trying to catch my breath, my initial panic at his anger fading quickly.

"Is that all you can do? Stand there and gape at me like a fish out of water?"

The insult stung me into a proper posture. Candidate for the position of lover or not, no one tells me I gape like a fish. I straightened up, closed my mouth, and glared out at him from under the angle of my hat. "You might better ask if I can still breathe after your manhandling has broken my ribs."

He grabbed my arm and dragged me to where Helena stood. "Walk," he ordered in a tone that I chose not to challenge.

We walked.

"May I inquire why you saw fit to remove me, without my permission, from the rally?" I asked as the ache in my ribs faded.

He kept a hand on my elbow, pushing me forward, the touch starting a wave of sensation that rippled over my torso, pooling in those deep, intimate parts that had been making themselves known whenever he was around.

"I thought that would be obvious even to you. A common brawl is no place for a lady." We reached the street, and he stopped and held up his hand imperiously.

Obediently, a passing hansom cab pulled to a stop next to him.

"I fail to see how you can interpret the throwing of one tomato as the desire to brawl," I commented, more than a little jealous since cabbies never seemed to stop for me. "Why you must misjudge everything I do—"

A muscle in his cheek twitched, keeping me from finishing the sentence. It took him a moment, but at last, he opened the door to the cab, and with a none-too-gentle hand, pushed me inside, giving the cabby my address before turning away, saying, "Helena, come with me."

He strode off, not looking back at us.

"Well," I said, peering out of the window. "He might be exceedingly gifted in kissing, but he is a *very* illogical man."

Helena choked.

I blushed, and said quickly, "I don't think you should mention our earlier adventure—your brother seems to be a little belligerent at the moment."

"I don't believe you have to worry about him," she drawled, then suddenly gave me a beatific smile before running after Griffin.

I pondered her comment for a moment, concluded emotion still overcame her senses, and since the demonstration had broken up, told the cabby to proceed to the nearest police station.

The visit went about as well as my previous call to the same organization—they pointed out that since we suffered no harm, it was likely a prank conducted by men who objected to the suffrage movement. I left somewhat mollified since the whole situation was more annoying than frightening, and I knew well how most men viewed the cause.

I had planned a quiet evening reviewing the household accounts so they might be ready for Mabel's return, but when I arrived home, Annie burst into tears upon seeing me and hurried away.

The evening post brought with it a large, stiff envelope with a prominent coronet. It turned out to be an invitation to the Duchess of St. Alban's annual masquerade ball a few days hence. It surprised me since I do not move in that circle of society, but a moment of thought cleared up the situation.

"Helena," I told Marmalade the cat. "She's a friend of one of the duke's daughters. No doubt she asked the duchess to add me to the invitation list, thinking I would enjoy the opportunity to parade around in an extravagant costume with the cream of society. The question is whether I should send my regrets, or indulge in the sheer waste of time and money that being costumed would require."

Marmalade, a wise cat, made no comment other than to purr and rub his teeth on my hand as we sat before the fire.

"I agree. It would be an insult to Helena to refuse. That just means I must come up quickly with an idea for a costume. Something simple, I think, like a toga. Emma will be able to help me design a Greek costume, elegant and graceful, draped in a flattering fashion."

I ousted Marmalade from my lap and left a message for Emma, asking for her assistance. As I entered the hall, Mullin stopped me with a note from Helena.

"Has there been any trouble below stairs?" I said as I took it. "Annie seems to be upset about something."

Mullin was an admirable butler, but he had one failing—he loved to gossip. I could almost see his ears prick up when I mentioned Annie's behavior. "No, miss. Nothing that I am aware of. Would you like me to make inquiries?"

"I'm sure it's nothing." I thanked him and opened Helena's note. My stomach tightened with dismay as I read the words.

Maggie Greene has invited me to take part in a protest tomorrow morning outside of Bosworth's club. I feel I must go and would be delighted if you were free to join us.

"Of all the idiotic…" I muttered to myself as I marched back to the library. "Now I'm going to have to go with her just to keep her out of trouble."

I wrote another note accepting her invitation and was eyeing the account book when Theodore returned with the intelligence that Emma was not at home. "Her landlady says she's likely down at her club," he said in a slightly adenoidal voice.

"That's perfect," I said, brushing the cat hair off my lap as I gathered up my hat and bag. "I'll go there and see all the excellent costumes her club members have made up for their historical reenactments. Perhaps they will provide me with inspiration."

As I was about to leave, Mullin materialized at my side. I could tell something was wrong because his face was pink with excitement.

"Yes? What is it?" I asked wearily, wondering what catastrophe had befallen us now.

"Excuse me for interrupting you, Miss Alex, but you asked earlier about Annie, and now it appears she has locked herself in her room. We have tried to speak with her, but she won't answer. Mrs. Mullin is concerned she might have done some harm to herself."

"I see. Theodore, tell Jackson to put the horses away. I'll have to go to the Sapphist's Club later." Removing my hat, I ran up the three flights of stairs to the room Annie shared with another maid and spoke loudly outside her door. "Annie, let me in. I want to talk with you."

"She won't answer, miss," one housemaid said from behind me. "I've tried and tried, but she just won't answer me."

Most of the household staff were gathered with her, waiting to see what would happen. I heard noises from inside Annie's room and turned to the staff and shooed them away. "Go on, back to your work. I will take care of this."

Mullin's face dropped, but he herded everyone downstairs.

"Annie?" I tapped at her door. "Everyone is gone except me. Will you please let me in?"

There was a scuffling noise. Then the lock turned, and the door opened to reveal a haggard Annie, her face swollen and red from crying. She looked so miserable it almost broke my heart.

"My dear," I said, closing the door behind me. "Whatever is the matter?"

She wiped at her face with a scrap of handkerchief and mumbled something incomprehensible.

A firm approach was clearly called for. I shook her gently. "This sobbing will do you no good. Now dry your tears and tell me what is the problem."

"Oh, miss, I can't. I just can't," she wailed, squinting her eyes with the effort of crying. No tears came, indicating she had been sobbing for some time.

"I will not leave this room until you do so. Annie, look at me." I softened my voice. "There is nothing you can't tell me. I'm your friend. You know that, don't you?"

The words must have penetrated her misery, for she attempted to collect herself. "Yes, miss, you are a friend. And I know you won't think the less of me for my fall."

"You fell?" I asked, looking her over for signs of injury. "Are you hurt?"

"No, miss, not that kind of fall." She took a deep breath. "I have been ruined."

"Ruined," I repeated stupidly, not comprehending at first. My eyes widened. "Oh, *ruined.*"

Annie nodded, and a few weak tears straggled down her face. "What will I do?"

I sat down abruptly in an old rocking chair in the corner. "Oh, my goodness. Ruined. Are you—is there—will there be a baby?"

She nodded, her face puckered as two thin lines of tears stole down her cheeks.

"Oh, Annie, how?" I blushed as I heard my own inane question. "That is to say, how did you come to this? Did you not use a preventative device?"

"I used a sponge. That's what my sister told me would work. You soak it in lemon juice, and it...well, it keeps things from...happening. Only it didn't this time."

"A sponge?" I remembered the pamphlet I had hidden in my glove box, given to me by Emma once I had told her I intended on taking a lover. The pamphlet described a pessary device intended to prevent just this situation. I had planned on having one installed in my person once I had need for it. "I'm sorry it did not work. Is it... is Jackson responsible?"

She shook her head miserably. "Mrs. Garner will dismiss me as soon as she comes home. Oh, miss! Please don't let them send me away. I can't go home. The shame would kill my mum."

"You are my maid, not Mrs. Garner's, so she cannot dismiss you. And I am not likely to," I said in response to her panicked look. "Who is it who has led you to this situation?"

"Mr. Jones." She snuffled into my skirt.

"I don't think I know him. Has he offered to make an honest woman out of you?"

She shook her head.

"Have you had a discussion at all about marriage?"

"No, miss."

"If he were agreeable, would you wish to marry him?"

"No, miss."

Her answer surprised me. I was sure she would feel the situation was serious enough to make her desire marriage over an illegitimate baby. "Damnation." I sighed to myself, at a rare loss for words.

Annie looked up with a wretched expression. "You won't turn me out, will you?"

"I've already said I wouldn't, and I mean it. Let's get you into bed. You've had a terrible day, but don't worry. We'll work things out somehow."

I spent another ten minutes reassuring her and getting her tucked into bed before I pressed her for details about the father.

"William Jones, his name is. I met him when we first came to London. He was ever so smart, and I was the envy of all the housemaids for having such a beau." She smiled at the memory of her domestic coup. "He took me to the Music Hall on my evenings off. We had such larks, you would laugh to see the way he went on."

"Do you know where he is employed?"

"Self-employed, he said. He was on a very important job that he couldn't tell me about, but he was never mean with his money, not like some I could name."

"When did you last see him?" I asked.

Tears pooled in her eyes again. "It's been over four days now. He used to call for me every day, faithful like, but now he's stopped calling for me and won't answer any of my letters."

"Four days isn't very long. Don't worry, we'll find him," I said, wondering how one went about finding a recalcitrant suitor. "What does he look like?"

"He's ever so good-looking," she said, sniffling. "Brown hair and eyes, not too tall, and dresses sharp. And he's got a lovely gold tooth."

An image rose in my mind, but I shook my head at it. There must be hundreds of people in London with gold teeth. Perhaps thousands. "A gold tooth? Where?"

"In the front. It shines when he smiles."

Mullin was lurking around the stairs as I descended, my brain whirling with speculation.

"Everything is fine, Mullin. No need to worry," I repeated the platitudes. "Tell Mrs. Mullin that Annie will do herself no harm. She is just a little upset over a bit of trouble in her family."

I set off to meet Helena the following morning. The ride to the club was short, too short for me to ply her with a few subtle questions about Griffin—his favorite authors, preferred foods, whether he liked to don skin-tight bathing costumes and cavort in the water in a manner that highlighted all the sleek lines of his flesh—so we confined ourselves to unexciting conversation until we arrived.

I put my hand on her arm as she started out of the carriage. "Helena, let me caution you about becoming too involved with Maggie Greene's group. I know you are determined to do your part, but please allow your good sense to guide your actions."

She flashed a smile. "I won't do anything you wouldn't do."

I followed behind her, far from reassured.

Maggie stood in a cluster of about twenty women. She

was a little perturbed to see me, but took my appearance in stride. "Ladies, this is an important protest that we will make today. Has everyone a sign?"

Helena held up her hand, and one of Maggie's minions brought over two signs. Helena's read *Women Demand Equality*, while mine mysteriously proclaimed to one and all that I was *Ignorant No More*.

The bulk of the women, including Helena, were clustered at the front of the club entrance. Maggie sent me down the street about half a block with the instruction to wave my sign at every passing vehicle. I was rather hesitant to leave Helena, but her assurance that she would not act foolishly still rang in my ears. Giving her one last warning look, I took my assigned position.

A few minutes later, a pair of constables arrived and shooed away Maggie and the others.

I moved closer, expecting the worst, but she surprised me with her acceptance of the inevitable. Gathering the group together, she herded us across the street. "The club clearly has the local police in their pocket," she informed us with a determination that filled me with foreboding. "We are forbidden to demonstrate directly in front of the entrance. They said nothing about demonstrating across the street, however, so this is where we will make our stand!"

As we took our new positions, vehicles poured into the street from the far end. I peered into a few of the carriages and motorcars as they stopped alongside the curb, but they were all empty. A suspicion took form when the first group of men exited the club.

Maggie and her contingent were in a knot directly across from the club exit. As the first gentleman stepped out onto the pavement, the militants increased the volume of their chants and waved their signs vigorously. The man ignored them and marched down the street to where his motorcar was waiting.

Uneasy, I started for Helena. As I dodged one protestor who was shaking her sign vigorously, I saw Maggie's hand flash and heard the impact as a stone smashed the window of the motorcar parked opposite.

"I knew it!" Horrified, I dropped my sign and ran forward as the women began flinging stones with abandon. Torn as I was with the desire to haul Helena away, I was more concerned about Maggie harming someone. I launched myself at her from the side, hoping the others would stop if I could down her. We fell together, hitting the pavement with a force that made my teeth rattle. Hats flying, we startled a few of the women closest, but the rest seemed to think nothing as we rolled in the street, Maggie screaming curses and trying to gouge my face with her fingernails.

Rocks and debris dug painfully into my back as I did what I could to wrest a large stone from Maggie's right hand and, at the same time, keep out of reach of the talon-like left. A sharp elbow to my jaw made me see stars, but had the benefit of reminding me I wasn't a helpless victim.

Gritting my teeth against the pain of Maggie's knee in my ribs, I made a fist and punched out blindly. Luckily, I connected with her face, snapping her head back into the curbstone. I hauled myself upright, breathing heavily as bent over to examine Maggie. She was dazed, but not seriously hurt.

"Helena!" I yelled, trying to get her attention. She seemed oblivious to me.

Several other women in the street yelled oaths and profanities at the men as I pried the stone from Maggie's fingers. They continued to pelt the club members, most of whom had taken refuge within the safety of the building. Two of the men stormed out into the street intending to stop the attack. As I straightened painfully, a stone whistled past my ear and struck a man as he approached.

Maggie kicked out at my leg just then, and I went down painfully on top of her. My fall seemed to knock the wind out of her, for she stopped struggling and lay inert, gasping for air. As soon as I could stand, I ran forward to help the injured man up off the street.

"Are you all right, sir? Let me help you—" My voice died as the man looked up. "Oh, my... Lord Sherringham."

A shadow fell over me as I tried, despite his incoherent sputtering, to help him up. I stepped back and bumped into a large, hard object.

"I beg your pardon," I said automatically, stepping around the object. A hand descended upon my shoulder and spun me around to face Griffin.

"Is this the sort of activity you champion, Miss Whitney? The stoning of men has a biblical quality, I grant you, but it is not one I would've believed you to condone." His face was hard, but his eyes immediately eased my spurt of anxiety.

"No—of course not—" I stammered, at a loss for an explanation. "I do not condone it... In fact, I was trying to stop the women from throwing any more—"

Griffin looked down at my hand, which still held the stone I had wrestled from Maggie, then up at me with an eyebrow raised quizzically. "Do you often find it necessary to carry a large rock with you?"

I flushed, knowing full well I could never explain the events. The thought crossed my mind that someone, somewhere, was having a good deal of fun at my expense. "Yes, Mr. St. John, I often carry a large rock around with me. I find it comes in handy when I am called upon to knock someone silly with it. Perhaps another time I can show you the technique."

A flash of blue to the left caught my eye. I groaned and turned on my heel as two constables rushed up. Having executed their plan with brutal success, the militants had scattered when they'd heard the bobbies' whistles. I trotted across the street to where Helena was standing, her arms limp at her sides, her mouth forming an O as she watched Lord Sherringham assisted back into the club.

"Don't worry," I told her with false confidence. "I'm sure your brother is all right. I suggest you go home and wait for him there."

She didn't move, but went a shade paler. I put a gentle hand on her shoulder.

"Helena?"

"Oh, Alex," she wailed suddenly, flinging herself on me. "What have I done? Why didn't I heed your warning? I could have killed Harold with that stone! How could I have done it?"

I felt Griffin's presence behind me. I was confident he would shield Helena from the wrath of the police, but knew he wouldn't go to any trouble to keep me from being arrested. Not even the fact that we had shared a very pleasing kiss would be enough to excuse what he believed to be my latest folly.

Helena suddenly noticed the policemen arriving in large numbers. She gave a gigantic gulp and looked like a scared rabbit. "What—what will they do with me?"

"Nothing, if you leave now. I'm sure your brother will tell them you are innocent of any wrongdoing."

Helena was plainly terrified at the results of her violent actions. That pleased me for a moment, and then, without warning, I was furious. I spun around and faced Griffin, angry at myself, angry that he would never believe my innocence given the evidence against me, and angrier still that I hadn't been able to keep Helena out of trouble.

"Just so you know—what Helena did wasn't her fault. She was under the influence of an extremely persuasive person, and if you say one word of criticism to this poor girl, I will take great pleasure in doing you a bodily harm, no matter what effect it might have regarding your candidacy for position of lover."

One bobby, seeing me wave the stone at Griffin, ran over to where we were standing and placed a restraining hand on my arm. "Now then, no more of that, miss. You'll have to come with me, you and the other lady."

"I will do nothing of the kind," I said primly, ignoring the stunned look on Griffin's face. "I have committed no crime and do not have the time to spend discussing the issue with you."

He tightened his grip and would, I believe, have forced me to accompany him had Griffin not regained his wits and stepped in.

"You are mistaken, Constable," he said. "This lady and the other were simply passing down the street and attempted to stop the attacks."

Helena and I looked at one another, she with terror written plainly on her face and me with astonishment at Griffin's action.

"Is that so?" the constable asked, clearly harboring some suspicion.

He looked from my stone to Helena's sign.

"Er... she just picked that up," I said, pointing to the sign.

She squeaked and dropped it.

"And that?" the constable asked, nodding at the rock in my hand.

"She took it from one of the women," Griffin said. "I saw her do so."

"Did she now? And yet this lady looks as if she's been fighting," the policemen told him, eying me dubiously.

"You can't take a rock from a woman bent on stoning people without some sort of struggle," I said with a righteous frown.

It took another five minutes of Griffin waxing eloquent before the policemen finally accepted our stories.

"I'll be taking your names as witnesses," the bobby warned, doing just that. "I'd advise you to be on your way and stay away from any such disturbances in the future."

He moved off to join his colleague, leaving us alone. Feeling there was nothing more to be said, I squeezed Helena's arm reassuringly as Griffin handed her into his motorcar.

"I will take you home," he said to me. "I can come back for Sherry afterward."

"That's not at all necessary. Your brother should probably see a doctor as soon as possible. I'll take a cab."

"Stay here," he told Helena and escorted me down the street to the nearest available vehicle.

The silence hung heavily over me for a good two minutes before I broke it. "Thank you for what you did back there. I know it must have gone against your wishes to protect me as well as Helena, but I do appreciate it."

"I just hope you both learned something from it," he muttered, seemingly distracted. It wasn't until another few minutes passed he found a cab and handed me into it. He leaned in, the oddest expression on his face. "Er… what you said a few minutes ago—"

"That I was sorry you had to protect me?"

"No, not that."

Chagrin flashed across his face as he ran a distracted hand through his hair

"What then?" I asked, desperately fighting the urge to kiss him.

"What you said after that. You said something about being your lover." His eyes were softly luminescent, warm pools of amber that snared me with no difficulty at all.

"Oh. That." Beneath my chemise, my nipples hardened. They'd never done that before, not in response to a man's look, but it certainly was Griffin that had them behaving in such a distracting manner. No doubt it was also his presence that left me short of breath, my heart pounding uncomfortably, my skin suddenly extremely sensitive. I licked a slight cut on the corner of my lip. Griffin's gaze pounced on the movement. "Yes. I… I feel that we have a certain… affinity despite our differences, and wondered… er…"

He dragged his gaze back to my eyes. Oddly enough, he looked as bemused as I felt. I decided it was the lack of oxygen to my brain that was making him appear so. Men of the world like Griffin did not bemuse easily. "Yes?"

"Well… it was an idea I had…" I said, distracted by his nearness. "I wondered if you had ever thought about the idea… if you'd ever considered the possibility… You seemed to enjoy kissing me, and I enjoyed it very much, and I thought…"

"What did you think, Alex?" he asked, brushing his thumb along my lower lip.

"I thought you might want to do it again," I said, my mind giving up the battle.

He leaned forward and gently caressed my lips with his. Heat pooled inside me, deep within me, radiating outward in waves of anticipation. "Say it."

"Would you consider filling the position of my lover?" I asked.

"No, say what you really want."

"Oh, I *really* want that," I said earnestly.

He laughed and kissed me again. "Tell me what you want."

"You. I want you."

His tongue touched the bruised corner of my mouth before sliding between my lips. I was shocked and surprised and thrilled all at once, my brain and body reeling at the intimate touch of his tongue against mine.

"Yes," he said finally, after he stole away my breath.

"Yes?" I asked, befuddled to the point of incomprehension.

"Yes, I will become your lover."

"Oh, thank you." I couldn't keep from smiling, relief filling me. "I was so worried about asking you, but it really wasn't as bad as I thought. And I believe having you as a lover will be very nice."

He gave me a look that sent my entire body tingling, his amber eyes filled with a passionate promise that had my heart speeding up. "It will be much, much more than nice, Alex."

The door to the cab closed, and I sank back against the cushions, whooshing out a breath that I didn't remember holding. It was only when I arrived at home that I noticed I still carried the stone.

EIGHT

"Annie," I said, as the woman in question muttered softly while struggling to force my hair—recalcitrant at best—into the semblance of a fashionable hairstyle. "I believe the time has come to make you aware of a situation."

"What would that be, miss?" she asked, glaring at a curl that refused to be pinned into place.

I arranged my expression into one that spoke of confidence in myself. "I have taken a lover. Or I will have taken him when he allows me to do so, but assuming that time will be soon, I believe we can use the present tense."

Annie's jaw dropped, the hairpins scattering all over the carpet. "You *what?*"

I tried to look nonchalant about the whole thing, as if taking a lover was a trivial act, one I did every day. "New Women take lovers. I am a New Woman. You know this."

Her eyes narrowed on me even as she knelt to gather the hairpins, her expression suspicious. "Would you be talking about Mr. St. John?"

"As a matter of fact, yes. I felt he was the best candidate for the position." I tried on a lofty expression. I looked vaguely constipated.

"Oh, well, then." Annie's shoulders sagged in relief. "That's all right."

I frowned, a little annoyed by her attitude. "What do you mean by that?"

"Well, he's a gentleman, isn't he?" She finished with my hair and gestured for me to stand.

I did so, and she eyed my dress, looking for anything that needed adjustment. "Yes, but any man I chose to be my lover would be a gentleman."

"There's gentlemen and then there's *gentlemen*," she said sagely, tugging at a sleeve. "Mr. St. John is a proper gentleman. He won't see you hurt."

"I am a grown woman, Annie," I said with complete disregard for the fact that she had seen me at my worst. "You are feeling vulnerable at the moment because of your situation, but I assure you I won't allow myself to be so burdened unless I desire it."

"You won't?" She looked like she wanted to smile, but didn't dare.

"No. I have the name of a doctor who will install a device that will prevent such things. Also, I believe there are things men can do. I will discuss the matter with Mr. St. John, and we will come to an understanding."

A slight noise escaped her, something sounding remarkably like a titter. "I'm sure you will. That's done, I think."

I looked into the mirror and was pleased by the dress and Annie's skill. I have no pretensions to any beauty, but the sapphire blue satin gown, with its accompanying midnight blue gauze tunic studded with crystals, set off my red hair and made my skin look paler than it really was.

Grimacing only slightly at my freckles, I took one last unsure look at the low neckline of the dress, gathered up my bag and velvet coat, thanked Annie for her work, and ordered her to bed before departing for my aunt's house, since I would accompany them for the evening.

The opera house was dazzling with flashing jewels, the shiny silks and satins of the ladies' gowns, and the brilliance of starched white against the black of the gentlemen's evening clothes. I was halfway up the grand staircase when my aunt jostled my arm. "Isn't that Lord and Lady Sherringham by the door?"

I turned quickly and scanned the crowd. Just coming in the door, Lord Sherringham was laughing jovially with a white-haired man in a military uniform.

"Yes, I believe it is." The entire family was present—Lady Sherringham in a horrible orange chiffon gown, Helena in pale mauve, and Griffin looking devastatingly handsome in evening clothes.

Watching out of the corner of my eye, I felt very aware of my body. Various parts tingled, while others became highly sensitized. I reminded Inner Alex that we were in public, and I would not shame myself, no matter how much I wanted to grab Griffin and rub myself all over him.

My uncle's box was next to last on the left side of the theater, offering a good view of both the stage and audience. Once we arrived in it, I turned my chair away slightly from the stage to watch the audience, all the while trying to calm myself so I felt less like I was being eaten alive by fire ants. Before long, the opening refrains of the overture quieted the conversation somewhat, and resignedly I turned to face the stage.

Directly to my left were the Sherringhams. Helena sat closest to me, talking to someone over her left shoulder. Lady Sherringham sat next to her in the front, and I could see the stout form of Lord Sherringham behind her, in muffled conversation. Etiquette wouldn't allow me to turn around and stare into their box, although I desperately wanted to.

The opera was lost on me. I spent the time indulging in impure thoughts so scandalous that when the intermission brought the house lights up, I was flushed, and badly in need of an ice bath.

"I'm just going to say hello to Helena," I told my aunt, and was rising when my uncle stepped into the box. "My dear, I believe you know this gentleman. He was most desirous of having a few words with you."

Griffin stepped forward and offered his hand. Inner Alex—who was responsible for the more lurid of my fantasies—immediately cheered, and made plans for entertaining his personal parts.

"How nice to see you again, Mr. St. John," I shook his hand, my breath caught in throat as his fingers lingered a moment on mine. "Are you enjoying the opera?"

"Not particularly. Helena wanted me to attend. She thought it would be good for my uncivilized soul. I'm glad to see you have suffered no ill effects from this morning's trial."

His eyes laughed at me, and I felt giddy with happiness. It was too public a place for me to discuss the subject of just how and when we were to become lovers, so I confined myself to speaking with obtuseness. "I had imagined it would be a good deal more trying than it was. I find that happens now and again—the anticipation of a much awaited event becomes almost too much to bear."

"Indeed." His gaze dropped to my lips, and my entire body tightened. "Sometimes anticipation can become almost painful."

"And exciting," I said somewhat breathlessly, gesturing toward my torso. "Body parts can feel…needy."

He took a step closer to me, his voice dropping to an intimate level. "What do those body parts need, exactly?"

"I'm not sure," I said, leaning in toward him. "Hands, I think. Hands are good."

His eyes glazed over a little, and he shifted uncomfortably. "Hands can be very good. So can mouths."

"Really?" I tried to process what he was saying, but it was hard to focus when, as I took another step toward him, I could smell the lemon of his shaving soap. "Used in substitution for hands?"

"That or in conjunction. They can be very good together."

"Oh." The word came out as a near-sigh. "I believe this is something I will have to investigate further."

"Alex—" he said, his voice a low rumble that positively thrummed inside me.

"Yes, to the mouth and hands together—" I started to say, and would have flung myself on him had not my uncle, who was outside the box speaking to an acquaintance, turned to call for my aunt.

The spell—highly charged and filled with sensual promise—was broken. Griffin took a step back, and I mentally told Inner Alex we would have a lengthy talk at a later time about proper behavior when in public, and after willing my breasts and lady parts to settle down, I changed the subject. "How's Helena?"

He had to clear his throat twice before he could answer normally. "Fine, now. I gather from what she said that you warned her against this Greene female. I apologize for my hasty conclusion earlier. Helena informed me you were against the protest from the beginning."

I accepted his apology, basking in the warm glow of admiration in his eyes as I asked after his brother. Griffin scratched at his collar as he answered. "Sherry's all right. Nothing more than a cut to the forehead, although he isn't aware of who threw the stone."

He looked at me meaningfully.

"And I'm sure he never shall be."

"Yes. Well." An awkward silence fell. Griffin waved in the general direction of my torso. "That's attractive."

Instantly, my breasts were back on full alert, and became two strumpets just barely confined by a Rational corset. It was as if they were horses, straining at the bit to be released into his hands.

I dwelt for a few moments on that mental image, feeling simultaneously hot and cold.

"Alex?" he asked.

"Nipples. What?" I blinked and realized that my imagination had run away again. Really, I was going to have to insist that we consummate our loverhood soon, or else risk permanent damage to my psyche.

His gaze dipped to my breasts, and seemed to remain there, mesmerized. "I said your dress looks attractive."

I eyed his shoulders, mentally imagining myself pressed up against his chest. "Ah, my gown. Yes, I am wearing one. Your chest is very nice as well."

He blinked twice at my strumpets, then hauled his gaze up to mine. "What was that?"

"Yes," I said, wishing I had my fan. "There doesn't seem to be enough air here tonight, does there?"

"On the contrary, there appears to be quite a bit of it," he answered, his gaze dropping back to my exposed cleavage. "It's delightfully ample, if you don't mind me saying."

I shot him a steamy look. He took a step closer to me, his eyes bright with heat and passion and desire, so much desire, a veritable opera house full of desire…

"My dear, you're standing on my wrap. Alex?"

I became aware my aunt had been speaking to me while I was busy trying to work out how to get Griffin alone and naked.

"My apologies," I said, moving to the side before fetching my aunt's silk wrap. She shot me a warning glance I didn't want to interpret. Instead, I turned back to Griffin, and with yet another change of topic, asked, "Will you go away soon?"

A fleeting look crossed his face, one that so resembled pain that my heart constricted at the sight of it.

"That is," I corrected myself, ignoring the pounding of blood in my ears, "will you be going abroad soon? I asked you earlier but did not hear plans of your further travels."

"I haven't made up my mind yet. There are certain obligations I have recently undertaken." His eyes were molten enough to set the entire building on fire.

My knees wobbled. My breasts insisted I release them right then and there. My New Woman parts demanded out-right *demanded* time with Griffin. "I imagine you would be eager to be on your way—after you attend to your obligations, of course."

"Do you really believe my…obligation…will be over so quickly?"

"Well, I know how men are," I said, adopting a world-wise mien.

"Do you?" His gaze searched my face, leaving me feeling as if I was standing in a bonfire.

I glanced at my aunt. She was thankfully in conversation with someone in the box to the right. "I thought that sooner rather than later might be good for your obligations. Unless, of course, you need some time to prepare for them."

A slow smile curled his delicious lips, once again stripping the air from my lungs. "If you believe I need time to prepare, you cannot be as familiar with men as you think."

Inner Alex wanted to both swoon at his nearness, and argue with him I was worldly, indeed, but before I could pin him down to a specific date and time, the third act of the opera began. With much regret, I tucked away the lurid seduction scenes playing in my head and turned my attention to the stage, avoiding the box to my left. During the fourth act, I was indulging in a pleasant daydream about just exactly how Griffin would respond to my seduction of his person when a sudden shout from below broke my reverie. I peered over the edge of the box and gasped with horror at the sight.

Six suffragettes with *Votes For Women* sashes draped over their fronts marched down the two side aisles, shouting slogans and hurling vegetables at the stage. The audience sat shocked for a moment. Then a handful of men ran forward and grappled with the women to remove them. Ushers raced down the aisle to assist as two protesters gained the stage and began shouting at the audience. Speechless with horror, I turned to my aunt. She watched the proceedings with some interest, pausing now and again to glance questioningly at me.

"I'm sure we have you to thank for this travesty," Lord Sherringham's loud voice echoed off the balconies. I turned, surprised at his comment. He stood at the front of his box and leaned forward to address my uncle. "If my niece exhibited such dangerous tendencies, Benson, I would take a horsewhip to her. She does you much discredit."

"My niece would have nothing to do with people who take action in such a disruptive manner," Uncle Henry said mildly. "I have implicit faith in her judgment and sensibility."

"As for you," Lord Sherringham continued, his eyes narrowing on me until they were slits of pure malice, "I shall take steps to ensure you and your foul organization do no further damage."

"I know nothing about this," I said in a small voice to his retreating figure. My eyes sought those of Griffin, but when I found them, they gave me no pleasure.

The audience's collective shock fizzled away as the suffragettes were extracted. Voices rose, expressing their astonishment, amusement, and disapproval. Wishing I knew how to swoon properly, I turned to my aunt. "You know I had nothing to do with this."

"Of course I do, my dear. I fear, however, that you will have a difficult time persuading other people of your innocence."

"I have a horrible headache," I said truthfully. "Would you mind if I left now?"

"Not at all. Let me tell Henry we're going."

"No, please." I put a hand out to stop her before she could turn in her seat. Shame mingled with ire, but neither one of those emotions lent themselves to being in the company of others. The memory of the doubt in Griffin's eyes...I fought the urge to cover my face and said quickly, "It's unnecessary for you to leave early. I'd rather be by myself."

It took some persuading, but at last I secured my early release. I slipped out of the box, my cheeks hot with embarrassment as I ran down the stairs. There were a few people about, mostly ushers who were clustered together in excited groups, but the atmosphere was close and stifling. I couldn't bear it. I bolted for the exit.

Outside, the night air was cool and soft, washing over my heated cheeks like cold water. Brushing away a few rogue tears, I glanced up and down the line for my uncle's carriage.

Unable to find it, and desperate to get away from the site of my humiliation, I decided to walk the distance to my sister's house. Clutching my cloak against the chill night, I set out.

NINE

I love Covent Garden in the evening, after the night has settled and the tradesmen have rolled away their carts. Although wary after my experiences with the purse thief and the men in Hyde Park, embarrassment over the debacle at the opera house made walking through the empty streets seem like a frolic in comparison.

My spirits sank as I strode along, miserably contemplating my emotions. "The sad truth is that you're perilously close to falling in love, and now you're paying the price of such folly."

My voice echoed off the closed shops, making an eerie counterpoint to the sound of my shoes on the cobblestones. I stopped. Frowning with concentration, I held my breath and listened. From somewhere behind came the unmistakable sounds of pursuit: strong footsteps moving quickly. A vision of the man with the bowler and gold tooth rose before my eyes, followed by a sharp bite of fear. I slipped into a dark doorway and peered out into the blackness, telling myself to breathe through the need to curl into a ball.

"Father is dead," I whispered to myself with far more bravado than I felt as the footsteps grew louder. "He has not come back to punish you for defying his wishes. You need not fear anyone anymore."

The footsteps paused for a moment, giving me hope they had nothing to do with me. But a minute later, a figured loomed up in a pool of light from a distant lamppost, passing quickly and silently into the darkness.

Relief swamped me for a few seconds, such a powerful emotion that it took me two tries to speak when the man passed my hiding spot. "Out for an evening stroll, Mr. St. John?"

He let out a startled exclamation of surprise and spun around to grasp my arm with a ferocity that had me flinching. "You damned fool, woman! Don't you have any better sense than to leap out at a man unexpectedly?"

"I thought it better to see who you were first," I explained, wincing when his fingers tightened. "You're hurting me."

He released my arm immediately, but I was so happy to see him I smiled.

This is, of course, the wrong way to greet a freshly startled man.

He took my arms in his hands, but gently this time, giving me an even gentler shake. "What the hell are you doing out here by yourself? It's not safe for a female to march through the city after dark by herself. I thought you'd learned that lesson."

"Don't yell at me. I don't like it. My father always yelled at me," I said, wanting to both grasp his head and kiss him, and shrug him off so I could scurry home and pretend the night never happened.

"I'm not yelling," he yelled. His jaw worked for a few seconds, then he added (in a much lower volume), "All right, I was, but it's only because you're driving me insane."

There was so much I wanted to say, but the horror of the exhibition overrode all pleasanter emotions. I simply shook my head and tried to leave.

He held on to me, watching my face before saying in a low, intimate tone, "Did you have anything to do with that display back there?"

"No." I gathered my courage despite my wish to run. I had to know if Griffin was the sort of man I could trust. Not just as a lover, but as a man. "I knew nothing about it, Griffin. They as appalled me as they did everyone else."

"You ran away," he said, close enough to me that his breath caressed the little strands of hairs that broke free from my coiffure.

"Only because I was so ashamed. It seems I'm always shamed in front of you," I admitted, looking at his neck because I couldn't stand to see into his beautiful eyes. "No matter what I do, it all seems to go wrong."

"On the contrary." His voice was a deep, sensual rumble in his chest. He released one arm to tip my chin upwards, leaning forward to say against my lips, "You do many things very right indeed."

His lips were gentle on mine at first, caressing, persuasive, yet demanding. I breathed in his scent, waves of excitement buzzing down my body. My vision blurred as I looked into those deep, endless pools of amber, eyes that glowed from within as he touched the back of my neck lightly. It electrified me; I felt his touch all the way down to my toes.

He nipped my lip until I gave him what he wanted, allowing him to sink into my mouth, his groan of pleasure matching my own. My fingers curled through his hair, soft as silk, tugging him closer when my body clamored to feel him.

He pulled me tighter, one hand on my behind, the other tangled in my hair as he thoroughly, leisurely, wantonly explored my mouth.

Just when I thought I would faint with the delight of it all, he ended the kiss, his mouth shifting to caress my jaw.

"Why, oh why, didn't I think of taking a lover before?" I murmured to myself.

He laughed, breaking the mood of the moment. I pulled away, desperately trying to catch my breath.

"I believe, madam, that we have an appointment?"

His raised eyebrow sent little shivers of delight down my back as I understood what he was asking. "Yes, we certainly do."

He held out his arm. I took it, and we walked in silence to the nearest cab.

I waited until the cab had set off for my house before turning to him. To my surprise, he held me off. "No."

"I'm sorry," I said, suddenly flushed with shame that quickly faded to annoyance. "I shouldn't have—"

"Yes, you should, but not here in the cab. It's going to be difficult enough to walk without you making it worse."

"Are you injured?" I asked, my embarrassment turning to concern. "You weren't walking with a limp. If you are in pain, I can summon a doctor."

"I can just imagine what he'd say. You have no idea what I'm talking about, do you?"

"No, but if you've had another accident—"

"I suspected that was the case, despite your claim earlier." He took my hand and placed it on his lap, pressing my fingers into his groin.

I froze for a moment. Inner Alex gasped with pleasure. I tried to imagine the size of the fig leaf needed to cover what his trousers contained, and failed. "Oh. I see."

"You don't, but you will. It's painful for a man to be so aroused, and if you were to kiss me like you obviously were about to, you might push me over the edge."

I felt strangely proud of myself, enough so that I took the liberty to explore the apparently vast lengths his arousal rose to.

So to speak.

"And that will definitely do the job if kissing you didn't," he said in a tight voice, prying my hand off his groin.

Heat flushed up from my chest, making me feel sticky and uncomfortable. "I'm sorry. I won't do it again."

"I pray fervently that you will, but not in a cab. Have you considered the ramifications of what this will mean to your home?"

I frowned despite the darkness of the cab. "I hardly see how the size of your…er…fig-leaf-bearing parts concerns anyone but us."

There was a noise suspiciously like a stifled snort of laughter. "I was referring to our rendezvous."

"The servants, you mean? I told Mullin that I would let myself in. My maid will be discreet, of that you have no fear."

He shifted slightly in the seat as if he had shrugged. "I have no fear of servants, but I don't want you being uncomfortable."

"I am a New Woman," I reminded him. "Everyone knows that we have lovers fairly dripping from us."

He said nothing to that. The ride home seemed interminable since I couldn't spend it kissing Griffin, or groping him through his trousers, or even admiring that derriere that I knew was going to be outstanding, but at long last I closed the door to the library and sighed in relief.

"Are you sure you want to do this?" Griffin asked, eyeing me, then bent his head so he could feather a kiss to my bare collarbone.

"Merciful heavens, yes," I breathed out, arching my back so my breasts were pressed against him. "Although it will be a long time before I forget the shocked expression on Mullin's face when you followed me in here."

Griffin pressed me against the library wall, his eyes almost glowing with desire, his hands stroking down my bare arms to my waist. A brief spurt of panic had me pausing for a moment, but there was nothing in Griffin's face that caused me to worry.

"You dragged me in here, madam. *That* is what he was staring at."

I smiled and brushed his lips with mine, feeling terribly wanton, but knowing this was right. I was meant to be here, meant to be with Griffin, meant to do all the things that had so consumed my thoughts. "I wish I could yell at him for waiting up for me, but he looked so concerned. Until he saw you, that is."

"We could go elsewhere," Griffin murmured, his mouth closing on mine. The wood was cool against my back, but Griffin was fire against my front. I slipped my hands up his waistcoat and over his shoulders, pushing off his evening jacket.

"No. It'll be all right. We'll stay here." I panted a little when I spoke, but felt he would forgive me since he was the one who kept me breathless with his kisses.

His tongue was bossy, pushing mine around until I suckled it. Then he moaned into my mouth. My fingers danced down the line of buttons on his waistcoat, pushing it off after his jacket.

His hands slid around to my front and finally closed around breasts that had been screaming for his attention. I leaned into his palms, leaned into all of him, reveling in the hardness of his body as he plundered my mouth again.

I plundered back.

"No corset?" he asked when we came up for breath, the wicked glint in his beautiful eyes lighting all sorts of fires around various parts of my body. I pulled off his tie as he nibbled at a sweet spot just behind my ear.

"Yes, but it's a very light version," I murmured, tugging on his hair until I could suck his lower lip into my mouth. I wrapped my arms around him, releasing button after button on the back of his shirt.

"I like women who wear light corsets." He groaned as I spread my fingers wide on the smooth bare skin of his back.

With a move that was so quick it was over before I was aware it began, he whisked my sapphire gown over my head and tossed it toward a chair. There wasn't much more of me to be exposed in my underfrillies, but it felt scandalously naughty to stand there in front of him in nothing but my rational corset, chemise, and combinations.

I reveled in every moment.

"I like a man who likes a woman who wears a light corset." I kissed him with every ounce of desire I possessed, my fingers tugging and twisting until I had his cufflinks off.

His hands fumbled on the hooks that ran down the front of my corset before allowing it to drop, and moving to the back of my chemise, pausing just long enough to shed his shirt. I stared hungrily at his chest, his magnificent chest, his wonderful, fabulous, breathtakingly beautiful chest, a veritable wonderland of muscle and sinews and dark, curly hair that suddenly made my legs go boneless.

"Chest," I squeaked, spreading my fingers across it, tracing all the contours that swooped and bulged in amazingly wonderful curves.

"Yes, it is," he answered, having unhooked enough of my chemise that he could tug it down over my hips, until it fell with a soft whisper of silk and lace at my feet. "And it's the most beautiful chest I've ever seen."

I arched my back when his hands closed on my bare breasts, my eyes closing as I gave myself up to the wonderful fires his fingers started. His breath was hot on my skin as he kissed a trail from my neck down to where my breasts tightened and grew heavy. His kisses were warm, steaming me as his lips caressed the sensitive flesh. I wanted to move, wanted to touch him, but with every brush of his lips against me, I lost more of myself to him.

"You're so beautiful. You taste of fire." His mouth closed around one aching nipple and I groaned with my pleasure, my nails digging into his shoulders. "You're soft and silky, and I want to taste all of you."

I clung to him as his mouth moved over to my other breast, too overwhelmed with the sensations he stirred to speak.

"You make me mad with desire. I've wanted you since that first day, wanted to touch you and fill my senses with you."

I whimpered my pleasure at both his words and actions, unable to pull enough coherent thoughts together to speak. With a murmur against my breast, he scooped me up in his arms and set me down carefully on the rug before the fire, propping himself up on his elbows, his chest pressed against mine as he kissed me again.

"Griffin?" I breathed against his shoulder, squirming delightedly, kissing the tanned column of his throat as he divested me of the rest of my garments. I knew I should remind him to lock the door, but all thoughts left my mind when his mouth followed his fingers as he kissed a path down my belly. His hands traced serpentine designs on the flesh of my thighs until I parted them for him. Then suddenly he was down there, in the tingliest of all my tingly spots, his fingers dancing a seductive waltz that left me aching for more.

"My beautiful Alex," he rumbled, his eyes alight with passion so hot it scorched my skin. I traced the line of his jaw until he looked up, his gaze holding mine.

"The door," I said, aware of nothing but the magic in his fingers as they caressed and teased, tension coiling inside me, winding tighter and tighter with each stroke.

"The door," he said, his mouth closing over my breast, suckling hard at my nipple until I almost came off the floor.

"Yes, yes! Oh, Griffin, the door!"

"The door is beautiful," he murmured against my other breast, teasing it with sweet nips that turned all the fires within me into raging infernos. One long finger sank within me, causing my hips to arch beneath his hand. "I've never seen such a beautiful, luscious door in all my life. It is soft as silk and so hot it burns me. I want the door. I crave the door. Let me have the door, Alex."

"It's all yours," I shrieked as something inside me exploded into chaos, a wondrous chaos of joy and ecstasy that had its beginning and ending in Griffin.

His fingers slid from my body as I lay panting on the rug before the fire, one side of me warmed by the flames, the other scorched by Griffin. "Before we do anything else, I have to ask you...erm...I've heard there is something that women can use."

I stroked a hand down his chest. "The pessary? Yes, I was planning on having one installed as soon as I have need of it."

"Ah. Then you don't have anything. I assumed not, but I thought I would check. I have a preventative."

"A what?"

There was a rustle of cloth against skin, and then he was over me, the male part of him covered in a flesh-colored garment that had a little ribbon tying it onto him. I had seen nothing like it before, and was more than a little confused. "What...uh...what..."

"It's a rubber," he answered, an odd expression flitting across his face. "It's not my favorite thing to wear, but it's better than nothing."

I was oddly pleased that he had taken precautions since did not, as yet, have my device installed, and gave a little wiggle against him. He leaned down to kiss me again, his mouth hot on mine as he nudged my legs wider, his chest hair teasing my aching nipples.

"Tell me you want me," he said, his eyes molten with passion. "Tell me you want this as much as I do."

"I do," I promised, kissing his beautiful throat. "I want it. I want you. Let me have you, Griffin."

He groaned as my fingers sculpted the contours of his back. Then he was pressing against me, nudging his way into my body, entering me in a way that suddenly had me worried.

"Um. Griffin?"

His head sank to my shoulder as he kissed my neck, nibbling on me while the solid length of him pressed slowly inside. He was hot and hard and filled me, stretching me until I squirmed beneath him. He groaned again, mumbling something about me not moving until he caught his breath.

"Griffin, I think I've changed my mind. I think there's something not quite right about this situation. You must be built too large or perhaps I'm too small or maybe I just over-anticipated this actual event, but you're beginning to hurt me and I think I'd like you to—"

He lifted his head, his big chest heaving. "I will stop now if that is what you want, but I can assure you that there is nothing wrong. We will fit together, even though this being your first time, you will feel a little pain."

"I don't like pain," I said, my mind at war with my body. The latter very much wanted him to stop, but my mind—and heart—oh, they wanted him to continue.

"I'm told it's brief, but if it's too much, we can stop. I may die in the process, but the choice is yours."

"You promise it'll be a brief pain?" I asked, wanting the intimacy, but fearing the unknown.

"I can only tell you what I've heard. I can try to go slowly, if you think that will help."

"No," I said, bracing myself. "Do it fast. I never did like prolonging unpleasant acts."

He laughed then, but groaned when I shifted beneath him in an attempt to get comfortable. To my surprise, the sensation of him being too much for me had eased a little. "If it hurts too much, tell me, and I'll stop."

I tried to don a brave, martyred expression, but then he kissed me again, and while my mind was swooning over the fact that his mouth was as hot at the sun, he plunged forward, a burst of pain flaring to life deep within me. He surrounded me, filled me.

He was everywhere, leaving me no escape. Panic swamped me, the familiar flame of fear licking the edges of my mind, and I was just about to scream when he murmured sweet words in my ears.

"I'm sorry, sweetheart. It will be better in a moment. I'll wait until you're ready for me to move again."

Somehow, just the sight of his eyes, full of concern, full of desire and yearning, calmed me. The panic and fear faded as I kissed a line across his jaw, and slowly, the pressure of him filling me took on an extra dimension, one of pleasure, one of need that only he could satisfy.

I moved my hips just a little to experiment with this unfamiliar sensation, capturing his groan in my mouth. "Alex, no, for the love of God, don't move—"

I shifted my hips again, and he slid deeper into me.

He moved then, a beautiful rhythm that sent me soaring, thrusting in with long, deep strokes that joined his body fully with mine until there was no way to separate us. His movements quickened, his kisses becoming harder, more demanding as his body moved. I wrapped my legs around his hips and matched his kisses, taking his heat and returning it with a fire of my own. We burned hot, hotter than I thought possible, our flesh bound until, in one brilliant moment, Griffin's back arched as he shouted my name.

A long time later, after our hearts stopped pounding, and our breathing changed from ragged gasps to a more regular pattern, and the fire we created burned down to deep, satisfying embers, Griffin lifted his head from my neck and looked down on me.

"Did you say something about the door?"

I smiled and kissed the tip of his nose. Men were such amusing creatures. "Don't be silly. Why would I choose such a moment to talk about architecture?"

I suppose I ought to have felt some shame or regret for losing my innocence, or at least embarrassment that I all but seduced Griffin, but all I felt as we assisted each other into our respective garments was the sadness that I wouldn't be able to spend the night lying in his arms.

Oh, there was satisfaction that I'd chosen my lover well, and there was the knowledge that our time together would be pleasurable beyond what I believed possible, even so, there was a faint sense of loss that tainted the moment.

When he adjusted the last button on my gown and I slipped his cufflinks back into place, we faced each other silently.

"May I see you tomorrow?"

Just looking at him made me want to fan myself. "I thought I would visit the doctor Emma recommended, for the installation of the pessary. It seems like it would be a good thing to have."

"Ah. Yes, that is important. The next day, then?"

I looked at him solemnly, slowly regaining control of myself. I wondered if I would ever be the same. "Unfortunately, I'll be busy then, too. There's the march to the Houses of Parliament at noon."

His jaw tightened as he dropped my hand. "After tonight's episode at the opera, you still intend on joining that group of misguided women?"

"Of course," I answered, surprised that he thought I'd give up such an important cause over a regrettable event. "I knew nothing about the demonstration tonight, and I had no part in the terrible attack this morning, but I *do* know the Women's Suffrage Union does not condone violence. The women who acted tonight were a small faction, a minority. The rest of the Union isn't like them."

"Whether your group sanctions their actions or not, can't you see how foolish they look? What a mockery they make of your cause? Is that how you want to appear to your family and friends?"

It didn't worry me that his amber eyes flashed with emotion. Griffin was as full of passion as I was, but I doubted if he would ever turn that against me.

All men turn in the end, the dark side of my mind said.

I ignored it, refusing to believe that Griffin was like my father. I said slowly, wanting to placate his anger and yet make my devotion to the cause clear, "I regret the fact that they disrupted the opera, and in such an uncouth manner, but that aside, I can't help but applaud their intentions. They were trying to bring awareness to a valid effort. It takes bravery to face an audience who doesn't agree."

"Bravery? What those women displayed was nothing more than cowardice, attacking a group of unarmed musicians and singers." Griffin's nostrils flared in a manner that I normally would have found enticing, but now I just viewed with sadness.

This wasn't a battle I would win standing in the library while the taste of him still lingered on my lips.

"Thank you for escorting me home," I said, giving his fingers a little squeeze before releasing his hand. "And for everything else. It was enlightening."

His hands closed around my shoulders, his voice low and urgent. "You are playing a game with adversaries who will show you no mercy, Alex. Do not doubt that they will win, no matter the cost to you, to Helena, and to all the women involved in your group."

Ire mingled with the warm, sated feeling from our lovemaking; for a few moments, I wasn't sure which emotion would gain the upper hand. In the end, it was humor that saved me. I kissed him on the tip of his nose and said, "Thank you for your warning, but I have no fear about any danger befalling us."

The muscles in his jaw flexed a couple of time. "It would please me if you did not take part in the march."

"A great many things would please me," I said with a little smile, one that made me feel like a cat who had just eaten an entire dairy's worth of cream, "up to, and including, seeing you naked in my bed, but alas, if wishes were horses, and all that. I appreciate your warning, and will make sure that I take every precaution to safeguard myself at the march tomorrow, but if you are asking me to cancel it, I'm afraid the answer is no."

He snarled a rude word under his breath, then rubbed a hand over the lower half of his face before saying, "There's nothing I can say to make you change your mind?"

"No," I said, watching when he obviously struggled with his temper. The fearful part of my mind had me stepping back a pace, but unlike the only other man in my life, he simply threw a glare at me, then spun around and stalked out of the room, slamming the door behind him.

I touched it, still feeling the remnants of his anger, marveling that although he was clearly furious with me, he hadn't so much as spat out an invective. I turned to lean against the door, the cool wood of it contrasting with my still-heated flesh, marveling at a man who had such powerful emotions, yet did not use them to harm others. Despite the moment of pain, he had been nothing but gentle with me, and I knew then that I was right to trust him.

"Now if he could only see the rightness of the Union," I told the empty room. Was my love doomed even before it was requited? Were a few stolen moments together between arguments all we were to have?

"Enough of this." I shook myself and went upstairs to bed.

TEN

The sun was out the day after the pessary insertion—the experience of which I refuse to recount, since it was unpleasant until I demanded a strong pain medication, which the doctor reluctantly provided me—reminding me how lovely the sky could be when freshly washed with blue.

Helena was waiting for me in a mouth-watering kingfisher blue walking skirt and matching coat that once again put my ensemble to shame. Her radiant smile greeted me as we clasped each other's hands like excited schoolgirls.

"What a fine day for a march," she exclaimed happily. "And what a lovely skirt! The color matches your eyes."

"Thank you." I hesitated. Fortunately, I was feeling no further ill effects of the experience the day before, and was very much looking forward to telling Griffin that I was once again in control of my fate. "Are you sure you're willing to go through with this? After last night's display, I doubt if your family would be pleased with your participation."

She waved off my warning. "Wasn't that exciting last night? I couldn't believe the bravery of those women to march into the middle of the opera!"

"Yes, they were brave, but I believe they could have chosen a different event and manner to protest. I am sure Maggie Greene was behind it."

Helena looked down at her hands for a moment, her lovely face clouded. "Alex, I owe you an apology about yesterday morning. I acted foolishly and ignored your warnings. I don't know what came over me, but I know I won't do it again. Thank you for being there with me."

"I have to ask you one question, and then we will let the subject drop. Did you know your brothers would be at the club?"

She nodded her head, worrying her gloves. "Maggie asked when Harold would be at his club, and I mentioned they were having a vote about a troublesome member. She thought that would be a good time to have our protest. Griffin seldom visits it, but because of the vote..." Her voice trailed off.

"I see. Never mind." I took her arm as we walked towards the gathering women. "It is a sorry person who cannot learn from her mistakes. Now, as for last night, while I applaud the intentions and bravery it took to demonstrate at the opera, I am opposed to disruptive methods such as the militants used."

"It must have been beastly for you with Harold being so rude. Were your aunt and uncle offended?"

"Shocked more than offended, I believe."

"I hope they paid no heed to what Harold said." She looked at me from the corner of her eye. "Griffin left shortly after you did... You didn't see him, by any chance?"

"Helena, you need not be coy with me. I am sure your brother told you he accompanied me home."

"Oh, no, I wasn't being coy, I assure you. Griffin told me nothing last night, except—" She smiled. "He was throwing things around his study and muttering something about you when I went in to say goodnight."

It was inevitable. I blushed. The feeling of being held in his arms, our bodies joined, wrapped in ecstasy, had quickly become my most cherished memory.

"There is nothing really I can tell you. I left early after the disgraceful scene. Griffin met me outside, and he kindly accompanied me home."

"Ah," she said, still smiling. "I wonder he was in such a curious mood, one moment elated, the next frustrated. You didn't argue with him?"

I cleared my throat and watched a clutch of children skip by. "We had a discussion, yes. You know how unreasonable he is about the cause. He may have interpreted the discussion as an argument."

"I'm sure that's it." She frowned briefly as she watched the Union leaders consult with one another. "The oddest thing happened this morning. I was passing the telephone room, and I thought I heard Harold mention something about the march today…" Her voice trailed off as the leaders beckoned us forward. "Look, I believe they are starting."

A short, energetic woman in her thirties passed among us, distributing *Votes For Women* sashes to those who did not possess one. Helena and I each obtained a sash, and I couldn't help but notice the excitement of the march brought color and animation to her usually pale cheeks.

"This is a truly a glorious moment. To be here with our sisters in bondage, marching down Parliament Street side by side, proud to be women, proud to strike a blow against tyranny, proud to be a part of this noble cause."

I smiled and said softly, "You really are a romantic."

"We both are," she said with a little squeeze to my arm. "After all, that's what makes our friendship so strong. Without you as my sister in suffrage, I would be lost. It is you I have to thank for unshackling me from the bonds of my slavery!"

"Good lord, you *have* been reading the pamphlets." I laughed at her dramatic speech.

"My dear friends," Mrs. Heywood said, drawing our attention. "We are about to undertake a great protest. Our march today to the Houses of Parliament will go down in history as one of the greatest demonstrations against male tyranny."

Helena nudged me, almost dancing with excitement.

"You will be able to tell your daughters of your courageous fight for your freedom, for *their* freedom. Do not give in, no matter how dangerous or difficult the battle is. Stand tall! Stand strong! Stand firm for your rights!"

The inspiring words enthralled me until I wondered if Helena had heard correctly. Since my notebook hadn't reached Lord Sherringham's hands, if he really *had* said something about today's march, there could be only one person from whom he could have acquired the details—Griffin.

"We are women of the twentieth century. No longer are we bound to the rules and laws of our grandmothers—our future can be one of equality, but to obtain that future, we must be willing to work."

My heart sank. What happened last night wasn't as profoundly important to Griffin as it was to me—men being what they are—but somehow, I had thought he differed from other men, superior to them, trustworthy where others were not.

"No," I whispered to myself. "He *is* different. He wouldn't do this to us."

"Our path will not be easy, it may not even seem to go anywhere, but along it we must tread if we are to secure for ourselves and our children those basic rights denied our sex for so long."

The surrounding women cheered and applauded Mrs. Heywood, but I ceased to hear as conflicting emotions swelled within me. Did our intimacy indicate Griffin had deep feelings for me, or was I just a pleasant diversion to be used and discarded when he tired of me? I found it impossible to believe he would betray us, but if his brother had the information about the march, where else could it have come from?

"Today we will present before the House of Lords a petition containing ten thousand two hundred signatures. As we march, you will, under no circumstances, respond to any comments or jeers from the crowd, nor will you commit any acts of violence, such as throwing stones. Stay in formation until the deputation to the House of Lords has returned, at which time we shall continue the march to Westminster Abbey, where we will hold a brief rally and disband."

"I won't believe it," I told myself. "There has to be another explanation."

"Pardon?" Helena leaned in to whisper. "I didn't hear what you said."

"Nothing important," I said slowly, unwilling to continue my unpleasant train of thought. I reminded myself that at last I was involved, part of the cause and taking action with the others. I needed to focus on that, not the worries of my heart. "They're forming up. Shall we take our places?"

Horses, carriages, and motorcars moved out of our way when we marched as a group down the middle of the street. The passers-by tossed the usual taunting and slurs at us as we passed, but we ignored them. Several women were singing a new suffrage song, and although I didn't know the lyrics, I kept a smile on my face as I hummed along with the others. In no time, we came to a halt in front of Parliament.

Unfortunately, the local police had the same idea.

Several ranks of constables had formed a blockade across the front of Parliament. When the deputation of three women approached the constables, showing them the petitions and asking for admission, they were rudely pushed back and summarily refused.

"Oh, dear. This looks somewhat ominous," I told Helena as we exchanged glances, my spirits sinking. "This many policemen... Perhaps I was hasty in dismissing Griffin's warning. These men look as if they would have little mercy."

We stood together, watching silently as the deputation continued to plead with the police. My thoughts were dark as a crowd gathered.

"Surely they cannot arrest us for simply marching down the street?" I asked Helena. "We have committed no violence, nor performed any illegal act."

Her face was pale as she watched the Union officers arguing with the constables. "I can't see how they could arrest us. We are being peaceable and orderly."

"Oh, no!" Suddenly, a cheer went up from the gathering crowd. Their arms pinned behind them, the three members of the deputation were pushed through the crowd toward a row of police conveyances. Cries of concern and distress broke out in our group, and several members rushed forward to help. Without warning, Helena and I found ourselves pushed from behind up against the wall of constables.

Details about the brutal treatment we suffered that day at the hands of the police are common knowledge, but I can't read them without memories rising, ones I would sooner forget. My old fear gripped me when I saw policemen attacking women with a brutality that I knew well. And then the nightmare became all too real when a constable grabbed me and wrenched my arms backwards before hauling me toward the police vans. I went limp, as I always did in that situation, until I saw Helena struggling with another constable. I tried to tell her to not fight him, but the shrieks and screams from the other women drown out my warning.

To my relief, we were flung into the police vans.

"Thank god," I said on a sob, crawling over another woman to get to where Helena had been thrown as well.

"Thank god for what?" Her hair tumbled down about her shoulders, her was gown torn, and tears streaked her now-dirty cheeks.

"The beatings stop once the confinement starts," I said without thinking, moving aside when two more suffragettes were tossed toward us.

"What are you talking about? Did that constable beat you? Are you hurt?"

"No," I said, and clung to her when she hugged me tightly. "I'm fine. What about you?"

"I'm not hurt either." She hiccuped with the result of tears.

I wanted badly to tell her it would be all right, but couldn't say more than, "I tried to tell you not to fight, but I don't think you heard me."

She shook her head, her frail body trembling violently against me as the police hurled another woman into the van. The doors slammed shut, and we were left in darkness. The only sounds audible were that of gentle sobbing and groans.

"Alex, what are we going to do?" Helena asked me softly.

"I wish I knew." I reminded myself that I had survived worse, and to my amazement, the fear eased. "We'll just have to see what we're charged with."

We were driven to the local police station, where our pitiful group was herded into a room. Helena held fast to me as we were escorted into the police station, then brought forward to be interviewed.

"Name?" a burly constable asked.

I gave it to him, as well as Mabel's address.

"Husband's name?"

"I'm not married."

The constable dismissed me without a second glance and turned his attention to Helena. The police facility was overwhelmed with our numbers, and I later found out that many women had been sent to other districts.

They sent our group of ten to share a hideous room with six wooden cots, no blankets, and I suspect many vermin.

After the noise of the march and subsequent arrests, the women in our cell were quiet—stunned, like myself, many of them bearing scratches and bruises, but none of us were hurt seriously. A few shared a bed; others sat on the floor, the very pictures of dejection.

Two hours after the march began, Helena and I sat on a bed together, comforting one another as best we could. I had fully expected that she would become hysterical in such a situation, but once again she surprised me.

"Don't worry, dearest Alex," she said, attempting to comfort me. "Griffin will have us out in no time. I told that police constable who interviewed us who I was and to contact Griffin for our release."

The woman in the bed next to ours lifted her head. Helena gasped in surprise at her face. The bruised jaw and a small trickle of dried blood gave the appearance of a battle-weary warrior; I recognized her as a devoted suffragette who had been arrested a year ago for attacking a policeman.

"Release you?" The woman's voice pierced the room. "You can't ask for release—it's our duty to serve the sentence, for it is only through our martyrdom that we will achieve our goal. This is our chance to protest through deed, not through mere words. Imprisonment is a fact that cannot be disputed or wiped from the record."

I will admit my spirits dropped even lower at those words. We could not, in good faith, abandon our sisters now and expect to be welcomed back at our convenience. I slid a glance toward Helena, convinced she would never hold up under such a strain as prison would afford, and also worried about what my family would say. Mabel was due to arrive home the following day. How would she take the news that her sister had been sent to prison for participation in a suffrage march? My stomach lurched at the thought of it.

There was very little talking during the day and night that followed; when there was talk, it was mainly by the women who had first-hand knowledge of life in prison.

"Your sisters before you have all committed themselves to a hunger strike. They have sworn a solemn oath that they will not eat until they are released from their unjust imprisonment," one woman said.

"I've heard a rumor that hunger strikers are horribly abused," Helena whispered to me, her expression stark.

A little tremor shook me until I got it controlled. I was no stranger to going without food, but thought such horrors were behind me. I pushed aside the memory of the endless, gnawing hunger, and reminded myself that I had wanted to belong to this group—now I must heed their wisdom.

"The Union is fighting to have our sisters labeled as political prisoners rather than common criminals, but the government refuses to listen to reason," another suffragette explained. "You see now why it is so important that we continue our protests, whether jailed or free."

The warders brought in the evening meal, a repulsive gray stew that we all refused. Even if I hadn't wished to honor the hunger strike, I'd never have eaten such unhealthy food.

How Helena and I made it through that long night, I can't honestly say. We cried, hugged each other for support, and slept very little. The other women were in similar situations, worried about their families and friends who would, in turn, be horrified at their imprisonment. Uppermost in our minds, however, was what would happen when we were brought before the magistrate.

Morning came at last, and we were taken, unwashed and bedraggled, before the Thames Police Court, where we were charged with the crime of assault upon a policeman. I stared around the court as suffragette after suffragette was brought before the bench, charged, interviewed briefly, then sentenced.

"Courage," I whispered to Helena as she gripped my hand, feeling myself oddly bereft of any emotion but exhaustion. She squeezed my fingers in response.

When my turn before the magistrate came, I pled not guilty, but could not make any statement or ask questions. I received the standard fine of half a crown. Acting in accordance with my fellow suffrage workers, I refused to pay the fine and was sentenced to three days in jail. The jailers took me away before I could see Helena brought up, but later she told me her experience had been similar.

Those of us who had not been arrested before were sent back to the foul cell from which we had emerged, while the other women—the ones who had been previously arrested in service of the cause—were sent on to prison for longer sentences.

"If you behave yourselves, I'll let you keep your clothing," the wardress told our motley group. Two of the women struggled and refused to comply with her demand we return to our cell. They were taken to separate cells where they were stripped of their dresses and left to sit in their chemises.

"We can be devoted to the cause and still maintain our dignity," I told Helena when she looked at me with wild eyes as the two were dragged away screaming and kicking. "We will cooperate with the officials."

And we did. The wardress allowed us to stay together in our cell, where we were later joined by two other women who were also scared, worried, and didn't wish to precipitate any further trouble.

Our thoughts that day were understandably dark. Mine were particularly so, for I carried the additional burden of having involved an innocent girl in a situation with grave ramifications. Sick with worry what my family and Helena's would go through when they learned we were imprisoned, I'm not ashamed to admit that fleeting doubts about involvement with the cause rose.

"It looks fine on paper," I said quietly to Helena. "But when you sit on a filthy wooden plank, sharing a chamber pot with three other women, with no hope of release for two more days, no food, and no water to wash yourself, your perspective changes."

Helena was curled up at the bottom of my cot, trying to comb her disheveled hair with her fingers. She glanced at the other two women, but they appeared to be sleeping. "Do you think we should give up the cause?"

"I don't know," I answered, aware of the lines of strain around her mouth. I had the feeling Helena was maintaining a tight control of herself, only just keeping from indulging in a fit of hysterics. "I still believe in the right of women to vote. I still believe in the Women's Suffrage Union, but this... Well, I just can't see how being dirty and miserable for three days is going to further the cause. The police and public won't respect us any more for it, will they?"

"I think they might—if they knew how we were abused, that is. Perhaps we could interest a newspaper in our experiences?"

I shook my head, too tired, confused, and scared to reason it out.

By afternoon, I was also exceedingly hungry and bored with my own dark thoughts. Helena and one of the other women were sleeping, and conversation with our remaining cellmate had proved disappointing. I was mentally writing a strongly worded letter to *The Times* about our treatment at the hands of the police when the wardress opened our cell.

"St. John and Whitney, you are to come with me to the Inspector's office."

Surprised and worried, we followed her through a maze of corridors to the Inspector's room, Helena in front of me as the wardress stepped aside. She paused in the doorway briefly before flinging herself forward with a glad cry. My vision was blocked by the wardress who entered after her, but I assumed the cause of Helena's joy to be her brother.

I wondered briefly how Griffin had affected our freedom and toyed with the idea of refusing to leave before my time was served, but that thought vanished quickly. I had enough of imprisonment and looked forward to going home, even if it meant having to listen to Griffin's lecture about the folly of ignoring his advice.

Relief flooded me as I peered around the wardress into the room. It *was* Griffin that Helena held so fiercely. I'm ashamed to admit that, even in that horrible place, under such excruciating circumstances, it filled me with jealousy to watched Helena cling to him. I knew just how strong his arms were and how safe I felt in them. I envied Helena her protector.

"You, wardress!" Blinking back a few tears, I turned toward the strident voice only to see Lady Sherringham being escorted down the hallway. "Who is that woman standing there? She looks familiar."

I twirled around in the other direction and scurried in a most cowardly fashion to a chair a short distance down the hall. I had little hope she wouldn't recognize me, but at least I could keep out of her way. After a day of imprisonment with little sleep and suffering the results of a horrible assault, I was in no shape to withstand Lady Sherringham's venomous attack.

I put my head in my hands and watched through my fingers as she entered the Inspector's office, only to reemerge a few seconds later with a reluctant Helena in tow. Helena looked for me, offered a weak smile over her shoulder, and allowed herself to be walked briskly away.

I closed my fingers around my eyes with the thought of what she would have to endure from her sister-in-law and wondered idly if she wouldn't be better off in prison. My musings were brought to a quick end by the feeling of strong fingers on mine. I took my hands from my eyes and looked up, trying to gauge the situation.

"Hello, Griffin." He stood like that for a moment, holding my hands in his, looking down at me from what seemed a very distant height. "We thought you might come. Helena was sure of it. I thought perhaps you might like to let us stew for a bit."

He said nothing, just heaved a big sigh and pulled me to my feet and into his arms. I would like to say I pushed away from this unseemly position in such a public place, but I did the opposite. I buried my face into his collar and clung to him tightly, kissing his neck and his jaw, turning my head until I found his mouth. His lips were gentle, almost tentative, as if seeking reassurance. I slid my hands up his chest and opened my mouth to him, my heart beating wildly as he stroked my tongue, building passion deep within me.

His hands were gentle on me, touching my hair, my back, my face. I wanted to stay like that forever—loved, protected, wanted. Instead, he pulled away from me and, with an unreadable expression, marched me out of the building and into a cab.

Mullin tried to say something to me when we arrived home, but before he got more than a greeting out, Griffin hustled me through the hall to the library, slamming the

door shut with an echo that I knew would resound through-
out the house.

He stood staring at me for a few minutes, breathing
hard, his hair looking as if he'd been running his fingers
through it.

I was mildly annoyed at that. I wanted to be the one
with my fingers in his hair.

"You are trying to drive me insane, woman. Admit it."
His kisses had a fire in them I had not experienced before.
They were everywhere, bruising my lips, burning my eyelids,
and branding my neck. "You drive me mad with desire. Tell
me you are trying to make me insane."

Waves of passion swelled within me, setting my skin
alight and making my heart pound although I very much
wanted a bath and an opportunity to brush my teeth.

"Griffin, please," I begged, returning his passionate em-
braces with a fervor I didn't know was possible. I buried my
fingers in his hair as I pulled him to me, the hunger within
me frightening in its intensity. "Please…"

"Please what?" he asked, kissing the answer off my lips.

"Please don't stop," I breathed out, slipping my hands
down his back to his wonderful derriere.

"I was mad with worry," he growled as he nipped my
earlobe, his hands cupping my breasts. The warmth of his
palms seeped through the three layers of my clothing and
scorched my flesh.

"So was I," I answered, desire overwhelming me as I
tasted his mouth. The feel of his hard body crushed against
mine sent my senses reeling. As I breathed in his masculine
scent, shivers of sensual delight rippled down my back. The
power of my desire was literally breathtaking, leaving me
giddy and helpless against the ache that threatened to con-
sume me. He was everywhere, everything to me. I felt him
in my blood, heating me to a fever pitch. Deep, primitive
urges cascaded until my head swam.

He looked deep into my eyes, his own a hot, burning
brand of passion and need. "I don't know if this is madness

or rapture, but I can't stop thinking about being with you. Being in you."

"I had the pessary installed two days ago," I said on a gasp as he lifted me up and pressed me back against the wall, pulling my legs up and wrapping them around his waist. "You needn't use the rubber device on yourself. Touch me, Griffin. *Now!*"

The sound of cloth tearing was muted as he ripped my drawers off, and then he was there, hot and hard and surging into me with sure, strong strokes, filling me, *thrilling me* with his touch.

"You're so hot," he groaned against my mouth. "So hot. I'll never have enough of you."

Words were meaningless sounds on my lips as I kissed him, kissed his jaw, curling my tongue into his ear as he pounded into me, my hips lifting to meet each thrust. I yanked his collar off, tearing at his tie until I bared his throat, that delicious strong throat, and scattered kisses along it as tension built within me.

"Ah, sweetheart, you're so good. You're everything I need." He moaned as I flexed my legs, nibbling that sweet spot beneath his ear. "I can't take it. I can't stand any more. Oh, God, Alex, tell me you're ready. Tell me you're with me."

"Always," I whispered against his lips, sinking within them to fire his frenzied emotions even higher. "I will never leave you."

He slammed me against the wall, his body moving in short, hard, fast strokes that matched our breath, his eyes wide with rapture as his muscles strained, my body answering by tightening around him as he sent us both flying to the stars.

He stood holding me for long minutes, the wood behind my back as hard as the man pressed against my front, our chests rising and falling in desperate attempts to get air, our hearts beating wildly. I let my legs slip from him, holding tight to him when they refused to bear my weight. He leaned against me, still struggling for breath, his voice low and deep, resonating deep within me.

"You infuriating woman."

I looked at him with surprise. This wasn't the lover's speech I was expecting. Instead, it had the hint of the lecture I expected earlier.

"You exasperating, impossible... lovely woman."

I smiled at the last words, but it was a short-lived smile. Griffin quickly adjusted his trousers as I made what repairs I could to my drawers, halting when he wrapped his hands around my upper arms.

"Do you have any idea what hell I've gone through the last day?" He shook me slightly to emphasize his words. "Do you know how worried I was?"

I tried to raise my hands, but my arms were pinned down tightly. The door to the library opened. "Are you all right, miss? I thought I heard—"

One look at Griffin's face was all it took. Mullin spun around and closed the door quietly behind him.

"I'm sorry—" I started, but was cut off.

"What were you thinking?" he asked on a growl. "You could have been seriously hurt. They could have hurt Helena. You could both be in prison!" He stopped, let go of my arms, and sat down on the leather couch, one hand over his eyes. "You are the most maddening, unreasonable, delectable woman I have ever met."

I sat next to him and placed my hand on his, pressing a little kiss to his ear. "I truly do appreciate the trouble you've gone to. I know my actions have caused you much grief, and in the future, I will do my best to keep Helena from any further participation—"

He snatched his hand away from mine and looked at me in horror. "Do you have the audacity to tell me—do you mean to say that you—that you can even *consider* further involvement with this group—" He choked to a stop.

I brushed a strand of hair back off his brow. "Of course I will consider further involvement. What happened today was a bizarre mischance. There's no reason I shouldn't take part in future events."

He glared at me, then took a deep breath, and allowed his shoulders to relax. "Do you not see," he began in a more reasonable tone, "that there are… *feelings*—"

"Yes, there are feelings," I said slowly, more than a little adrift regarding what point he was trying to make. "But I am a New Woman, and you are a modern-thinking gentleman, and what we do in private can be of no concern to anyone else. If you are worried about my reputation, it doesn't bother me at all."

He ran his hand along the back of his neck, his jaw working a few times before he said, "No, damn it, I'm not talking about that. Or maybe I am. I don't know. You have everything so twisted up, I can't tell what I'm thinking anymore."

I realized then that I loved him. I wasn't just falling in love, or in lust, or even fascinated with him—no, I'd fallen tip over teakettle in love with the man, and he knew it, and now he expected me to make a declaration. "Griffin, if you are worried about me putting demands on you because I asked you to be my lover, I can assure you I won't. I understand that, to a man, the act of lovemaking can give physical pleasure without emotional engagement."

"Damn it, woman, what I feel for you is not just lust!" he exploded. His hair, an unruly tangle, now stood on end.

"Oh. I'm thrilled to hear that. You, too, are more than just a lustful pleasure to me." I chewed my lip, hesitating to put anything more into words.

"Alex," he growled out again, pulling me to him, taking my chewed-upon lip into his mouth. I was just about to reciprocate when one of the library doors was flung open, two golden-haired girls romping into the room, accompanied by two large, reddish-brown dogs. The dogs leaped upon Griffin with a display of tongues and tails, while the girls threw themselves upon me.

"Auntie, Auntie, we're home!" they shrieked together, quickly abandoning me to chase the dogs.

"So I see," I said, looking with dismay at Griffin.

"Alex, my dear, we have had the most tedious journey. Amanda was seasick the entire way—" Mabel walked in and kissed me on the cheek, then paused when she saw Griffin. She smiled and held out her hand to him. "How do you do? I am Mabel Garner, Alex's sister."

"Mabel, this is Mr. Griffin St. John. He is… a friend," I finished lamely, feeling Mabel wasn't quite ready for my New Womanhood just yet.

Griffin shook Mabel's hand, then sat down again at her request.

"Forgive my daughters, Mr. St. John," she said, shooing them away. "We have been at sea for the last four weeks and they are a bit energetic. Oh, there you are, Joshua."

Two men stepped into the room, one of whom was Joshua, Mabel's husband. He was a round, short man with a pleasant countenance, and he held out his arms to me when he saw me.

"Alex, my dear! How long it's been since we've seen you!" I hugged him, kissing him on the cheek with great affection. He waved his hand toward his companion. "And you know Robert Hunter."

"Robert?" I said, turning to the second man. "Can it be? Robert?"

He stood behind Joshua, grinning at me. It *was* Robert! His skin was a dark tan, his blond hair whitened by the sun, but his cornflower-blue eyes were the same as when we were children. I squealed and threw myself into his arms, hugging him as tight as I could. He laughed and spun me around once before setting me back on the floor.

"Alex, you haven't changed a bit." He surveyed me from head to toe. "Well, I amend that statement—you have changed, and for the better."

I blushed and clung to his arm, gazing at him with admiration. Not a tall man, he was slight of build, but strong.

"You have changed, though, Robert." I touched the end of his golden mustache. "That's new."

"Alex!"

I turned to see why Mabel was outraged. Griffin stood awkwardly behind her.

"Oh, I'm so sorry," I said and introduced Joshua to Griffin.

"And this"—I grabbed Robert's arm and led him to Griffin—"is an old friend, Robert Hunter. Robert and I grew up together. Next to Emma, he's my oldest and dearest friend and one whom I haven't seen for many years."

The men shook hands while I beamed at first at Robert, then at Griffin, delighted that the two men I loved most were together. Griffin was pleasant, but I noticed he watched Robert closely.

"I met Mabel and Mr. Garner in Joburg," Robert said, turning to hold my hands. "I was on my way back to England when they convinced me to delay my trip and travel with them."

"Now, Robert, let's not have any more of that discussion. You will stay here with us," Mabel told him before saying to me, "He wants to go to a hotel. Come, girls, I want you to wash up. It was very nice meeting you, Mr. St. John. Will we have the pleasure of having you dine with us one night?"

Griffin bowed stiffly. "Thank you, I would enjoy that."

He excused himself and started for the door.

"I will be back in a moment," I told Robert and hurried after Griffin. I caught his arm at the front door and stopped him.

"I am sorry about the interruption," I said with a wry smile. "I want to thank you again for having me released. I will always be grateful to you for your kindness."

"No gratitude is necessary," he said coldly, not looking at me.

I gazed at him with dismay. One minute he was making love to me with a fire that would put hell to shame, the next he wouldn't even look at me. Who could explain the minds of men?

He stepped forward to leave, then apparently thinking better of it, turned and looked towards the library door. In one swift, violent movement, he gathered me into his arms and kissed the breath right out of my lungs. Releasing me just as quickly, he left.

I stood with one hand on the door, the other around my bruised ribs, out of breath and surprised.

"Will someone," I asked the empty hall, "explain to me what goes on in the mind of that man?"

The sound of my unanswered echo sent me running upstairs, where I had a quick wash and changed my dress.

ELEVEN

We were in the drawing room after breakfast the next morning when Helena came to see me. Mabel was talking about South Africa, describing the many trials (as she called them) with which life had forced her to deal. I gave little notice to her chatter, paying attention only when she described some place of beauty. She had turned the discussion to my attendance at the evening's masquerade ball when Mullin announced Helena.

I jumped up at the sight of her unhappy face. "Helena! Whatever is the matter? Have you been crying?"

She looked with distress at Mabel. I introduced her, and Mabel, with a knowing glance, excused herself to look over the household accounts that I had so long neglected. I gave her a grateful smile as she left. Whatever else her faults, Mabel had a kind heart.

Helena gulped a few times, then grasped my hands in hers. "Oh, Alex, I've had the most awful row with Griffin. He had a terrible argument earlier with Harold about you—"

"About *me*?" I interrupted, astounded.

"Yes. Harold…it was horrible, and Griffin said terrible things to him. I've never seen them so angry with one another."

"What were they arguing about?"

"Nothing! Everything! You, me… Oh Alex, Griffin has forbidden me to take part in the candidate's meeting next week. He has forbidden me to attend any more of the Union's meetings, and—" She choked to a stop. "He has forbidden me to see you anymore! I had to tell them I was going to my costume fitting to come here now. What shall we do?"

She sobbed uncontrollably as I did my best to calm her. I sat her down and ordered strong coffee, feeling we could both use it.

"I have to say that I am not surprised, although dismayed by Griffin's attitude. However, after the events of the past few days, I can hardly blame him for not wishing you to involve yourself with another protest. I think it would be best if you stayed away from the candidate's meeting at Exeter Hall."

She dabbed her eyes with a lovely and completely useless lace handkerchief. "You will be there, won't you?"

I hesitated, thinking of my family. "Yes, I will," I said slowly, trying to put into words my conflicting emotions. "Griffin's anger…to be honest, I can understand some of it. He has a point regarding the potential danger that could result from demonstrations. I certainly don't wish to repeat our recent experience, and yet, I support the Union cause whole-heartedly. But you are different. It is much harder on you, given your family's opinion."

"If you are attending the meeting, I will be there as well," she said firmly and wiped her nose discreetly. "There is… something else I must tell you."

"Oh?" A sick feeling crept over me.

"Griffin came home last night in a terrible temper. I've never seen him so angry, so cold. He frightened me. I couldn't find out what had happened, but oh, Alex, he's planning on leaving! He wants to sail in three days for Brazil. He even refused to go to the St. Alban's ball tonight after I told him you would be there."

"Oh, that annoying man," I said softly to myself. "That annoying, adorable man."

Helena clutched my hand. "Alex, you have to stop him. You're the only one he will listen to."

I gave a hard little laugh. "On the contrary, at this moment, I fear I am *persona non grata*."

She looked at me curiously. "Why do you say that?"

"It's a long story—"

I stopped as the door opened. Robert stepped in, saw Helena, and apologized. Or rather, he started to, but one look at Helena sitting in a canary chiffon day dress with ruffles at the neck and sleeves seemed to bewitch him. He stammered and finally dragged his eyes off her to me.

"I was about to visit some friends." His eyes went back to Helena. "But if you wished for me to stay…?"

I watched him with interest. "I do, and more. I'd like you to meet my dear friend Lady Helena St. John. Helena, this is Robert Hunter, an old childhood friend who is staying with us."

Helena blushed prettily and held out her hand.

"Helena is Griffin's sister," I said, wondering if Griffin was truly so angry that he would abandon our new arrangement. Blast the man, I'd have to be the one to make him see reason since he was clearly feeling slighted.

"How fascinating," he breathed out, never once taking his eyes off of her.

"Yes, she is," I said, prodding Robert. "And I'm sure you'll see her again, but right now you have a call to make."

Robert blinked at me. "I do?"

"So you said." I made little shooing motions, eager to get rid of him.

"Ah yes, I have a call I must make." He gazed longingly at Helena. "I hope to see you soon, Lady Helena."

I pushed Robert out of the room and turned to find Helena wearing the same dreamy expression. Sitting beside her, I asked, "Did Griffin say anything else to you last night?"

"Last night?" Her thoughts were evidently a million miles away.

"Yes, last night. The evening we most recently had. *That* last night."

"No." She sighed happily. "You've known Mr. Hunter for a long time? Does he… is he here with his family?"

"He has no family other than a brother in South Africa," I answered, watching happiness spread across her face.

I could see I wasn't to get any further information out of Helena today, so I gave her a summary of Robert's life, told her I would think of something regarding Griffin, and sent her on her way to her fitting. I hesitated between trying to telephone Griffin or writing him a note, but my own time was at a premium, and I left shortly thereafter to meet Emma for the last fitting of my costume.

"I still think one of your simple Greek outfits would have been lovely," I told her an hour later.

"Yes, but just think how unique this will be," Emma said as I turned for the dressmaker. "There are always Greek women at a costume ball, but how many Scheherazades will there be?"

I had to admit that she had a point. After consultation with a scandalous version of the *Arabian Nights*, not to mention a good deal of money in the form of incentives to Madame Depui, the dressmaker, I had devised a costume made up of golden gauze embroidered with faux precious gems.

"I like the sashes," Emma said approvingly. "Green, blue, and purple—very dashing. But Alex, your midriff! Won't your aunt be scandalized?"

I looked down at the daring two inches of bare midriff peeking through the sashes that swept from my left shoulder to my right hip. "Madame Depui insists it is perfectly suitable."

"Oui," Madame said, adjusting one of the veils that hung from a small, close-fitting cap. "It is perfect the way it is. Very catching to the eye."

"What jewelry will you wear?" Emma asked as I disrobed and changed into my regular clothes.

"Nothing. I think jewelry would detract from it. Thank you, Madame. You will be sure to have the hem raised by this afternoon?"

"Yes, it is minor, the hem. I should have it done in time."

"Excellent." I tipped her generously and invited Emma to take a walk with me in Hyde Park. "I have so many things to tell you. Robert is back from South Africa."

"Robert Hunter? How interesting. I haven't seen him in about ten years."

"He's matured nicely, I think. And is a fair way to being smitten with Helena," I said.

"Really." She pressed me for details. As we strolled to the park, I told her first about Robert and Helena, and then about my own troubles.

"It sounds to me like Mr. St. John is jealous," she said after a few minutes of silent thought. "Is there any reason he should be?"

"Of Robert?" I gave a little shake of my head. "I'm sure you're wrong there, and of course not. He's just angry because I won't immediately roll over and agree to his wishes."

"No, I meant he wouldn't be jealous unless there was some sort of emotional relationship."

"Oh. Well, as to that…" We had reached the park and started across its expanse. I cleared my throat and paused a moment to find the right words. "You know it was my intention to offer Griffin the position of lover."

"Yes."

I glanced at her to see if she was laughing at me. Her face was averted as she leaned over to admire some flowers.

"Well, I offered him the job, and he accepted."

"I see." She turned to me, her smile knowing. "And I take it you approve of him in that role."

"I would have to be mad not to," I said, unable to keep from smiling myself at the memories that threatened to scorch my mind. "I just knew he would have the most outstanding derriere, but it has exceeded even my highest hopes."

She laughed and squeezed my arm. "So you have had your first lover's squabble and now must find your way clear to making up?"

"I would hardly call this our first squabble."

"Perhaps not, but this is the first one where your relationship has entered the fray. I have no advice for you other than to talk to him. I find that most things work themselves out if you just take the effort to talk."

I explained to her the nature of the argument. "It's going to take more than a conversation, I fear. You know how much my involvement with the Union means to me. You know what my emancipation has cost me."

"I know, but does Mr. St. John?" she asked, her head tipped to the side as she considered me.

That made me pause. "What do you mean?"

"I know what being a New Woman means to you because I know what you've suffered. But have you told your Griffin about your past?"

"No," I said slowly. "You know I don't like to dwell on it."

"An understandable sentiment, but in this case, I believe it would be good for him to know just why it's so important for you to feel that you are part of something."

"It's more than just being a part of the cause—" We had reached the edge of Rotten Row and paused to admire the horses as they cantered past.

Just as we were turning away, I noticed a small man in a brown check suit standing at a little distance next to the railing. He turned, his eyes meeting mine, whereupon he smiled, politely tipping his hat in greeting.

"Is it, though?" she asked, and would have continued, but at that moment, connections were made in my poor confused brain.

"The man with the gold tooth!" I gasped. "Or, as I suspect, Mr. William Jones!"

"Who?" Emma's brows pulled together as I dashed over to the man.

"Good day, miss," he said, gold flashing as he spoke.

"It *was*. Would you tell me, please, who you are and why you are following me?"

"Me, miss? Follow you, miss?" He did a credible job of appearing confused, but it did not mislead me.

"Yes, you, sir." I allowed one eyebrow to raise a fraction of an inch.

"I don't know what you're on about, miss. I haven't been following you. I'm just out for a stroll on a lovely morning." He smiled amiably before moving off.

"Who was that?" Emma asked.

"I'm not quite sure, but...Emma, would you mind if we had tea another day?"

"Not at all," she said, giving me a smile. "You go talk to your Griffin. I'm sure things will look better after that."

I didn't correct her, but took off as quickly as I could without drawing attention to myself, hurrying down the side street where I had last seen Mr. Jones.

I caught sight of my quarry a block ahead, rushing to a corner. I ran after him, just in time to see him disappearing into a shop between a bookstore and a Cook's travel bureau.

"There's nothing for it," I told myself and plunged into the store. Blinded by the dimness of the shop after the bright day, I was startled when a voice spoke directly behind my right shoulder.

"May I... *serve* you in some way, madam?"

It was a shop clerk, looking more than a little astonished at my appearance.

"Thank you, no. I'm just browsing." I strolled nonchalantly over to a counter and prepared to interest myself in its contents. Once rid of the clerk's attention, I would casually work my way through the rest of the shop in search of my prey.

"Good lord," I cried, staring in horrified shock at the products of an intimate and thoroughly masculine nature held in the case. "Does that do what I think it's supposed to do?"

"Erm..." The clerk squirmed next to me.

I looked closer, reading the label with astonishment. "It does! It is supposed to increase the size of a gentleman's apparatus. Who knew such things existed?"

"Madam—"

"Surely such a procedure must hurt," I exclaimed, peering closely at the item in question. "All that suction cannot be good for one. Have you ever tried it yourself?"

"Eh—"

"I can't imagine how it could be effective. Perhaps if I could just see it demonstrated. I would get one for my lover, but he is quite sufficient in that regard."

"Madam, please!" The clerk looked like he was about to faint. Unfortunately, the second clerk arrived and was duly scandalized by my presence.

"This is a gentlemen's outfitter," he said, hustling me to the door. "Ladies are not allowed in the shop!"

"I don't see why not." I argued, but it was in vain. The door was closed firmly in my face.

I stood in thought, watching the shop. I could see the dim figures of the clerks move to the rear and partook of the opportunity. Casually, I leaned against the glass, ignoring a display of men's apparel shading my eyes as I peered into the shop.

I am not a skittish creature, but the sudden blast of a raucous motorcar horn being blown in proximity had me jumping. Unfortunately, I collided with a person as I did so, but was righted before I could fall. I turned to thank my benefactor, only to find myself face-to-face with Griffin.

I blushed. He scowled. We both looked at the motorcar, which was proceeding down the street, making a horrible racket.

"Do you need assistance?" Griffin asked with a coolness that seemed to dim the sun.

"Thank you, no," I said with dignity, gesturing toward the shop. "I'm perfectly fine."

He glanced at the items displayed in the shop window and back at me. "Doing a little shopping?"

I colored deeper at the inference. "No, of course not. I was looking for a man."

"Just one?" One of his glossy eyebrows rose in a manner that made Inner Alex want to swoon, and Outer Alex want to grab his head and kiss the mockery right off his eyebrows.

"Yes, just the one." I told my inner self to behave herself. "A man with a gold tooth, as a matter of fact. He has been following me for days now." The expression of incredulity that he wore would have led to an excellent exit line, but I didn't have time for unnecessary drama in my life. "Griffin, I need to talk to you."

"I'm afraid I have an appointment," he said, bowing before turning on his heel and marching off.

I wanted to yell after him he couldn't run from me for long, but there were too many people around, and although I had gained much courage, I didn't feel up to courting more scorn from strangers.

Robert was in the library when I returned home, staring moodily into the fire.

"What happened to you?" I asked, slumping into the nearest chair regardless of manners.

"The contact I hoped would be interested in hiring me has reconsidered. But you look downright glum. Is all well with you?"

"Nothing is well other than you and the family being home," I said, giving in to dark thoughts about what I'd do if Griffin was so willing to throw aside our blossoming relationship. Robert was caught up in his own misery, so after a depressing half hour, I went to prepare for the ball.

TWELVE

Later, as I was dressing, I told Annie about my plan for her to have a cottage on my father's estate while she had her confinement. When she came back to work, as she professed she wanted to, the servants would know nothing of what happened.

"Are you certain you want to leave the child with your sister? I'm sure we could work out a way for you to keep the baby with you, although it would mean leaving Mabel's house."

"That's all right, miss. My sister said one more mouth wouldn't make that much difference, and I can visit whenever I like."

I thought the arrangement sounded sad, but Annie was happy, and I had confidence in her family. "What about Mr. Jones? Have you told him?"

"I've written to him, but he won't reply," she responded grimly.

I decided—for the present—not to push her further, but I was determined to see her happily settled. Mulling over a way to achieve this goal, I sat before the dressing table and braided my hair to prepare for donning a black wig purchased from the dressmaker. Certain that red hair was out of place on Scheherazade, I planned to wear the wig and the veils as my disguise, finding the thought of moving about in company completely unknown strangely thrilling.

Annie twined faux pearls through the wig while I played with my braid and tried to work up enough nerve to bring out the item I had purchased earlier. I took a deep breath, opened a drawer, and removed a small black object. Consulting the (somewhat scandalous) *Arabian Nights* I borrowed from Joshua's library, I carefully outlined my eyes with the kohl stick.

"Oh, miss!" Annie gasped. "You look ever so foreign!"

I looked at my heavily ringed eyes. "I don't know about foreign—I certainly look as if I've been up a chimney."

"It's a lovely touch, miss. Do leave it," she said as I made a move to wipe it off. "No one would recognize you with the black wig and the dark eyes."

Anonymity had its charms, so I left the kohl and finished dressing. I stood in front of the mirror, swathed from head to foot in floating veils, the embroidered jewels sparkling, and the long dark tresses of my wig reaching to my waist. I felt exotic and mysterious behind the veils and relished the thought that no one would know who I was.

The walk downstairs to the library was a sensuous experience, the lightweight gauze swinging against my bare legs (Scheherazade didn't wear stockings). I couldn't help but think of Griffin's kisses and touches as the material rippled around me, caressing my skin. Robert grinned and let out a low, long whistle as I came into the library.

Mabel fussed about the sheerness of the material and almost had a fit when she saw my two inches of bare midriff. By the time Uncle Henry called at the front door, Joshua had to physically restrain her from hustling me upstairs and into a sturdier ensemble.

Although his eyebrows went up at my appearance, Henry had nothing but compliments for me as I donned my sapphire velvet coat. "You look charming, my dear, charming."

"Thank you. Are you not going to wear a costume?"

He pulled out an order from his inner pocket and pinned it on his chest. "I shall go as a diplomat."

"And what a very good costume that is," I replied, smiling.

As I entered their carriage, my spirits sank as I beheld the figure of Wellington.

"Mind my ruff, dear," Caroline said as I took my place next to her. She had worked wonders in the short time and was dressed in an Elizabethan costume complete with a large, white ruff, and pearls down to her knees. "I'm supposed to be one of Henry's ancestors, since ours were not as prominent as his."

"Cousin, you are the epitome of beauty. I love you as a redhead, but as a brunette, you will break the heart of every man at the ball. Please promise me the first dance," Freddie cooed.

"If you like. Aunt Caroline, you look lovely, regardless of whose ancestor you are supposed to be. How on Earth did you get the costume made so quickly? It has much more detail than my own, and I had to spend a fortune to have it made in time."

Uncle Henry coughed delicately. "It seems your aunt was planning to go to the ball all along, my dear. She thought it best to spring it on me suddenly, knowing my resistance to such social events."

"I ordered my costume from Messrs. Nathan," Freddie offered, referring to a popular theatrical supplier. "Do you like it? I think I make a dashing Wellington."

"You are, as always, very handsome, Freddie," I told him.

We chatted about Mabel and Joshua on the way and were soon at the St. Alban's townhouse. For a moment, as we walked up the curved drive to the doors, I remembered a week past when I was on the outside of such a ball, trying to chain myself to a fence.

And now I had a lover who was ready to throw me over at a moment's disagreement.

The house was brilliantly lit, the lights gleaming off of sparkling chandeliers and glittering jewels. Great vases of flowers filled the rooms with their heady perfumes, while distant strains of music promised dancing in the ballroom. A babble of conversation rose and fell as guests sauntered down the grand marble staircase into the reception rooms below.

We left the men to shed our coats and inspected our costumes in the ladies' withdrawing room, while maids in black dresses ran back and forth, assisting guests, adjusting costumes, and bringing restorative cups of tea. The costumes themselves were almost overwhelming. Real jewels—not faux ones like I wore—clung to almost every surface. Billowing waves of satins and silks accompanied each movement as women primped before several large mirrors. There were allegorical and historical figures ranging from queens to milkmaids, as well as fantastic creations, which had their inspiration in the fertile imagination of their wearers.

Aunt Caroline and I, each on one of Uncle Henry's arms, sauntered down the curved marble staircase with Freddie following behind. The crush of people was tremendous as we made our way down the reception line, but once we were finally released into the ballroom, I stood back and watched the parade of society before me.

Freddie led me onto the floor for the first dance, attentive as ever, but it was another man who consumed my thoughts. "You've been avoiding me, my sweet cousin."

"Not intentionally," I said, wondering what Griffin would do if I forced him into a conversation. "I've been busy."

"With more of those suffragette activities? My dear, if you must go to them, at least allow me to accompany you. I wish only to protect you and keep you from upsetting yourself."

His objection annoyed me. "I assure you I am in no way upset by the cause. And if you are about to offer for me again, please consider this a refusal."

His eyes glittered with a bright, strange emotion. "You make light of my worries."

I couldn't keep from frowning a little, noting the sharp edges of his words. "No, I'm just assured of my own judgment."

"I can only hope nothing befalls you to shake that confidence, my dearest one. Promise me that should you ever need me, should you ever find yourself in danger, you will seek my help."

I murmured a polite response, and chatting inanely about nothing for the rest of our dance before Freddie returned me to Caroline's side and moved off. I searched the crowd again for Helena, watching everyone from over the top of my veils. Despite the disappointment that Griffin wouldn't be in attendance, I very much looked forward to seeing Helena's reaction to my daring ensemble.

One lady, also dressed as Queen Elizabeth, proceeded past me, followed by eight Yeoman of the Guard, all handsomely clad in scarlet and gold tunics with white ruffs and matching scarlet tights. As the group made its way to an improvised throne, the Yeoman disbanded. One of them, a tall man with light brown hair, came my way.

"Might I request the honor of a dance?" he asked.

I glanced over at my aunt, who was holding court with her bevy of friends, and made a quick scan around the room, but saw no one who would fit Helena's description.

"I would be delighted," I told him and accepted his hand.

"Lieutenant Angus Bell," he said, bowing as he led me onto the floor. "May I say, ma'am, how charming I find your costume?"

The dance was almost as pleasant as the lieutenant himself. He talked about his life in the army, asking me for another dance.

"Thank you, but I feel the need to keep an eye on my aunt."

He glanced at Caroline, clearly amused, but was polite enough to not ask why. "Perhaps later in the evening."

I murmured something vague, and he went on his way. I spent the next hour alternately dancing and watching for Helena. It quickly became apparent to me why I had never sought invitations to such functions, for I had little in common with society and less tolerance for their airs and mindless chatter.

"Honestly, Aunt," I told Caroline in a moment of privacy, "the men all talk about their hunting lodges, horses, or military careers. The women have even less of interest to discuss and seem to focus on who was seen with whom, what they wore, what they were worth, and who their parents were."

"I'm sorry you're not enjoying yourself," she answered, nodding to a passing acquaintance.

I felt guilty at complaining since I'd foisted myself on them. "Ignore me. I'm being out of sorts and petulant."

In an attempt to find diversion, I danced with a German princeling dressed as some character from a Wagnerian opera (I never determined which one), who tried his best to impress me with tales of his bravery and courage. He found me a dull partner and returned me as soon as possible to my aunt. He bowed, clicked his heels, and kissed my hand, followed by the same niceties to Aunt Caroline. As he stepped back, he bumped into an Arab sheikh who approached.

The Arab salaamed before me and asked in a thick accent for the next dance. Bored, I agreed and watched idly as he strode off. The way he walked caught my attention. I took a few steps away from the wall so I could watch him better.

I knew that back. I knew those hips. I knew that delicious curved behind. *Intimately*. There was no doubt about it; it was Griffin, disguised as a sheikh. "It can't be!"

"What can't be, my dear?" Caroline moved over to me, calmly fanning herself as she smiled at people strolling past us.

"That man. The Arab. Did you see him?"

She looked where I indicated. "Not really. Why do you ask?"

"I think it's Griffin. Mr. St. John. But why would he make an appearance here?"

"Why shouldn't he?"

"He told his sister he wasn't coming. And what's more important…" I hesitated a minute, glancing at my aunt.

She smiled.

"You know, don't you?" I asked her.

"There's not much that escapes me, Henry always says."

I sighed and leaned against the wall. "Griffin and I had an argument over my involvement with the Union. He told Helena he wasn't coming to the ball, which is why I'm so surprised he should be here now, asking me to dance. Unless… Oh, Aunt, do you think he recognized me? Prince Heinrich didn't leave me off close to you, did he?"

"Not particularly, no. But I am acquainted with Mr. St. John, and surely he would know me."

"But not me," I said thoughtfully. "Not in this wig and with my face hidden behind the veil. He must not have known who I was."

"If you say so, my dear. But what does that matter? If he asked you to dance, he will soon learn the truth."

"You're right." I chewed on my lip as I considered the matter. "As soon as I speak, he'll know me. What I need is an accent."

"Don't you think that's a little extreme?" Caroline asked.

"Not at all. He had one. He most definitely had an Arab accent when he asked me to dance. Therefore, it's only right I should have one. It's just that I only know one other language."

"I never understood why your mother taught you Russian," Aunt Caroline mused.

"She hoped that someday Mabel and I would meet our relatives."

"I have no desire to go back to the old country," she said with a little click of her tongue.

"I think it would be fascinating. Regardless, I think a Russian accent will do just fine. Please don't be offended, but I'm going to move away from you now, just in case Griffin suspects something."

She nodded, and I moved away, surprising a variety of people whom I didn't know while I chatted my way down the room.

As the music started for the next dance, Griffin came back to claim me, escorting me out to the dance floor. I alternated between outrage that he would invite a strange woman to dance while he was engaged as my lover, and yet, unwilling to reveal myself. It was with a horrible combination of jealousy, newly found love, and a dash of annoyance that I found myself in his arms.

For a moment, I doubted myself. This man had a huge, fierce mustache, and wore a blue and white burnoose, a white blouse, along with full, dark blue silk trousers tucked into long black boots. A length of red satin strapped a scimitar to his waist, and although his disguise couldn't fool me, I was glad for the anonymity of my veil and wig.

I'd let his conversation set the tone. If he knew who I was, then I would try to have a rational conversation about my plans for involvement with the Union. If not...well, I didn't know quite what I'd do then.

"You are Scheherazade?" he asked in a deep voice with a heavy accent.

My heart dropped at the accent. If he knew who I was, he wouldn't try to hide his identity.

"You guessed that well. Yes, I am Scheherazade," I agreed in a close approximation of my cousin Katya's version of English.

His eyes narrowed. "A Scheherazade that is a long way from… Russia?"

"Yes. St. Petersburg. And you, you are a sheikh? Where is your harem?"

The mustache quivered in a manner that indicated a smile, although I couldn't see his mouth beneath it.

He waved a hand toward the reception rooms. "I left them outside, where they wouldn't be in the way."

He replaced his hand lower on my back and touched my bare skin. A jolt of electricity skimmed up my spine, setting my whole body alight. I frowned into his chest to stop the strident clamoring of all my lady parts, parts which very badly wanted to reacquaint themselves with him. "Indeed. Your harem must mean little to you if you keep them outside, like animals."

"They are only women."

I looked up through my lashes into the lovely amber eyes that I would know anywhere, annoyed with his drawled words. "Is that the prevailing attitude towards women where you come from? Do they matter so little?"

"In Arabia, women do as their husbands tell them and don't question the men's wisdom."

"Which is probably why Arabia is sometimes viewed as being less than modern regarding women's rights," I retorted, fuming at his misguided perspective. "Arabs are part of an intelligent, highly cultured society, but about this, I must admit they sadly fail to gain my admiration."

"Could it be, Scheherazade, you would like to have more than one husband?"

"Certainly not!" I replied indignantly. The conversation wasn't going at all as I planned. "In *my* country, women desire the love and respect of only one man. As long as they are treated as equals and respected for qualities other than the physical, they are happy."

The mustache twitched again. "St. Petersburg must have changed since I last visited. I don't remember its society being so liberal," he commented in Russian.

I stared at him for a few seconds, keeping from outright gawking, and sent a mental thank you to my mother for having taught me her ancestral language before I responded in the same. "A good deal has changed, I am sure, since you last visited. Women are taking their rightful place in societies all over the world, not only in St. Petersburg."

He looked startled to hear Russian in reply. Then the mustache twitched and the corners of his eyes crinkled.

We danced without speaking for a few minutes.

"What of the men in your country?" he asked finally, returning to English. "What role would you have them play? Jester to their queen, perhaps?"

The music ended. He put a hand on my elbow and we made our way through the crowd to the side of the room.

"Men play fools well enough with no help from women," I said lightly. The conversation was moving entirely too close to home for my comfort. I tried desperately to think of a way to change the subject, but was compelled to meet his gaze when he turned me to face him before releasing my arm.

"What would you have us do, Scheherazade? Stand by quietly and watch as you women trample on our hearts?"

I wondered if my disguise had been as successful as I previously thought. Griffin watched me with an intensity that was almost intimate, waiting for me to answer a question that I didn't understand. I dropped my gaze at last, unsure of what he wanted from me. When I looked up, he was gone.

An enjoyable five minutes were spent a short time later in a conversation with Helena, who was dressed as a French shepherdess complete with stuffed lamb. I recognized her at once and waited until her sister-in-law, dressed as Mary, Queen of Scots, was engaged before I approached.

"I can't talk to you long," she said nervously, looking over her shoulder at Lady Sherringham. "But I want to meet with you. Would tomorrow morning suit you? I'm supposed to return books to the library at ten."

I agreed to meet her and asked casually if Griffin had changed his mind about attending the ball.

"Oh, no. He wouldn't even see me when we left. He locked himself in his study and refused to come out," she said sadly.

The better to dress himself as an Arab, I thought. I wondered if Helena would know him when she saw him… if he was still here. I hadn't seen the tall Arab sheikh since our dance.

"I see your cousin is here," she said with a giggle.

"Yes, unfortunately he is."

"I must run, but I will meet you tomorrow morning. *Au revoir!*"

A short while later, as I stood at my aunt's side, I noticed a flash of blue on the dance floor. Helena was dancing with Griffin and the look of delight on her face told me she'd recognized him.

The house had a long hall that ran the length of the building, with doors to the various rooms opening off it. As I came down the stairs from the water closet, a man's voice floated up from below. Surprised by the name that was mentioned, I peered over the banister, noting Freddie tucked behind a large palm, engaged in conversation with a man dressed as a giant white rabbit, complete with a fancy waistcoat and pocket watch.

"Scheherazade? What's that?" the white rabbit asked.

"It doesn't matter," Freddie said with an abrupt gesture. "Just don't botch things up again."

"Nothing will go wrong. Not this time. Not when I have this with me." The man in the rabbit suit pulled out an object—what I couldn't identify—from his waistcoat and showed it to Freddie.

"Make sure it doesn't." Freddie moved off, leaving me with a distinct sense of unease. I hesitated for a second, then followed, but quickly lost them in the crowd.

Suspicion boiled within me. What on earth was Freddie up to? Did it have something to do with the odd feeling I had regarding him earlier?

The ballroom was even more crowded than earlier, with people clustered in small groups along the walls, talking, laughing, and watching those who were dancing. As I squeezed by a large woman dressed as Catherine the Great, I came face to face with an American cowboy who was laughing with a tall, amber-eyed sheikh.

Abruptly the sheikh turned, and much to the surprise of the Columbine standing near him, whirled her into the dance. Annoyed to the point where I momentarily forgot Freddie, I cast only the briefest of indignant glares at Griffin and his partner before I spotted a familiar face. "Lieutenant Angus! How nice to see you again. Are you enjoying the dancing?"

Excusing himself from a conversation with one of the other Yeomen, he replied in the affirmative. I batted my lashes and waited expectantly.

"Are you engaged for this dance?"

"Not in the least," I replied, my eye on the colorful Arab where he was still dancing with the Columbine.

As we stepped into the dance, the music ended.

"Shall we wait for the next one?" Angus asked politely.

Far across the room, two tall white rabbit ears bobbed and headed out a door, which led to a courtyard. "I—I suddenly feel the need for a little fresh air," I replied, curious where Freddie's friend was going. I took hold of Angus's arm and tugged him toward the door. "Perhaps you would be so kind as to escort me outside for a moment or two?"

I gave the poor man no choice, but he was nice enough to fall in with my wishes without complaint. Outside, stone steps led down to a pleasant shrub-lined path, running the length of the house. Large stone urns were interspersed between the tall shrubs, affording many choices should a person wish to avoid being seen.

One glance at Angus and I realized my mistake. He assumed I wanted to stroll outside for amorous purposes and moved closer in preparation. I considered my options and decided that an appeal to his sense of chivalry was the answer, so brushing aside my remorse at prevaricating, I spun a quick tale.

"Did you see the man in the giant white rabbit suit? No? Well, he came this way, and he has been… Well, let us say, he has made himself objectionable to me. I wish to locate him to make sure he's not doing the same thing to another woman, and I had hoped you might help me confront him."

Angus, a typical example of his gender, puffed up importantly as I appealed to his masculinity. "Of course I will help you. The nerve of the bounder!"

I turned to face him as I spoke, simpering in a manner that I found repugnant, but which was so effective on those of the male persuasion. "I appreciate your help. There is no one else to whom I can turn."

As the words left my lips, Griffin passed by, the Columbine clinging to his arm. His stony gaze left little doubt in my mind that he not only guessed my identity, but had also heard me utter the puerile drivel to Angus.

"Let's start down there." I pointed in the direction opposite to the one Griffin had gone and started off towards a dark corner. Annoyed with my draperies, I detached one side of the veils so I could search without encumbrances.

I sent Angus along the far wall as I started down the side next to the house, examining behind and in each urn as I passed them, only to reach the far corner without success. A small metal gate led out to the street beyond. I looked out, shivering in the chilly evening air, but couldn't see beyond the pavement directly in front of the gate.

"Well," I said, turning around to see why Angus had been so quiet, "I guess we will have to look at the other end."

"If you like," Griffin replied, his voice noncommittal.

I blinked at him for a moment before demanding, "What have you done with Angus?"

"The gentleman was needed elsewhere," he answered, frowning. He must have thought the horrified face I made was in response to his statement. "I realize he is *the only one you can turn to in a time of need*, but are you really that despondent at his departure?"

"Not in the least," I answered truthfully. "But I am concerned about the man standing behind you, pointing a pistol at your head."

Griffin spun around and would have lunged had not a voice from behind me ordered him to halt. Something cold and sharp pricked my jaw. I turned my head slightly and saw the open gate and the furry white suit of a giant rabbit behind me.

"One move towards my friend there, Mr. Sheikh, and the lady loses more than a veil."

Griffin turned back slowly, his face impassive. The short, stocky man behind him reached around and removed the scimitar, then nudged Griffin with the pistol and ordered him to walk. A hand gripped my shoulder painfully, forcing me to follow, the knife moving to press up against my shoulder blades. Fear faded to anger as we passed through the gate and towards a closed carriage parked a short way down the street.

"This is ridiculous," I said as they herded us along. "Kidnapped in the middle of a masquerade ball. And by a giant white rabbit!"

Only the sight of the very real pistol held firmly against Griffin's back kept me from saying more. We stopped next to the carriage.

"Get in." The man with the gun pushed Griffin.

"No," he replied in a low voice.

I started forward as the thug shoved Griffin, slamming him with brutal force into the side of the carriage. The knife was back at my throat, digging in with a pain that caused me to gasp. Warmth trickled down my neck as the man in the rabbit suit pulled my head backwards, the wig loosening under his grip.

"Now, do you get in nicely or do we have to cut up the lady?" the rabbit asked Griffin, his voice striking a chord in my mind. I was sure I'd heard it before.

Griffin glanced at me. His eyes focused on the trickle of blood creeping down my neck onto my bosom before they lifted to meet mine. A second later, he leaped on the man with the gun, sending him flying backwards. I had enough wits about me to push backwards and down, slipping out of the rabbit's grip, leaving him staring in surprise at his handful of long black wig and veils. Wishing I had my walking shoes on so I might impair him more effectively, I kicked him as hard as I could in an area that disables gentlemen. It certainly gave the rabbit pause for thought.

"Alex, get out of here!" Griffin bawled as he lunged onto the rabbit man. I looked around for some sort of weapon and spied the man with the pistol pulling himself up to his feet. Without even a thought of what I was doing, I threw myself on him, knocking my head against his as we tumbled to the ground. Gasping with pain, I sat up, shaking my head. The man beneath me groaned and tried to sit up as well.

I struck him as hard as I could directly on the temple and watched with satisfaction as his head snapped back and hit the curb.

"I am beginning to see the value of taking the offensive stance, rather than the defensive," I told the unconscious man.

Various oaths and strangled noises issued from the two men still locked in battle. Griffin had a hold of the knife, but the bunny-clad thug was slowly turning it towards his face. Having successfully dealt with one man, I thought I'd assist Griffin with his.

Sucking on a bleeding knuckle, I limped over to them and waved my fists at the attacker. Abruptly, the man released the knife, ducked down, and squirmed out of Griffin's grasp. Grabbing his semi-conscious partner, he leaped into the carriage, whipped the horses, and sped off into the darkness.

Griffin leaned against the wall, panting and holding his right shoulder.

"Well," I said, straightening my costume as best I could, feeling especially pleased at the villain's reaction to the threat I posed him, "there's another one for Caleb."

Griffin looked at me as if I were insane.

"Caleb was my father's stable boy. He taught me how to fight, and clearly that villainous rabbit saw I knew what I was doing when I waved my fists at him," I explained.

"Despite your prowess in brawling," Griffin replied grimly, peering under his hand, "I think the appearance of that bobby coming around the corner had more to do with them running than the terrifying thought of you attacking."

The sight of blood on his shoulder distracted me from a sharp retort. "Are you injured?"

I pushed his hand off and examined the wound. He had a long but shallow cut running across his shoulder.

"No more than you," he replied, straightening up to face the constable. I dabbed at his shoulder, then wiped off my own blood.

It took a good deal of explanation, but in the end we convinced the constable that we were not seriously hurt and couldn't identify our attackers. Griffin promised to report the incident fully in the morning.

"Will you stand still for one moment so that I might have a conversation with you?" I asked as we limped back to the house.

"No," he snapped and tugged me toward the stone stairs that led to the verandah.

"Of all the obstinate... Fine, will you at least listen to my theory of the unwarranted attack upon us? I have a suspicion about the identity of the man in the white rabbit suit—"

"No," he said just as shortly, and refused to say another word until he deposited me next to Caroline.

Despite our disheveled appearances, no one paid attention to our return. I had lost my veils and cap and had to pull my braid around the front to hide the dried remnants of blood. Griffin was dirty, but his costume fared better than mine. He escorted me to my aunt's side, then made a slight bow and excused himself. I was furious with him for refusing to speak on the subjects that weighed most on my mind.

"What a very dashing sheikh Mr. St. John makes. I take it from your frown that your disguise wasn't successful?" she asked.

"Not particularly, no," I replied, picking at a spot of blood on the delicate gauze as I fumed to myself.

She nodded. "Ah. Did you have a pleasant stroll with him?"

I looked at the well-meaning twinkle in her eye and couldn't stop the words. "Not really. He still refuses to speak to me. Two men tried to abduct us, held a pistol to Griffin's head and a knife to my throat. We escaped. I am a little sore and believe I will go home. If you don't mind me borrowing Geoffrey, I'll wish you a good night."

Anything I say seldom surprises my aunt, so the look of astonishment on her face was almost worth suffering the attack. I limped off to find my coat and Geoffrey, my uncle's coachman.

THIRTEEN

I met Helena the next morning outside of Westminster Abbey. After my success with the Scheherazade costume of the past evening, I was convinced I could look somewhat stylish, so I wore a new white suit with a blue and white striped vest and a white bolero jacket trimmed with blue braid.

I felt very proud of my smart new ensemble until I observed her in a pretty blazer suit of sky blue with rows of dark blue tubular braid.

My lips pursed as she drew close, causing her to burst into laughter at my jaded look.

"Well, really, Helena, it is too bad!" I said indignantly, circling her to get the full effect of the charming outfit. "Here I sit in my new white duck dress thinking that at last I can hold my own with you, and you insist on floating over to me looking like a rain-washed summer sky."

She raised her hand, still laughing. "I promise you, Alex, it is an old gown that I have had for two years."

"Hrmph." It was hard to be disgruntled with her when she looked so charming, so I gave her only a brief lecture as to the horrors of the feather industry regarding her hat, and we settled down on a nearby bench to chat.

"I have so much to tell you," she said breathlessly, having giggled through most of the feather lecture. "Someone ransacked our house last night!"

I stared at her, amazed. "For what purpose?"

"It's hard to tell. They tore apart the study, stole my mother's gold candlesticks, and made a terrible mess of Griffin's room."

"How awful! Did the servants hear anything?"

She peeled off her gloves and wadded them into a ball. "They weren't home, except for the under-kitchen maid. We were all gone, of course, to the ball, and we had given the servants the night off. Lucy, the kitchen maid, had a toothache and was upstairs in bed. She said she didn't hear a thing."

I sat down with no pretense at grace, wondering at such actions in the Sherringham home. "That's extraordinary."

"Griffin came home—did you know he was at the ball last night? Well, he came home early and found two men ripping his study apart."

I turned my horrified gaze onto her, fear clutching at my heart with barbed fingers. "How…is he…what happened?"

She stared down at her gloves, twisting them out of shape. "He tried to stop them, but they were too strong for him, and one of them struck him on the head."

My stomach dropped into my boots as a wave of dizziness threatened to make me sick. I closed my eyes to stop the world from spinning past me.

"Alex, are you all right? You suddenly went pale."

"It's just the sun in my eyes." I lied, wanting to run to Griffin at the same time. I needed more information from Helena. "Is your brother badly hurt?"

She smiled, and I felt my stomach move back to its accustomed location. "He is in good health, thanks to Clairmore."

"Clairmore?"

"Our butler. He returned home early and heard a commotion. When he went to the front of the house to see what it was, he found two men standing over Griffin, who was lying unconscious at the bottom of the stairs."

I must be in love with him, I told myself, wanting badly to shake Helena until she explained how Griffin could be unharmed and yet unconscious. Nothing but love would cause such agony. "But… you said he was in good health?"

"He is. Don't fret. The concussion was a mild one, and he suffered no other injury, only a slight cut to his shoulder. He had a slight headache this morning and no other adverse effects."

I clutched my shaking hands together, wanting to shout with relief. It was hard work trying to hide the love I felt for that obstinate man. "I am horrified, Helena. Do you know the motive for such an attack?"

She watched as a group of American tourists strolled by, reading aloud from their Baedeker. "Harold says they were out to rob us, but Griffin believes they were after something in particular."

I considered this. "He might have a point. How would common burglars know that your family would be gone for the evening unless someone told them? Did the police question your servants?"

"Harold wouldn't let us notify the police. He says it was just a random burglary, and one of the servants must have told someone the family was to be gone. Only…" She looked puzzled.

"Yes?" I prompted her.

"I would agree, except Griffin said he would be home that evening, so the servants couldn't have told anyone the house would be empty."

A dreadful thought occurred to me, but I felt it best to keep it to myself. "Perhaps the burglars thought he would be asleep and out of the way," I suggested slowly.

Her expression brightened a smidgen. "That would explain it. I suppose that must be what happened."

It seemed to me that the crime had been committed with one particular victim in mind, but I felt it wise not to share that opinion and instead changed the subject. "Is your brother still planning on leaving soon?"

Her shoulders slumped. "Yes, he is. I tried to talk him into staying a little while longer as I thought he might have a reason to, but he seems adamant about leaving in two days. Alex, isn't there anything you can do to keep him here? I know he admires and respects you. Perhaps if you talked to him—"

I looked at the Abbey, the two magnificent spires, the colored windows, the warmth of the stones. It seemed so unmovable, so sturdy, so permanent. No doubt a great number of unhappy lovers had passed through its doors, yet it had survived since Norman times.

"Your brother is many things, but of them all, he's stubborn. I tried to speak with him, but he refuses to listen."

The look she gave me left me feeling ashamed for my part in driving away her beloved brother. "Then all hope is lost," she said, her eyes filling with tears.

I fought the urge to sigh, but in the end, gave in to a heartfelt one. "No, not all hope. Emma suggested that I... well, explain about my family to Griffin. If I can do that, perhaps he will feel differently about...things."

"Your family? Your sister, you mean?"

"No," I said, miserable. The last thing I wanted to do was to explain to Helena, lovely, bright Helena, what fanaticism was. Desperately, I steered the conversation into a subject guaranteed to distract her. "Did you enjoy the ball last night?"

Her glum expression faded, and she smiled with a warmth I felt in the coldest part of my soul. "I did. Wasn't it wonderful? I must admit, I was jealous of your costume. It was so very daring! I didn't see you later, though. Were you not feeling well?"

"I was fine, just tired of trying to dodge Freddie. He would insist on dancing with me at every opportunity."

"I thought he danced nicely," she replied absently, picking at a piece of trim.

I looked at her in astonishment. "You don't mean to say that you danced with him as well?"

"Yes, I did. Shouldn't I have?"

"Well, no," I said after a moment's thought. "I'm just surprised that you would want to."

"He was speaking with Harold and asked me if I would care to dance, and as he was your cousin…"

I made a face at that. "Please don't feel you must tolerate his attentions if you would rather not. He has become rather intense of late. It's beginning to worry me."

We sat for a few minutes in silence, enjoying the late spring sun, each wrapped up with our own thoughts.

A sudden intrusion into my contemplation of Griffin's character had me asking, "What on Earth was Freddie doing speaking with Lord Sherringham?"

Helena shrugged and pulled on her gloves. "I have no idea. I apologize for not being able to meet you at home, but the family… Well, I thought it best if we met here instead."

"Ah." I was still puzzling over what Freddie would have to say to someone of Lord Sherringham's circle.

"The reason I wanted to see you this morning," Helena spoke slowly, "is because I have received a note from Maggie Greene. You have seen the newspapers, I am sure?"

"I have. Some of the Union members have not yet been released. To be truthful, I fear for the future of the Union with them in prison. What did Maggie want with you?"

Helena peered at me from the corner of her eyes. "After my appalling behavior the other day, you must surely think me foolish to accept a letter from her, but she sounds so repentant that I cannot help but believe she has seen the error of her ways."

"You endow Maggie with attributes I fear she lacks," I said with an almost overwhelming urge to snort. "Has she asked for your support in a campaign to take over the Union?"

Helena blinked a couple of times. "Yes, how did you know?"

"I thought she might make a play for control after Mrs. Heywood and the other officers were arrested. This means the end of the Union. The conservative members will never accept Maggie's leadership, while the militant faction will not accept otherwise. I wouldn't be surprised if they formed their own society."

Helena opened her bag and handed me a note written on cheap paper. It was from Maggie, asking for Helena's support, encouraging her to consider joining a new organization if the Union refused to endorse the militants.

I smiled grimly at Helena's astonishment and handed her back the note. "What will you do?"

"I'm not sure." She looked at her hands for a moment before glancing up and noticing my obvious disappointment. "Dearest friend, of course I will do whatever you think is best. Please advise me."

"Oh, no, you are a grown woman; you must make your own choices. If you believe you can do some good by joining Maggie's forces, then you must do so. If you find you cannot wholly support her program, then you must tell her so."

We spent a long time debating the situation, and I believe she had convinced herself of Maggie's unsuitability to run the Union by the time Robert strolled up.

Helena blushed madly at his appearance.

"Ah, Robert, there you are. Helena, you remember Robert Hunter," I said, amused despite the fact that my own romance had gone sour.

She shook hands with him in a self-conscious manner. For his part, Robert could not take his eyes off Helena.

"I asked Robert to meet me here so he could accompany me later with some shopping," I explained, delighted with my foresight. "As you have a little time before you must go to the library, perhaps you will chat with Robert for a few minutes. I have the most overwhelming desire to visit the Abbey and see the crypt again."

"Certainly. I would be delighted," she answered, gaze cast down demurely.

"Excellent. I will be back shortly." I strolled off to the Abbey and joined a throng of tourists. I spent as long as I could admiring the Lady Chapel, then went below to tour the crypt before slowly making my way back outside to tear Robert away from Helena.

I hadn't the heart to separate the two. Robert insisted on escorting Helena to the library, fearing for her safety on such a hazardous mission, so I went about my shopping on my own. I returned home a few hours later to find Robert, the girls, and the hounds playing in the square across the street. I retired to my room, and spent the next two hours alternately writing an explanation to Griffin of my past, and then tearing it up because everything came out so stark.

"I'm just going to have to tell him in person," I told my reflection.

She made a rude face.

Later in the evening, I had the chance to find out how Robert's day with Helena went. "You look sad," I commented, running him to earth in the library.

He sighed. "I was thinking of Miss St. John."

"Ah." I watched him carefully, sure of what was to come.

"She... I... I have nothing, Alex, nothing which I could offer her. I spent all those years working for Wallace on his coffee farm for nothing. He wouldn't even give me the parcel of land we agreed upon in exchange for my apprenticeship."

"Your brother has always been... Well, we won't go into that now. Couldn't you raise the money to purchase a farm through some other means?" I sat next to him on the leather sofa, wishing I could help him.

His Adam's apple bobbed. "No. I managed to raise a sum of money and purchase a small, inferior farm, but I lost it."

The poignant note in his voice made a lump come to my throat. "How did you lose it?"

"Wallace bought up the note." He stared gloomily into the fire. "When the first crop yield failed my expectations, I couldn't meet my obligations, and he foreclosed."

"There must be something we can do," I said, determined to help my friend. "I would be happy to loan you whatever sum you need."

He smiled and kissed my hand. "Dearest Alex, what a good heart you have. Thank you, but no. I will find a way by myself."

"But surely a loan would solve all of our problems. I would be part owner, and you could marry someday and take your bride to live on the coffee farm."

"What a fine husband I would make." He laughed bitterly. "Borrowing money to be married, then dragging my poor wife out to live in the wilds of Africa. No, my dear, I will find my way without your generous offer of help, don't worry."

Joshua came in at that point and I said no more on the subject, although I resolved to have a chat with him later about Robert's situation.

The following morning, I decided I'd tackle Griffin later in the day when Helena indicated he would be home. A glance at the clock set me into motion; dressed in a navy and white checked day dress, I ran downstairs before any of the family was up, and spent the morning at the hall devoted to my favorite charity. There I helped assemble clothing, books, and other donated items in boxes to be sent to needy women. It was a soothing task and mindless enough to allow me to continue mentally rehearsing the things I would say to Griffin.

"Off home, are you?" one woman asked as I was leaving the hall.

"I'm not sure…" I hesitated as I stood on the front steps, trying to decide what I should do next. "There is a meeting to discuss the leadership and future of the Union scheduled for noon. I suppose I should attend to that, although… Oh, I'm just being silly. I'll go."

There were numerous women in the meeting hall when I arrived. As I feared, the militant group presented their case with brilliance, sweeping up the audience up with a vision of women's suffrage, playing on our sense of duty, adventure, and outrage.

The meeting ended in confusion, nothing having been decided, although sides were clearly being drawn. The future of our protest at the upcoming election speeches at Exeter House was in question, with both sides claiming proprietorship.

I returned home intending to change before I presented myself at Lord Sherringham's house, but when I entered, Mabel pounced on me as soon as I took off my hat and coat. "Cousin Freddie is here to see you. He is in the library with Joshua. Where have you been all day?"

"Out and about." I gave her a summary of the day's activities.

She gave me a look that all older sisters have in their repertoire. "Really, Alex, I think you might have a little more concern for us. We were worried when you left no word of where you would be."

I murmured another apology, and listened to a brief lecture on the duties of unmarried women to their good name, hoping all the while that Freddie would leave, but as luck would have it, he found me at last. Mabel gave me a pitying look and excused herself.

"Dearest cousin," Freddie said, taking my hands to kiss them. He was his usual handsome self, his eyes filled with warmth and concern. "You positively radiate charm and grace."

His fingers tucked a loose curl behind my ear. I suppressed a grimace at the touch and moved over to the couch, wondering how to broach the subject of what I'd seen at the ball. "I'm afraid I can't chat with you. I have an engagement that I must dress for."

Freddie dropped to his knees.

"Beloved Alex, most precious of all women, this time you cannot refuse me." He took my hand in his, his eyes glowing brightly. "You must see that I can offer you much, beloved one, not just my protection, but my heart, my devotion, my life if you wished it."

"I'm sorry, Freddie, I can't think of how to say no in a manner that you will accept, so I will simply say this: I have given my heart to another. I will never marry you. In fact, I'd like to discuss last night—"

His fingers tightened painfully around mine. I tried to pull my hand back, but his grip was too strong. "You would be wise to think twice about refusing me."

"Are you threatening me?" I asked, taking a step back.

"Of course not. I would never do such a thing," he said smoothly, his face earnest, but his eyes calculating.

"No, but you would talk to a man in a rabbit suit shortly before he attacked me," I said, pushing down my worry.

"Rabbit suit?" He did an excellent job of looking surprised. "Attacked?"

"Yes. At the St. Alban's ball—I saw you speaking with the man who later attacked a friend and me. I heard you mention my costume to him."

"My dearest cousin, you do me grave injury," he protested. "As if I could do anything to harm you. I mentioned you to several people at the ball that night. Many of my friends had very complimentary things to say about your outfit. That is no doubt what you overheard."

It wasn't, and we both knew it, but I didn't feel in possession of enough facts to challenge him on the subject.

He pressed another kiss to the back of my hand before I could get it away. "I am appalled that you were attacked, but this proves the validity of my concerns about you. You must see that to deny me any longer is the sheerest folly."

"I see nothing of the kind. I'm sorry, but I have made my decision."

There was a curious flat expression in his eyes that sent a sudden chill of horror skimming down my back. I had seen that look before, usually just before my father inflicted some new form of punishment. "I have it in my power to make you a very happy woman—or one who will think back to your days with your father with longing. Heed me, Alex. You *will* be mine."

"No," I answered, protesting both his statement and the fear that clutched at me. "I will never go back to that hell. I think it's time I told Aunt Caroline that you are making yourself obnoxious to me—"

His fingers bit into my arms as he jerked me forward, his face a few inches from mine, his eyes those of a stranger. A furious stranger. "You so much as whisper to her or anyone else a complaint about me, and I'll see to it that you're locked up in a lunatic asylum."

"What—" I fought the panic that filled me at the sight of his face, and what he was saying.

"Your father was as mad as a hatter. No one will doubt that his daughter is equally insane. Just remember that the next time you think to refuse me, Alex."

"You can't. I'm of legal age," I said, trying to quell the fear that followed panic. "You have no power against me."

"I have powerful friends, ones who would have no problem helping me shut you up so no one ever sees you again. Is that what you want, Alex? To be locked away like a rabid dog?"

"Go away," I said, my stomach twisting with nausea.

"Just remember what I said. I hold the cards, Alex. You'd do better to realize that."

Unable to speak in the face of his threat, I got my legs moving, praying as I left the room that he wouldn't follow me to the stairs. Luck, for once, was with me, for he simply gathered up his coat and hat, and departed.

I collapsed on my bed, wondering what I was going to do. I wanted to tell Griffin, but what would he think of me? I hadn't yet told him about my father—would he fear the taint of insanity had brushed me, too? Would he take Freddie's side in feeling that I should be locked away?

No, I couldn't tell him. I couldn't tell anyone. Aunt Caroline would fuss and get Uncle Henry involved, and then Freddie would retaliate against me. "But does he have the power?" I asked, unable to remain still any longer. I paced the width of my room. "He can't. I have agency over my own life."

The memory of Helena telling me about Freddie and Lord Sherringham stopped me. I clutched my hands, my mouth suddenly dry.

Griffin's brother would definitely have the sort of power to have me locked up—and he would no doubt take great delight in doing so.

"It goes against everything I've fought for my whole life, but I'll just have to keep quiet," I said aloud as I sat down on the bed. "Maybe if Freddie finds out about my relationship to Griffin, he'll stop proposing."

That idea didn't hold much hope for me, but it was all I had. Once I was in control of my emotions again, I hurried into the library to inform Joshua and Mabel that it was safe to come out.

"Did he ask you?" Mabel inquired.

"For the umpteenth time, yes. And I refused him. Please don't let him wait for me again," I said, trying to calm my still wildly beating heart. "He didn't take my refusal well. I would rather not be alone with him."

Mabel said nothing more, but I could feel her doubt even as I ran up the stairs.

Emma arrived shortly after that intending to visit Robert.

"Emma is going to Paris for a few days," I said a short while later, after they had greeted each other, and settled into the library. "I have never been. Perhaps we can make a brief trip there together sometime soon, just the three of us."

"That would be delightful," Robert said glumly.

I exchanged a glance with Emma.

"I hope you don't mind, but Alex has told me something about your current situation," Emma said. "Naturally, I am distressed that your brother has treated you so callously. Have you had any luck in obtaining a sponsorship?"

He stood with a hand on the mantelpiece, staring into the fire with a most forlorn look on his face. "No. Wallace seems to have done his work thoroughly. I can't raise the capital it would take to buy another farm. So my dear friends, it would be useless for me to make plans to go anywhere. Instead, I will begin preparations to remove myself from your sister's kind charity, Alex. I will find a job somewhere in town."

"You're not the sort of man to take things lying down," I told Robert, dismayed by his defeatism. "If you love Helena, then do something. Don't just fold up on yourself."

Robert looked at Emma for help. She gave a little shake of her head. "I'm sorry, but about this, I agree with Alex. No woman wants a suitor who sits around moping and bemoaning the fact he isn't worthy. Tell Helena of your feelings. Tell her of your situation. I'm sure she will understand."

"Yes, tell her," I agreed. "And then ask her to join you in a life that will be filled with love and fraught with difficulties, but for heaven's sake, stop mooning around and ask her."

Robert blinked a few times at our frank speech, but at least he stopped his wallow in self-pity. "But—but—"

I patted him on the arm. "You must trust that we know of what we speak. We are not naïve young ladies. We are worldly New Women. Emma is educated, and I have a lover."

"You do?" His eyes opened wide. "An actual...er...not just someone courting you? No, wait—don't answer that. It's none of my business."

"You are one of my oldest friends. I don't mind you knowing about my lover. And you needn't dance around the subject. Both Emma and I know all about men and what we want from them."

His gaze shot to Emma. "But surely you are—"

She raised a hand to stop him, making a wry face. "I think explanations about that would be best left for a time when Alex has a bit more experience being a New Woman."

"What explanations?" I asked her, distracted.

"Another time. Right now, we are here to help and support Robert."

"Very well." I narrowed my gaze at him. "Please tell me you will heed our advice?"

"How can I? I have nothing—"

"Oh, for heaven's sake!" Emma said, clearly at the end of her patience.

I knew just how she felt. "Have the decency to tell Helena of your feelings, or you will spend the rest of your life sniveling about what might have been."

It was probably the term "sniveling" that made the difference. I have found that gentlemen hate to be told they are snivelers.

Robert stiffened at the word, then turned stiffly and marched out of the room. When Emma and I, exchanging small victorious smiles, followed him, we saw he paused only long enough to gather his hat and coat before leaving the house.

"You don't think we've acted a trifle precipitously, do you?" I asked Emma as she collected her own things.

"Sending him into the lion's den with no protection and his heart on his sleeve, you mean?" she asked with a little laugh.

"When you say it like that, it sounds so hopeless." I sighed. "I pray it will be enough."

"I'm sure it will." She paused for a moment at the door, giving me a long look. "I wonder if you and your Griffin would like to join me at the club for dinner next week. Tuesday is a public night, and I would be happy to have you as my guests. There are a few things I would like to explain, and I think it might be best if he were there to help."

"I'm sure he would be delighted, as would I, but what sorts of things are you talking about?"

She patted my cheek. "We'll leave that for then. Good luck with your campaign to rally Robert to brave new heights. I will send you a postcard from Paris."

Mabel demanded my attention before I could make my escape. Sighing to myself that I would never bring Griffin to see reason, I gave her the attention she required for almost two hours. I dashed up the stairs to change into something suitable for visiting a lover, and just left my room when

Robert stepped emerged from his with a suitcase in each hand, his face haggard and worn.

I put a hand on his arm, worried by the stark nature of his appearance. "You look as if you have pulled backwards through a fence. Where are you going?"

He set down the suitcases and took both of my hands in his. "Alex, my dear, I want to thank you for your love. You are a loyal friend and one I will never forget."

"What's happened?" I asked, squeezing his fingers.

He closed his eyes briefly, then said, "I went to ask for Helena's hand."

"She has refused you?" I asked, awash in disbelief.

"No, her guardian has refused to allow me to present my case."

"Her—oh, you mean Lord Sherringham?"

"Yes. I can't blame him, of course. I wouldn't want a penniless man with no future asking for my sister's hand. But I had believed… Helena is so… I had hoped…"

To my horror, I saw Robert was on the verge of tears.

"Oh, Robert!" I said, my own eyes filling. "Don't listen to Lord Sherringham. You should have spoken with Griffin. He would be delighted to see Helena happy with you."

He shook his head. "It is to her guardian I must apply. He controls her—her—"

"Her fortune, yes, I know. I wondered if Helena would tell you about that." I bit my bottom lip, thinking. "It would certainly allow you to marry and be coffee farmers, if that is what you wished."

He slumped into a chair next to the stairs. "Even if I wanted to be the kind of man who lived off of his wife's money, I don't have the choice now. Sherringham has refused to allow me to call on Helena again."

"But surely Helena doesn't care."

"No, Alex. It's one thing to ask a woman to support her husband if she has the ample means, but it's another to ask her to forsake her rightful inheritance to live a life of genteel poverty."

I shook my head, wanting to shake him for giving up so easily. "Robert, you are being maudlin. There is no need for this. I am sure Griffin can help you—"

He stared at his suitcases, saying, "I have a friend in Chelsea. He will let me stay with him." He stood and kissed me on the cheek. "Don't worry, I'll be fine, and will let you know my address later."

"There will be no need," I said with much firmness. Until my father's death, I hadn't the chance to be firm with people, and I wasn't going to lose the opportunity to be so now. "You are staying here."

"Alex—"

"I will not hear another word about you leaving." I tried to wrestle his suitcase away from him.

"It's no use. I must go. I can intrude on Mabel's and Joshua's kindness no longer."

I argued, I pleaded, and in the end, I finally badgered Robert into staying put, feeling I had a better chance of helping him if I knew where to find him.

After a glance at the clock, I decided I'd send Griffin a note, requesting his presence, since it seemed as if I would never again leave the house. I didn't feel like I could tell him about the situation with Freddie, but I could—and should—give him details about my father. If he broke our connection after hearing the truth...well, I'd deal with that if it happened.

Shortly after I saw Mabel, Joshua, and the girls off to visit our aunt, a footman summoned me downstairs.

Griffin stood in the small front parlor, doing a very fine impression of a pillar of salt.

"I'm so glad you're here. I was worried you weren't going to answer my plea," I said, closing the door, and with my back to it, twisting close the lock. I felt as if I could burst into song with the happiness of seeing him again.

"You said you had something important to say to me." His words were clipped, but it didn't stop me from wanting to smile.

"Well, of course I do. I've wanted to talk to you for the last few days." I wondered what he'd do if I flung myself on him.

His look grew dark. "If it's about Hunter and you, I don't want to hear it."

"Robert? He has nothing to do with me other than being a dear friend."

"Then it must be that infernal organization." His jaw tightened.

"You are a very trying man, do you know that?" I walked over to him and slipped my arms around his waist, gently biting him on his chin. "It's unfortunate you don't want to hear what I have to say, but I'm going to say it, anyway. I want to tell you about my past."

His glorious eyes narrowed. "What about your past? You're not going to make me believe you've been with other men, because you were most definitely a virgin."

I eyed him for a moment, calculated how long my sister and her family would be gone, ran over a quick list of the servants' duties in the afternoon, and decided there was time. "I want to tell you why I am the way I am. Or rather, the way I was."

"A virgin?" he asked, looking adorably confused, but his shoulders relaxed.

"No. Well, yes, because I was before you, but I want to tell you why I am...well..." I waved a hand around vaguely. "Why I'm so determined to be a part of the Union."

He looked like he wanted to sigh, but at a gesture from me, sat on the sofa. "I've heard what you have to say on the subject, but if you are determined to tell me again, I will listen."

I thought of sitting next to him, but Inner Alex was mentally listing the things she wanted to do to him, so I thought it best I remain at a distance. I sat on the edge of a nearby chair and surreptitiously wiped my palms on my skirt. I bit my upper lip for a few moments, trying to sort out in my head what to say. "What do you know about fanaticism?"

He wasn't expecting that. He leaned back and rubbed a finger on his lower lip.

Instantly, I wanted to kiss that lip.

"Are you referring to a specific type of fanaticism, or just the subject in general?"

"Religious fanaticism. Or rather…" I thought for a second. "A fanaticism based in religion, but which was uniquely its own."

Both of his eyebrows rose as he looked at me, obviously waiting for me to continue.

I took a deep breath and rubbed my hands on my skirt again. "My father was a gentleman by birth, if not deed. He was a deeply religious man at first, or so my sister told me, but after my mother's death when I was seven, he seemed to…change."

"How old was your sister?" Griffin asked, now watching me in a manner that reminded me of a panther spotting prey.

"She's eight years older. Her mother was my father's first wife, and when my mother died, her maternal family took her in. I saw her occasionally, but not much until…until my father died at the end of last year."

I couldn't sit there with him watching me so closely. I rose and moved over to the coal fire, absently poking at it with the fire tongs. "My father become convinced that I was the source of all the evil in his life—he blamed me for the death of my mother, for losing his friends when his madness became intolerable, for everything in his life. He was determined to fight the devil in me, or so he said."

"Did he beat you?" The words were spoken softly, but I felt Griffin's breath brush the tendrils of hair that escaped my chignon. He stood close to me, so close I could feel his heat, but he didn't touch me.

"When he thought that would work, yes." I stared at the dull red glow of the coals, trying to quell the panicked beating of my heart. "He was a most inventive man, and he delighted in concocting trials, as he called them. Torture would be another word—"

Griffin grabbed my arms and spun me around, fury twisting his face, and making me gasp and take a startled step back. "He *tortured* you? His own *child?*"

I realized that the anger wasn't directed at me, and moved forward again, placing both hands on his chest. "He was a monster, Griffin, but I survived. The servants did everything they could to help me. They fed me when he demanded I go without food or water. They let me out of the closets and chests when he slept. I owe everything to them, for I was too cowardly to face my father alone."

"Cowardly." He almost spat the word, then his gaze gentled on me, and he kissed my hands. "You are the strongest person I know, and you believe yourself to be cowardly."

"I'm not strong, but I am resolute," I said, smiling to myself when he pulled me against his chest, his lips now caressing the corners of my mouth. "When he died, I swore I would at last live the life I had dreamed of since I was a child. I would do what I wanted, go where I wanted, live where I wanted. Most of all, I would fight for other women, so they, too, could escape their shackles."

He was silent for a moment, his eyes still filled with warmth, but now a wariness had tinged their edges. "You would give up your life for this cause?"

"No. Or rather, I thought I would at one time, but now there's you. And it may make me the worst sort of suffragette ever, but I find I don't want to sacrifice myself to the cause if it means losing you. I don't want you to leave me, Griffin. I'm falling madly, incredibly, derangedly in love with you, and I want you to stay here. With me."

He froze at the last of my words, and for a few seconds, fear gripped my gut with a cold, gruelly hand.

"You love me?"

"Yes." I didn't think I had enough air in my lungs to say the word.

"Do New Women fall in love?" he asked, his eyes still searching mine.

A spurt of irritation had me responding, "They do when they engage the right person. Honestly, Griffin, I don't understand why you are having such a difficult time accepting this. Did you think I'd give the job of lover to you if I didn't have strong feelings for you?"

He had the grace to look abashed. "You never mentioned you were going to fall in love with me. All you said is that you were looking for a lover. And, I believe, a cigarette."

"Yes, well, I've given up on the latter," I answered, waving away that idea. I slid my arms around his neck, threading my fingers through the cool silk of his curls, tugging on them gently until his mouth was against mine. "And what about you, my gallant savior? Do you make a habit of dallying with women for whom you feel nothing but a mild interest?"

His lips did all the answering I wanted, but it wasn't with words.

"I locked the door," I told him a few breathless minutes later.

His eyes could have steamed a plucked chicken. "I am tiring of quick trysts, Alex. I want more. I want much more."

"As do I, but for the moment…" I nodded toward the clock. "Mabel won't be back for half an hour."

We had our clothes removed in record time.

"Are you sure about this?" I asked Griffin as he pulled me over him. He was sitting in the middle of the couch, his arousal looking large as I peered down at it. "Are you supposed to be that imposing?"

"I am the same as I have always been, sweetheart. Now if you would just… Oh, lord… not… not… narrrng!"

I wrapped my hand around the long, hard length of him, amazed when he twitched, delighted with his gasps as I slid my fingers along the underside.

"Fascinating," I said, continuing my exploration. His head lolled back as I used both hands, adjusting my movements until I had him groaning almost non-stop. "This really is fascinating. I did not know about all of this. Are you particularly sensitive here?"

He shot up off the couch, prying my hands off his nether bits. "Yes, yes, I am, and if you want me to see this through to the logical conclusion, you'll stop touching me there."

"Oh." We both looked down at the part I had been touching. It twitched. "What if I touch you just there?"

His eyes crossed.

"This *has* been an informative afternoon. Now, if I do this, what exactly do you feel—Griffin!" He pulled me over him again, my legs splayed along his thighs, his arousal nudging my intimate self, which, true to form, was tingling madly. I looked him in the eye. "You expect me to impale myself on you?"

"Yes. Yes, I do. Right now. This instant. Earlier, if possible."

I squirmed around on the very tip of him. "I'm not sure about this, Griffin. This seems rather an uncomforta-aaaaaaaaaah!"

He gripped my hips and plunged upward into me, taking my scream of pleasure into his mouth. "Ah, sweetheart, if you knew what you did to me."

"Well, I know what you're doing to me," I answered as he showed me the rhythm that pleased us both. On top as I was, I discovered I could control the depth and speed of my impalement and quickly found that if I tightened all my muscles as I sank slowly down upon him, it made him buck and groan in the most satisfying manner.

"Alex—oh, Lord, woman, don't stop. Move like that again."

I swirled my hips, enjoying my power, enjoying the fact that I had him babbling with mindless pleasure. *Men are such simple creatures under all the sophisticated trappings,* I thought to myself as I both tightened and swirled, which had the most amazing effect on Griffin. His hair stood on end and his eyes blazed.

"You're doing this on purpose, aren't you? You're trying to make me lose my mind with sheer, unadulterated ecstasy, aren't you? I know you are. I can see it in your face. Admit it!"

I smiled, rather smugly I'm afraid, and tightened, twirled, and sucked his tongue into my mouth. "You were babbling just a moment ago, my love. I believe that settles the question of superiority of the sexes."

I paid for my smugness.

"I accept your challenge," he said just before he flipped me over so my back was to the couch while he covered me. My legs wrapped around him as he kissed my breasts, laving them, suckling and nipping and scraping his teeth gently along my nipples until I thought they were going to catch fire. "Now we will see who babbles. Now we will see which of us has more control."

I stroked my hands down his back, scraping a gentle line down his spine with my nails before letting my fingers fondle his so very delectable derriere. I *loved* that derriere. "If you… Oh, Griffin!… If you think… Just a little to the right, love… If you think you are going to make me babble… you… you… Merciful heaven, Griffin, don't stop!"

"Never," he swore into my neck, his mouth hot on the tender flesh beneath my ear. His hands curved under to hold on to my behind, and if I wasn't enjoying myself so much, I might have been worried by the glint in his eye, but as it was, I didn't have any wits left with which to worry.

He plunged. I thrust. We kissed and sucked and nibbled, our fingers lighting fires that burned bright as our bodies moved together in a dance of such sweet joy, tears burned in my eyes as we found our pleasure.

"I believe I would call that a draw," I said lazily some long minutes later as I gently kissed his neck. "However, in the interests of a rational, scientific examination of the subject of which of the sexes is superior, it behooves us to continue this activity until we are satisfied with the results."

Above me, Griffin's chest heaved into mine as he panted out his answer. "It will probably kill me, but I agree."

"I can't think of a better way to die. Griffin?" He lifted his head just enough to look into my eyes. I kissed his nose. "What are we going to do about this?"

"About what?" He nuzzled my neck.

"This." I freed an arm and waved it around the room. "You and me. Everything."

"Oh, that." He nibbled on my earlobe as I traced the long sweep of his damp back down to the wonderful contours of his behind. So firm, yet so very soft. I let my fingers linger there.

"We can't go on doing this."

"Why not?" he said into my hair even as his lips caressed my forehead.

I tilted my head back and trailed kisses underneath his jaw. "What if we are out somewhere in public? With other people?"

"I don't see a problem."

Someone knocked at the door.

Griffin looked at me. I looked at him. "Caught!" I said in whispered exaggeration.

He pressed a gentle, gentle kiss to my lips and disengaged himself from me. "With our trousers down."

"One moment," I called over his shoulder to the door as we scrambled back into our clothing.

"I have a solution to the problem. Do you see my collar?"

"It's under my boot. Would your solution involve a house where no one is likely to interrupt us?"

"In a manner of speaking. It would involve you marrying me."

"Forgive me," I said as I buttoned up my skirt. "I am a little lightheaded from our activities, especially that last bit. Did you say marry? You and me?"

"That's the idea. Here, I believe this is yours."

I took the undergarment. "But I don't wish to marry!"

One of his delightful eyebrows rose, just as I knew it would. "Why not?"

"I am a New Woman. We believe in lovers, not marriage. Well, not marriage right away. I would like to marry you some day, Griffin. But not yet. I wish to fully explore loverhood first."

"Your objection is ridiculous." He dismissed my concern even as he pocketed one of his socks that I handed him. "We will do the same things when we are married."

"Possibly, although you can't deny there's a lovely sense of illicitness that makes everything that much more exciting." I peered into the small mirror next to the door and tidied my hair.

"There's also the fact that it limit us to only having brief moments together."

"Yes." I sighed and buttoned up the last few buttons on my shirt. "But if you were to come to my house in the country, we would have time together."

He gave me a look that let me know he didn't like that idea much. "We will marry."

"You don't approve of me!" I felt obligated to point out.

He stepped back and raked me with his eyes. I blushed at the look. "On the contrary, I very much approve of you."

I reached over to touch a curl lying against his ear. "That is, you do not approve of my political views any more than I approve of yours."

"That is easily arranged. You give up your participation in the suffrage movement, and I will give up my opposition to the subject of women's votes."

I gave him a look that I felt said many things. "I spent my whole life in servitude to a man. I will not go willingly into that state with another, not even you."

"I didn't think marriage to me constituted servitude," he said slowly. "But I see that from your view, it might well be taken as such. Very well. We will negotiate a compromise. Draw up a list of your demands. I will do the same. We will compare lists and merge them into one that works for us both."

I opened my mouth to protest the very idea of making a list of marriage demands, but something about the idea tickled my fancy. I knew he was struggling to be true to himself, and yet allow me the same consideration.

"Very well," I said, holding out my hand. He shook it gravely. "I will commence making a list just as soon as I am able. Blast it, that's the girls. Mabel must be home early. Tomorrow?" I asked, unlocking the door.

"Tomorrow," he agreed, before turning to greet my sister and her family as the girls and dogs burst into the room.

FOURTEEN

"Why," I asked the following morning, glaring at the clothing spread out on my bed, "Have I spent an inordinate amount of time and money obtaining clothing, yet when I want something to wear, it appears I don't have a single, solitary garment worthy of being seen outside the house?"

Annie offered a mustard-colored dress. "How about this one, miss?"

I made a face at it. "It makes me look sallow."

"How about this blue one?" She pulled out one of the Reform walking dresses. "You haven't worn it yet."

"It makes me look lumpy," I muttered. I was acting childish, and I knew it. "Wait. I apologize. I'm out of temper this morning. Bring out the white lace blouse and the tan walking skirt. That will be good enough."

Before I went downstairs, I knocked on the door to Robert's room. He appeared, tucking his shirt into his trousers. I pushed him back into his room and ignored his shocked expression. "Can you be ready to go in five minutes?"

"Go? Go where?"

"I need to see Griffin."

He smiled.

"Stop smirking and just tell me whether you want to accompany me to see Helena."

His mustache drooped dejectedly. "What would be the good? I'm not worthy of her and can never aspire to give her the things she is accustomed to."

It took a great deal of forbearance, but I managed not to throttle him. "Robert, I am going to tell you something that will make your problem easy to solve. It took me a while to figure it out, but it is really very simple."

He looked at me with hope. "Yes? What is it?"

"This: either you can propose to Helena and live happily ever after on a coffee ranch—"

"Farm," he said morosely.

"—farm, or you can mope around until someone else who knows what he wants comes along and marries her."

"She deserves someone like that."

"Robert, I could strangle you! She deserves *you*! She loves *you*! You are the one she wants, and by heaven, you are the one I mean to see her have!"

It took more than a little arguing, but eventually he saw the wisdom of my reasoning and agreed to meet me downstairs.

"Cheer up," I told him, leaving the room. "I have a feeling this is going to be a delightful day."

I raced down the stairs and was heading into the library when Mullin stopped me. "Miss Alex, a cabby just brought this note. It is marked urgent."

Ignoring his look of curiosity, I took the note and read it on my way into the library. I stopped in the doorway and turned back to the hall.

"Mullin!"

"Yes, miss?"

"Is the cabby still here?"

"He said he would wait out front for an answer, miss."

I thought for a minute, then gathered up my coat and bag. "Tell Mr. Hunter to wait for me. I shouldn't be too long."

I dashed out the door, gave the driver the address listed on the note, and leaped into the waiting cab. Smoothing the note, I read it again. *Alex: Come to this address as soon as you can. It is urgent and concerns a matter of grave importance.–G*

Obviously Griffin must have news of the men who were so bent on harming him.

I was right, as I often am, only I had it twisted around, as, alas, I frequently do. When the cab pulled up at a decrepit-looking house, it was the man who had been dressed as the white rabbit who opened the door for me. He had gained another pistol, I noticed with horror when he pushed it into my ribs.

"Now don't give me any trouble, and I won't have to use this," he said in a low, mean tone, pulling me inside before I could do so much as squawk.

"Who *are* you?" I couldn't help but ask, my mouth going immediately dry. I had a few panicked seconds where I wanted to scream and run away, but worry about Griffin gave me strength. "And why are you doing this? Where is Mr. St. John?"

"You can call me Percy. As for your other question, all in good time. Now walk. No, upstairs."

We climbed a grimy and rotting staircase several flights to the top floor, stopping at a door blistered with age. I made a covert search for some sort of weapon that I might use to defend myself, but saw only refuse. The man with the gold tooth opened the door, rubbing his hands together gleefully at my appearance. "I've often said the best road is the straightest. You didn't have a problem with the lady, did you?"

"None, Merlin."

"Merlin?" I asked, startled by his name. "I thought you were William?"

He laughed and took a step closer to me. "Mum had her fancies, she did. As do I—"

There was a note in his voice that made my skin crawl, and my gut turn, but I fought down a brief sensation of nausea, and squared my shoulders. I had conquered worse than a few threats from someone like him. "Why have you been following me? Why you have twice attacked Mr. St. John? And why you have brought me here?"

"Ah," Merlin said, stepping even closer and running a finger along my ear. "Now that is a complicated story. It may take some time to tell, a very long time."

I recoiled at his touch, but remembered I was a New Woman, and tried to slap him. Before I could, though, he spun me around with my arm twisted painfully behind my back.

"Fun and games later," he hissed in my ear. "Right now, I have a little business to take care of."

An entryway and several rooms led off the hallway, but Merlin ignored most of them as he marched me to the end and pushed me into a small, musty room, slamming shut the door and locking it quickly.

"I insist you let me out!" I yelled, rattling the doorknob and pounding on the door, but it did no good. My hand went automatically to my head, only to remember I had left in such a hurry I wasn't wearing a hat.

"Damn." I pulled out a hairpin and looked at it critically. It would not do as a substitute lock pick. "Now what?"

I examined my prison. The furnishings comprised a small iron bed with filthy bedding, a wooden chair that looked frail, and a chamber pot.

"Not a very inspiring collection," I mused, eyeing the skylight about ten feet above me. I had no ladder, unfortunately. "Obviously, the first order of business is to escape, so I can warn Griffin."

I looked again at the skylight. If I could reach it, I could make my way along the roof and climb down the building. It wasn't a pleasing idea, but it was the only one that seemed remotely feasible. I wasn't about to force my way past two men, one of whom was armed.

Before I formulated a plan, footsteps echoed down the hallway toward my room. I snatched up the chamber pot and held it behind me, intent on using it as a weapon if the unsavory William/Merlin attacked.

The door opened. "Here's some water for you, miss. We wouldn't want you to croak before you've been claimed, now would we?"

"Claimed?" I asked, ignoring the dirty bowl of water that Percy thrust toward me. "Claimed by whom?"

"By your betrothed, of course." He cackled in a manner that left me shivering in disgust, turning the key in the lock even before I could make it to the door.

I waited a few minutes to make sure he wouldn't be back, using the time to contemplate his comments. "Now is not the time to give in to fear. There is Griffin to think of. I must warn him."

Fifteen minutes later, I perched on the end of the bed, upended onto its foot and secured to a nail in the wall with strips of the filthy bedding. I used a plank from the bed to balance myself, straightening up slowly to my full height. The bed creaked and wobbled, but the makeshift rope held. I reached up the remaining few feet to the skylight and opened it. I took as firm a grip as I could manage, breathed deeply, and hauled myself upward.

It took several tries, but eventually I hoisted myself up. Bits of rock and debris ground painfully into my arms and torso as I pulled myself forward and sat panting next to the skylight. As I was assessing the situation, a cab rattled on the street, sending me over to the edge of the roof to peer down on the arrival. If it were Griffin, I would yell a warning before the thugs had him in their grasp.

Although my position on the roof made it difficult to see who had arrived in the cab, I could tell it wasn't Griffin—this man was much thinner and probably a few inches shorter. I was about to turn back to the door when I noticed an open window on the floor below.

"How very thoughtful of Mr. Jones," I muttered to myself as I avoided the pots and loose bricks until I stood directly above the window. I tried leaning over the edge as far as I could, but to no avail—I couldn't see in the window. A glance across the street relieved the worry that some concerned resident might come out to see why a woman was on the roof opposite. There were very few people on the street, and those present didn't look up.

The beginnings of a plan formed in my head. Before leaving the building, I felt it prudent to find out what Merlin and his friend had in mind regarding both Griffin and me.

"All well and fine, but if I can't get to it…" The words trailed off as I glanced down at the ledge that ran the length of the upper floor. It was about six inches wide—wide enough to walk along if I were very careful. I examined a nearby drainpipe. It seemed to be loose, but I thought it would hold me long enough to get to the ledge.

I don't recall the entire trip down the drainpipe to the floor below, although certain moments would live in my memory with brilliant clarity for many years. With my back to the street four stories below, I reached the open window, cautiously peering in it before I entered the room. It appeared empty, so I crept inside, tiptoeing to the door.

The hall was just as empty, although voices could be heard ahead of me, emerging from the sitting room.

"I'm not showin' you anythin' 'til you show us the money."

That sounded like Percy speaking. I expected to hear Merlin in response to his statement, but the voice that answered was the last I expected to hear.

"How do I know you haven't damaged her?"

My stomach turned upon itself as I struggled to keep from throwing open the door and asking Freddie what he thought he was doing. Only the thought of Griffin waiting to fall into this trap kept me silent.

"She's all right, although we had to give him a little tap on the head to keep him quiet."

"I don't care about *him* so long as he's out of the way. I just want to make sure there's nothing apparently wrong with the girl when the clergyman comes."

Girl? Clergyman? Freddie's words had me concerned, but I ignored them to worry over Merlin's reference to a man. Could it be that Griffin—

"She'll be right as rain. Locked up safe, she is, with no way out," said Merlin, interrupting my unpleasant musing.

"You have the stuff?" Percy asked.

"What stuff?" Freddie asked. "Oh, the laudanum? Yes, I have it here."

"Give it over. I want to give the gent another dose in case 'e wakes up. It took all we 'ad to get 'im up 'ere."

"You can have it later, after I'm done with the girl." Freddie sounded annoyed.

A horrible picture formed in my mind as I listened. The mention of the opiate, myself, and a clergyman settled into a nauseating scene in which they doped me just enough to be married to Freddie, apparently with my full consent. If Freddie had a clergyman in his pocket—and Percy and Merlin as witnesses—it would be difficult for me to deny my willingness in the ceremony.

I had to find out if Griffin was the man they were talking about. I crept forward silently and peered into the room. The men were sitting around a fireplace that ran perpendicular to the door. Percy was in a high-backed chair with his back to me, and Merlin was stretched out on a couch that faced the door, but he watched closely as Freddie gazed out of the window. Next to the door was a battered sideboard.

My spirits picked up at the sight of it, for on the top lay a ring with three keys. I knelt on the floor behind Percy's chair and inched my way forward, keeping one eye out for Freddie and Merlin. My hand snaked up the side of the furniture, touched metal, and closed over the keys with painstaking slowness. I held my breath, hoping the keys wouldn't clank together.

Freddie turned his head to speak with Merlin and I froze, not wanting any movement to catch his peripheral vision.

"Blast the man. When did you say he would be here? It's already half past and I don't have all day to wait around. If I don't get to Roget's by midday, I might as well leave the country."

Merlin laughed unpleasantly. "I've heard that old Roget employs men who know how to break bones without leaving a mark."

Freddie shuddered, then asked petulantly, "Are you sure the girl's all right? She has to look feasible, you know."

"I'm sure, I'm sure. If you like, we can check, although you aren't getting her until we're paid."

Freddie made an annoyed noise and turned back towards the window. Merlin tipped his head up to blow a smoke ring. With the keys grasped firmly in my fist, I crawled quietly out of the room into the hallway.

Down the hallway I went, trying the doors gently. There were only two locked—mine, and the one across the hall from it. I turned the key in the lock and slipped into the room.

There were wooden slats across the window, but enough light filtered in for me to recognize the still form lying on the floor.

"No!" I said with a whispered gasp. "Oh, Griffin, no!" I rushed to his side and examined his head carefully. He had a lump on his temple and a small trickle of blood, but no bones gave under the anxious pressure of my fingers.

I sighed with relief and hurried back to the door to look out into the hallway. No one was in sight, so I closed the door quietly and locked it from the inside. Tucking the keys into my bodice, I went back to Griffin and tried to bring him around.

Kisses and endearments didn't do him any good, but they made me feel better, although worry about the amount of laudanum he received soon had me gravely concerned. I'd seen people under the influence of that opiate, but never had I seen someone so completely unconscious.

"Forgive me, my love," I whispered as I smacked Griffin soundly on the cheek. He stirred briefly, then fell back into a stupor.

I slapped him again. His eyelids flickered, but nothing more. There was no water in the room, so I returned to slapping him, trying desperately to rouse him, but I couldn't wake him for more than a few seconds at a time. I tried sitting him up, thinking I could half carry him out of the room, but he was too heavy for me in his drugged state.

It must have been ten minutes later when a door banged down the hall and I jumped up, terrified. I ran to the door and listened, but heard nothing. Cautiously, I slipped out of his room, taking care to lock it before dashing to my room.

The key turned in the lock with a squeak, but I made it in and lock the door from the inside before I heard approaching footsteps.

I stood with my ear pressed against the door.

"'Ow do I know where the blasted keys went? I'm not the one as was in charge of them. That's Merlin's job."

The doorknob to my room rattled and there was a sharp knock. "You in there, miss?"

I moved back from the door and said in my most arrogant voice, "Yes, I am, and I am tiring of being held in here. I demand that you let me out!"

"Not yet, miss. Your time will come soon enough."

"What about the other door?" I heard Merlin ask.

"It's locked too."

"Well, come on, then. Don't just stand there like you have nothing better to do. We have to find those damned keys."

Their voices rumbled back down the hallway and I slumped against the wall with relief. I had been worried they might have a duplicate set, but was heartened by their response.

It was some time before I could go back to Griffin's room; Percy and Merlin were all over the top floor of the building, searching for the missing keys. Judging by the acrimonious comments being bandied about by Freddie, no one had yet thought of a skeleton key. Taking my chance at a rare quiet period, I left my room secured, and dashed into Griffin's, locking it as well.

I roused him by resorting to several sharp slaps and had him in a sitting position with his head between his knees when I heard voices outside the door. After unnecessarily cautioning the barely conscious Griffin to be quiet, I crept to the door and listened. What I heard turned my blood to ice.

"Well, someone must have a pass key! Go downstairs and check, you idiots."

"Now then, Mister Black, there's no reason to be calling us names. I'll just send Percy downstairs to the manager, like, and ask politely for a key. She likes you, doesn't she, mate?"

Percy sniggered.

"Good. Fine. Just do it! I'm already an hour late for my appointment, and Mr. Hope won't wait around here forever."

I assumed Freddie was talking about the clergyman. Crawling back to Griffin, I found him with his head sunk down on his chest, sleeping.

"Griffin, you must pull yourself together," I hissed, smacking him on the cheek.

"Huh? Wha'? Alex?"

"Yes, my love, it's me. You have to stay awake and concentrate."

He blinked at me groggily, and I slapped him again. His head snapped back, his eyes opened wide but unfocused. I reached out to slap him again, but his hand shot up and caught mine.

"Listen to me, Griffin. This is very important." I spoke with my face close to his, peering intently into his beautiful, clouded amber eyes. "We are being held prisoner. We have to get out now. Do you understand?"

He blinked at me a few times, then said thickly, "Prisoner. I understand."

I helped him to his feet, which were none too steady, and unlocked the door. There was no one in the hallway and only occasional sounds from the sitting room. I put both hands on Griffin's head and shook it until he protested.

"You must be silent. The men are in that room, and they are armed. We have to go past them without them seeing us. Can you do that?"

His eyes were still confused and clouded, but he nodded his head. I grasped his hand and led him from the room, but stopped when someone pounded on the door to the flat. Pushing Griffin back into his room, I held the door open a fraction and watched as Merlin emerged from the sitting room to answer the door. I expected to see Percy—my jaw dropped when I saw a familiar face.

"William Jones, I want to speak with you!"

It was Annie, *my* Annie, come to confront her paramour.

"Why haven't you answered my letters?" she demanded, shaking her fist and unleashing a torrent of angry comments.

Merlin backed up, his hands outstretched, obviously trying to defend himself against the tongue-lashing Annie gave him. He held up a hand, said something too quiet for me to hear, and went into the sitting room, closing the door behind him.

I didn't have time to dither. "Annie," I hissed, poking my head out of the door.

She looked up, her hands on her hips, the very picture of a righteous, indignant woman. Surprise flooded her face as she saw me.

"Shhhhh!" I cautioned. "Don't tell him you know I'm here, but I need you to help me."

The sitting-room door opened and Merlin appeared, his back to me as he carefully closed the door behind him. I ducked back, peeking through a mere inch of open door.

"Now, Annie, my love," Merlin said in a placatory tone.

"Don't you 'Annie, my love' me," she warned. "You have me in the family way! Why haven't you answered my letters?"

"Letters? I didn't receive your letters, my sweet—"

"Not much, you didn't! Oh! Oh!" She seized her chest.

"What's wrong, Annie?" Merlin seemed more concerned with watching the door to the sitting room than with Annie.

"It's my heart. The doctor said I should rest when it acts up."

"You go home and have a good rest love."

"I can't—" she panted, clutching her chest harder. "The doctor says I have to lie down right away when I have these spells. It might be fatal!"

If Annie ever went on the stage, I would be happy to support her endeavor by any means required. I did not know she was such a natural-born actress, but the performance she gave Merlin was outstanding.

Merlin settled her in one of the free rooms. "I'll look in on you in a few minutes," he said, returning to the sitting room. He didn't even glance toward our room.

A soft tap on the door alerted me to Annie's presence. "What are you doing here, miss? Oh, isn't that—"

"Annie," I spoke in a low voice, but with an urgency that was hard to mistake. "Your friend, Mr. Jones, has kidnapped us. Mr. St. John and me, that is. He's drugged Griffin, and I don't think I can get him out by myself. Please help us."

"William did? *My* William?"

"Your William. Will you help us?"

Her face set in a grim expression. "Tell me what you want me to do, miss, and I'll do it."

I hugged her. "I'm just worried that Percy will return from sweet-talking the manager before I can get Griffin out. I need you to cause a distraction that will focus the attention of the men away from the door so I can get him past without being seen. Can you do that?"

"I'll make a scene that William won't forget in a long time," she promised. "It will be a pleasure to tell him what I think of his ways!"

She slipped out and closed the door. I turned back to Griffin and alternately shook and slapped him into semi-consciousness. He staggered against me drunkenly as I tried to keep him awake and moving.

I could hear the raised voices even through the door. Opening it quietly, I gave Griffin one last shake and, putting my shoulder under his arm, led him down the hall. We came to the open door of the sitting room, where Annie was in action. She ranted, she yelled, she threw bits of crockery at the men. Bless her heart, she had all three men crouched in the far corner as she aimed a large jug at them.

Whirling around, she slammed shut the door to the sitting room. A loud crash showed the jug had fulfilled its destiny.

I grabbed Griffin and dragged him towards the door. He stumbled and fell against me heavily, but we got out of the flat before the door to the sitting room opened. I didn't stop, knowing that Percy would be on his way up at any moment. We started down the stairs, Griffin leaning on me and stumbling because his legs weren't working as they should. I worried that Annie might have put herself in danger by helping us and was relieved when I heard her voice echo down the stairwell.

"That's the last you'll see of me, William Jones," she shouted.

Griffin and I made it down two floors when I heard someone starting up the stairs. Annie was above, clattering her way noisily downward, muttering as she descended.

Panicked, I hurried down the passageway, pulling Griffin into the deepest shadows I could find. His head lolled sleepily, but he was still standing.

I roused him quickly. "Griffin, put your arms around me."

"Mmmm?"

I lifted one of his arms onto my shoulders just as Percy paused on the landing.

"Oooh, Basil, stop that!" I squealed with a high-pitched giggle and rubbed my hands through Griffin's hair. Poor man, he lifted his head and tried to focus his eyes on me, but failed. I peeked over his shoulder as Percy looked hesitantly toward us.

"Some people don't have nothing better to do than watch them that are enjoying themselves. Get on with you and let those two have some privacy," Annie sniffed in a disgusted tone as she passed him on her way down.

Percy, wilting under her comments, continued up the stairs.

With Annie's help, we stumbled our way down the remaining two flights and out the front door. Angry shouts and oaths from above informed us that the passkey had been used and our escape was known.

"Blast," I swore as Griffin tripped over the debris and rubbish that littered the street. He was leaning heavily on me as we stumbled along. "I'm not going to last for any great distance, Annie."

"What do you want me to do?" Annie asked.

I looked around frantically for a spot to hide. We half-dragged Griffin around the corner where I spied a side yard, similar to the one at my aunt's house, although this one was full of trash bins. "An excellent hiding place. You go look for a cab while I hide Griffin."

Ten minutes later, one street away from where I left him, I spotted a cab that was crawling.

"Thank heavens," I panted to myself and dashed up to it, ready to heap praise on Annie's head for finding it.

"Why, cousin—" a familiar voice drawled.

"You!" I gasped, snatching my hand back from the door.

"You look distraught," Freddie said, all charm and concern as he opened the cab's door. "Let me help you in."

He stepped out of the cab, his arm extended to me. Unwilling to let him gain control of Griffin or me, I grabbed the cravat around Freddie's neck and yanked him forward, throwing him off balance.

"Not in a million years," I swore, kicking him hard on the knee, then harder in another, more vulnerable spot.

"Here, now, miss," the cabby cautioned as Freddie screamed, clutching his groin as he toppled to the ground.

"This man is a criminal and a kidnapper," I cried. "You must help me. He attempted to abduct another man and myself."

"Well—" The cabby hesitated, watching as Freddie writhed on the ground.

"I'll pay you twice the standard fare."

"Get in," the cabby said, and we quickly drove the two blocks to where I had Griffin hidden.

"But ma'am, there's no one there," he protested when I scrambled out of the cab. "Just some trash."

I peeled the refuse off of Griffin's legs and moved one of the bins.

The cabby scratched his jaw. "Why, bless me, there *is* a man there."

I hated to do it, knowing it would bruise his cheeks, but I slapped Griffin a few more times. His eyes flew opened, but they were still out of focus. I shook his head until he protested. Then the cabby and I got him on his feet. Once we had Griffin settled in the cab, I told him to drive around the area.

"But that gentleman—" He pointed down the street to where Freddie was crawling toward us.

"He can take care of himself. I'm looking for my maid. She went to find us a cab and I cannot leave without her."

"No cabs around here, ma'am. If she's looking for one, she'll have to go up to the Crescent."

We set off for the Crescent. I watched fearfully out of the window, but only saw Merlin and Percy once, from the distance of a block. I doubted if they could see into the cab, but ordered the cabby to pick up the pace.

We found Annie about ten blocks away. She was exhausted and on her way back to help me, having been unable to find a cab.

"I think we did it," I said, sinking back against the ratty seat, finally able to relax. Griffin's head lolled over onto my shoulder. I stroked it and smiled to myself at his soft murmurs. Annie sat on the other side and watched us with just a hint of her dimples.

The debate about where to take him raged within me as we drove away from the slums. I was torn between tending to him myself and letting his family, who must surely be worried about him by now, take care of him. "I suppose it's only right to take him to his home," I said after much internal debate and gave the cabby Griffin's address.

"I can take you there, ma'am, but it's quite a ways away. Over two shillings. I'll have to ask you to show me you have the fare," the cabby said apologetically.

"Oh, money." I sighed. Percy had taken my bag, and I had nothing in my skirt pockets.

"Annie?"

She shook her head. "Just a few coppers."

We both looked at Griffin. I searched his pockets until I found a collection of coins that satisfied the cabby. What he must have thought of us, I shudder to think. I was disheveled, hot, and dirty from my experience on the roof and running around the streets. Griffin looked disreputable, with a bloodied head and drunken appearance. Annie alone was presentable.

The Sherringhams' footman flinched when he saw me standing on the steps with my tangled hair and a torn, dirty dress, but responded to my question. "Lady Helena and Lady Sherringham are out, but Lord Sherringham is in, Miss Whitney."

I looked at the semi-reclined figure of my hero in the cab, and my heart revolted at leaving him in the care of his brother. "Tell Lady Helena that her brother has been taken ill and is recovering at the home of Mr. Joshua Garner."

"Yes, miss," he said haughtily, sniffing in disgust.

I gave the cabby the address, and in a relatively short time, we were home. Mullin had the door opened before I could step down from the cab.

"Miss Alex! The family has been most distressed about your absence," he said with a look of strong disapproval at my appearance.

"It's a long story, Mullin, and not one I want to tell on the street. Is Theodore about? I need help. Mr. St. John is ill, and Annie and I are exhausted."

In the end, it took more than Theodore and Mullin to get Griffin in the house and into a guest room. The laudanum was wearing off, and it left him antagonistic, causing him to fight groggily, but with great strength. I did the best I could to calm him, but by the time we settled him in a bedroom, Theodore had a black eye, Mullin swore one of his teeth was loose, and Robert walked with a pronounced limp.

We propped Griffin up on pillows, and while we waited for the doctor to come, I sat on the edge of the bed and tried to pour coffee into him. More coffee ended up *on* him than *in* him, but we made a valiant effort.

Dr. Melrose, a darling man who was my sister's physician, came at once. After eyeing the footmen, he ordered everyone but Robert out of the room, saying he might need Robert's assistance to conduct a thorough examination.

I dashed to my room and had a perfunctory wash, then spent the rest of the time pacing the hallway. Periodic sounds of crashing and harsh yelling emitted from Griffin's room, sending me more than once to knock on the door and ask if my help was needed. Joshua did his best to calm my fears, but Mabel insisted on knowing exactly what had happened after I ran out so early and why Annie accompanied us home.

"That doesn't matter right now," I snapped. "Not until I know—until I know—oh, damn!" I kicked at a chair that insisted on getting in my way.

"Alex! I will not have such language in my house," Mabel lectured, but she was cut short when Joshua gently guided her downstairs.

Loud voices in the hall drew my attention, and with a reluctant glance at the door to Griffin's room, I went to the head of the stairs. Standing in an arrogant posture before Joshua, Lord Sherringham was bellowing at the top of his lungs.

"I won't have it! You have no right to hold my brother against his will. I demand that you hand him over immediately!"

The tone of his voice recalled memories of my father in his finest rage, but the similarity gave me strength rather than weakened me. I marched down the stairs, my jaw tight, my eyes narrowed, and my fists clenched. "Griffin is currently receiving the attentions of a doctor. You will kindly lower your voice."

The earl spun around at my words and turned a hideous shade of purple. "You—you—" he sputtered incoherently, stalking forward toward me, his lips curled in a grotesque mask of fury that washed over me like acid.

I stiffened my knees and refused to be cowed. I would not show this man anything but my scorn. "Until the doctor informs us it is safe to move him, Griffin will remain where he is. We will keep you notified of any changes in his status."

"How dare you speak to me that way, you harlot! You are to blame for my brother's attack! How dare you stand there and pretend to protect him? I am removing him this instant to my home, where I can be sure he will be looked after properly. Move out of my way before I take my whip to you." He raised his riding crop in a threatening manner.

There are a few moments in my life about which I feel an overwhelming sense of pride. This wasn't one of the brightest, but it was one of the most satisfying. I took two steps forward, snatched the crop out of his hand, and snapped it over the banister.

"If you dare to lift one finger towards Griffin," I said in a low, ugly voice, "*one finger*, it will be the last thing you do."

He spewed vile words at me, but Joshua—who told me later that at that moment he was afraid I would attack Lord Sherringham on the spot—calmed him into some sort of coherence.

I didn't remain to see. Ignoring the protests of my shaking limbs, I raced up the stairs and continued to pace endlessly along the hallway outside Griffin's room until the doctor emerged at last.

"His head—" I faltered.

"Ah, Miss Whitney." The doctor gave me a very incurious look. "The patient is fine, nothing more than a mild concussion and an extreme case of laudanum overdose. After he sleeps it off, he should be fit as a fiddle."

I wanted to kiss him and dance a jig at the same time. "Thank heavens. Is there something we should do? More coffee or other stimulants?"

"No, you've done just what I would have suggested. It's a good thing you got him moving when you did, though. The amount of laudanum he seems to have consumed, combined with the concussion, might have done him harm had you left him in a stupor."

My stomach lurched at the thought of my Griffin at Merlin's mercy.

"What he needs most is to be allowed to rest. He's a little hostile right now, so you must be careful. For some reason, he seems to think he must escape the house."

I thanked him and hurried into the room. Robert and Doctor Melrose had undressed Griffin and get him into bed with only minor damage to the various articles in the room. Robert was stooped down, collecting bits of a broken jug.

"Don't worry about that, I'll clean it up later," I told him as I stopped at the bed. "Have the doctor look at your leg."

Griffin lay with his eyes closed, a furrow between his brows. I tried to smooth it out, but his hand shot up and grabbed my wrist with a strength that was almost painful. His eyes opened at my gasp of pain. I was happy to see his lovely amber eyes were once again in focus, although it took a few minutes before he recognized me.

Robert slipped out of the room, saying he would get a compress for his knee, and I was left to sit with my fallen hero. I brushed back the hair from his temples and laid a hand alongside his cheek. "How do you feel?"

He looked at me for a few moments while the words filtered through his fogged brain. "Feel tired."

"I know, my poor darling. You lie there and rest. You're safe now."

I murmured endearments as he dropped into a restless sleep. After I was sure he was resting as comfortably as I could expect, I went downstairs to face the familial equivalent of the Spanish Inquisition.

Conversation stopped when I entered the sitting room, faces turning to me with ill-concealed expectation. I smiled wanly, refused a cup of tea, asked for one of coffee, and sank exhausted into a chair.

Mabel glared at me, evidently still annoyed at my rudeness earlier. Joshua watched me patiently while Robert stood gazing forlornly out the window.

"We were kidnapped," I said in answer to the unspoken question.

The response was more heated than I expected, and I closed my eyes until the exclamations were finished.

"Would you like to wait to tell us, my dear?" my brother-in-law asked.

I should my head. "Thank you, but I think I would rather tell you now. Griffin may need me later."

"Doctor Melrose said he would be fine in a day or two," offered Mabel, her anger apparently forgotten. "I don't think you have anything to worry about. Now, tell us about this kidnapping."

I went over the entire amazing episode, hesitating over telling the truth about Freddie, but deciding that I'd wait for Griffin's counsel before I revealed that information. I had a feeling that Griffin could control his brother if Freddie sought Lord Sherringham's aid in getting me out of the way.

"My one concern now is whether we should contact the police," I finished wearily.

Joshua asked, "We've already done so. They sent several men to the location, but said it was empty. Clearly, the miscreants had left as soon as they realized you'd escaped."

I stared at him in surprise. "How did you know where we were held? I don't remember the location at all."

"Annie," Robert said succinctly. "She gave Joshua the address she had for her...er...friend."

"Oh, yes, of course. Annie knew it." I clutched the chair tightly, my head swimming. Robert's words seemed to come from a very long way away. An inky, dark pool loomed up before me.

"Delayed reaction," I heard someone say and thought I heard Helena's voice just before my head went under the dark water.

FIFTEEN

"You startled me, you know. I've never had anyone swoon just because I entered a room." It *was* Helena I heard before I fainted. She stood next to me, speaking in a hushed tone. "You didn't say anything, either. You just toppled quietly to the floor, clutching a cup of coffee."

I summoned up a smile for her, although I had a feeling it wasn't a brilliant specimen. "I'm sorry. I must have been more overwrought than I imagined."

"Are you sure he's going to be all right?" Helena was almost panic stricken with concern about the state of her brother's health until we trouped upstairs together. Side-by-side we stood, watching him sleep.

"The doctor says he just needs to sleep. There's no actual damage." A thought struck me, causing me to giggle under my breath. Helena looked askance at me, horrified that I could laugh in the face of her brother's brush with death. "No, I'm not laughing at the situation. But can you imagine what Griffin would have to say if he knew we were standing here watching him sleep?"

A smile stole across Helena's lips, and after she delivered a last kiss to his forehead, she returned home.

Several hours later, the library was the scene of a domestic storm.

"No! I will not have it, Alex!" Mabel marched past me in a fine show of drama. "Even if he has asked you to marry him—and he certainly has not mentioned that to either me or Joshua, or even Freddie that I know of—it is beyond improper that you should spend the night in the same room with him."

I glanced at Joshua, hating to make a scene, but resolute. "The last thing I want is to give you grief, but someone has severely drugged Griffin. I won't be able to sleep knowing he might have some sort of reaction or relapse during the night."

She gave a ladylike snort and dismissed my concerns. "The doctor said he would be fine."

"I don't care. I'm spending the night with him." I rose from the sofa, marveling inwardly at my sudden bravery. I'd never before outright disputed Mabel's requests.

"I will *not* have it!" Mabel yelled, startling Joshua. "No sister of mine will behave with such impropriety!"

"He was almost drugged to death. The doctor as much as said so," I pointed out, wanting to yell as well, but knowing that would do little good. I refused to go down the path of my father by giving in to the need to shout when things were not going my way.

"I don't care! I refuse to allow you to shame us with such scandalous behavior. What if it got out? How would we hold up our heads?" she ranted, her hands gesticulating wildly.

"There is nothing we could do that we haven't already done," I said in a calm voice, one that sadly belied the inner turmoil gripping me.

Mabel gasped with shock and assumedly horror, and things went downhill after that, dissolving into hurtful accusations and slammed doors. I waited until she went to rail at Joshua for having such an unreasonable sister before slipping into Griffin's room, where I crawled into bed with him, my hand on his chest just because it made me feel better to have it there.

Griffin slept through the night and late in the morning. It wasn't until noon that I found him sitting up in bed, rubbing a hand over his stubbly cheeks.

"Ah, Sleeping Beauty awakens," I joked as I entered, turning to hail Annie as she left my room. "Send up some coffee, please. Lots of it."

"I thought I was dreaming," Griffin said, yawning, looking around the room. "What am I doing here?"

I sat carefully on the bed and ignored, as best I could, the large expanse of chest in front of me. I reminded myself sternly that he was recovering from a head wound and overdose of opiate, and although he might enjoy the expressions of affection I was so desirous of showing him, it would be better to wait until he fully recovered.

"Do you remember anything about yesterday?" I asked, keeping my eyes fixed firmly on his face.

He frowned and rubbed his head, grimacing when he touched the injured spot. "Not much. I remember you and a fat man who tried to take my clothes off." He looked down at himself, then pulled the blankets up when a housemaid came in with coffee.

"Do you remember anything about being drugged or hit on the head?" I asked as I poured him a cup.

"No. Just a bad dream about stairs."

I told him briefly what had happened. He interrupted my narrative frequently with several outraged comments and scattered oaths.

When I finished, he said just one thing. "Tell me again what you said to Sherry."

I repeated it. His scowl faded and a little smile curled his lips. "I wish I had been there. He must be furious. I can't wait to see him."

Our eyes met, and the smiles left both our faces. I placed my hand gently on his cheek. We sat like that for a moment. Then he pulled me forward and onto his chest.

"I owe you my life," he whispered, kissing me gently. "My brave savior."

"It wasn't quite as dramatic as that." My hands moved to his bare chest as his mouth claimed possession of mine, a moan of pleasure slipping from my lips as his tongue stirred the embers of a fire than never completely extinguished. Carefully, gently, slowly, I pulled myself away from him. "You're not supposed to overextend yourself. The doctor said you must not make any quick or strenuous actions, lest it cause your head to hurt."

He protested, but I left him to get dressed by himself. Ten minutes after he came downstairs to the sitting room, Mullin entered, murmuring, "Lady Helena St. John... er..."

"It's all right, Mullin," I said, climbing from Griffin's lap. I straightened my dress and tried to look like Griffin hadn't been in the middle of a detailed examination of my mouth, simultaneous with a tactile mapping of my upper person. "Helena! Here is the brave hero, all in one piece, as you can see."

"Yes, I can see he's feeling much better," she said with a smile as she kissed his cheek. Robert, who was behind her, summoned a smile of his own, although it was distinctly on the wan side.

"Mabel and Joshua have taken the girls to the zoo," I told Helena. "You'll stay for luncheon, I hope."

"The time has come for all of us to be completely honest," I told them a half hour later. Chicken, potatoes, and vegetables were all passed around.

"I've always been honest with you," Helena protested.

"I've never doubted that," I reassured her. "My comment was aimed primarily at your brother. It's time he tells us what he suspects."

Griffin grumbled a bit at that, but in the end agreed. "I will, but only after you explain what you think has been happening."

"Are you afraid you're wrong, or that I am?" I asked him, curious.

He went to shake his head, grimaced, and answered, "Neither. I just have a hell of a headache. No, I don't need another compress. Tell us what you think."

I sat down from where I was about to fetch him something to make his head feel better. "Very well. I shall begin by telling you all about my cousin's role in this."

"Your cousin?" Helena asked. "What does he have to do with it?"

I took a deep breath, reminding myself that I was amongst people who would not judge me for my father's sins. Quickly, I explained not only his part in the kidnapping, but the threat he'd made to me.

Robert and Helena were shocked and appalled. Griffin, as I suspected, was livid. He paced around the room, tossing out the most unreasonable comments.

"I'll kill him!"

"You won't," I said. My heart warmed that he wanted to protect me. "You'll just end up in prison, and then we won't be able to have connubial relations."

He checked for a moment at that thought, then continued pacing, but less vigorously. "In that case, I'll silence him. I'll tell him I'll knock his teeth down this throat if he ever so much as looks at you again."

"That would also likely end up with jail time," Robert pointed out.

Griffin shot him a look of fury.

"He's right. Beating Freddie isn't the answer," I said, getting up so I could hug Griffin before gently pushing him back toward his chair. "He has, as he said, powerful friends. Er...you don't think that what he said was true, do you?"

"About what?" he asked, frowning.

I smoothed out the wrinkle between his brows. "About me inheriting my father's madness."

"Hell, no. The idea is ridiculous," he said, looking thoughtfully at the cutlery at his place setting. "Helena, do you remember where I put that Abyssinian gelding knife?"

"Thank you for that," I said, retaking my seat.

He glanced up. "For wanting to geld your cousin?"

"For not thinking I could go mad like my father."

"But...what are we going to do?" Helena asked, looking worried. "We must protect Alex."

Griffin shrugged and reached for a bowl of marinated tomatoes. "That's easy enough. We'll be married soon. He won't be able to do anything then."

"You are engaged?" Helena gasped, leaping up to hug me. "Now I shall truly have you for a sister. Oh, I am so happy!"

I stared at Griffin as Robert congratulated us both, and Helena kissed her brother. I had my own thoughts about when we would marry, but I could see Griffin's point. A speedy marriage would nip Freddie's intentions in the bud, so to speak. I took a bite of chicken and said, "I suppose we should. It seems quite clear that Freddie's plan regarding the kidnapping was to marry me after he drugged me just enough to make me not quite lucid."

Griffin muttered a few choice phrases involving the gelding knife that I ignored.

"But that's illegal," Helena pointed out.

"Of course it is, but there is more to it than that. There's his connection with Lord Sherringham."

Helena laid down her fork. "My dearest friend, just because I saw your cousin speaking with Harold, it doesn't follow that he had a part in your kidnapping!"

"I'm lost. What does the earl have to do with you two being kidnapped?" asked Robert.

"Nothing," I said, trying to put facts together. "At least...I think the kidnapping was tangentially related to Griffin."

"I don't understand," Helena said, back to looking worried.

Griffin and I exchanged glances, his thoughtful, mine suspicious.

"There isn't any proof," Griffin said to me, acknowledging the dark musings that had finally come together in my mind.

"No, but the connection is there. Helena saw Freddie and your brother talking at that costume ball."

"But why would Harold want your cousin to kidnap Griffin?" Helena asked.

I took another deep breath, hating to upset her, but knowing it was for the best that she understand what was going on. "It's been my belief for some time that someone means to… well, to be blunt, to kill Griffin."

Helena gasped in horror, but took the news better than I expected. "I say again, why? Why would anyone want to harm him?"

"The most common reasons are for gain, love, or revenge," I mumbled as I fought with a tough piece of chicken. I looked up and saw I had the attention of the table. Turning to Griffin, I asked, "Who would benefit by your death?"

"Helena mostly, and probably Harold," he answered.

I thought for a second. "Do you have a will?"

"No." At my questioning look, he continued, "I've been meaning to make one, but just haven't found the opportunity."

I pushed the chicken around my plate before setting down my silverware. "If you were to die in your current state, your brother would likely divide equally your estate between Helena and himself. At worst, it would go to Lord Sherringham in its entirety."

"Possibly." He stared sightlessly at nothing in particular, his brows pulled together.

I turned to Helena. "You told me you inherited money from your mother. Who controls your fortune until you are of age?"

She swallowed hard, her fingers working absently on a bit of a roll. "Harold does, and another trustee, Oliver Hope."

"And if you marry, is your fortune settled on you?" I asked.

She blushed and only just refrained from glancing at Robert. "No. I won't have it until I'm twenty-five."

Something niggled in the back of my mind, but I couldn't pinpoint it.

"I don't understand the purpose of your questions, Alex. What are you trying to say?" Robert leaned forward to pin me back with a curious glance.

I ignored it and turned back to Griffin. "Why would he want you dead? He's got everything—a title, an ancestral home, respect, position, a house in town."

"Debts up to his knees," Griffin interrupted. "There is no money from Rosewood, and he has run through what little money Letitia brought to the marriage. The house in town is mine, not Sherry's. I bought it when his creditors forced him to sell it."

"The house is yours?" I asked, sitting back in surprise. "Does your brother have a house?"

Their heads swinging in unison between Griffin and me as if they were at a tennis match, Helena and Robert watched us in silence.

"He had Rosewood," Griffin answered. "But that was destroyed, and all that's left is three hundred acres of land leased for the next forty years."

"If the house had not burned," I said absently, toying with the mustard pot, "it might have kept him from coveting your income."

He looked at me oddly. "You should know the worst. I don't have any proof, but I've always believed that Sherry burned the house down himself."

"Griffin!" cried Helena, clearly flabbergasted.

"It's time you know the truth, too, Helena." His fingers spasmed as he spoke, turning to me to explain. "Sherry always was a little different, and he loathed having to share Rosewood with us. My father specified in his will that Rosewood would always be our home, as well as Sherry's. He hated that. It wasn't too bad when I was at school, but when I came home—"

"I can't believe it. Do you know what you are saying?" Helena asked.

"He knows, Helena," I said, wishing I could shield her from this heartbreak. "But you must admit, it fits. Lord Sherringham is an important person in the House of Lords but has no means and no house living in his brother's home. I can only imagine what that would do to a man of his immense pride."

Helena had tears in her eyes. "But to kill Griffin—our own brother—he couldn't do that!"

"No, I agree with you there. That's why he had to find someone to do the job for him. With Griffin out of the way, he would inherit... a sizable fortune?" I set down the mustard and looked the question at Griffin, who nodded wearily. I forestalled the urge to kiss him silly. "I have a suspicion your brother has been less than honest with your inheritance, Helena. When was the last time you had an accounting?"

"I—I don't pay attention to those things," she mumbled, avoiding my gaze.

I felt like she had deflated in the last few minutes, and was troubled by my role in her unhappiness.

"What about the other trustee? Wouldn't he notice if Helena's brother were embezzling funds?" Robert asked.

"I hardly ever see him," Helena answered.

Griffin pushed his plate back. "I think it's time someone had a look at your trust, Helena. I'll speak to Hope about it in the morning."

She smiled gratefully at him. We talked the situation over for a while longer, but didn't come to any conclusions. Robert and Griffin were all for immediately confronting Lord Sherringham, but Helena and I cautioned them against doing so.

"After all, we don't have any proof," I pointed out, passing a bowl of grapes to Helena. "Nothing but a few suppositions and coincidences. The police would laugh at such an unsubstantial accusation, especially when it targets an important person like Lord Sherringham."

"What we need is evidence," Griffin said, glaring at the innocent orange he held in his hands, just as if it had personally offended him. "I believe I can get that."

"How?" Helena and I asked together.

"I'm fairly certain I know the reason you were kidnapped, as well as me. Yesterday—no, it was the day before yesterday, I told Sherry we were engaged."

"I take it Lord Sherringham wasn't pleased with this news?" I asked.

"You could say that." Griffin's eyes glittered as his lips curled at the corners. I felt suddenly ten degrees warmer. "He was enraged and tried to forbid me from marrying you, but I told him to mind his own business."

"So, he would want to get rid of Alex as well as you? Why?" Robert asked.

Griffin tore off a bit of orange peel, deftly extracting a bit of orange and offering it to me. "Because he knew one of the first things I would do was make my home ready for my bride. That would mean he and Letitia would have to leave, since they would refuse to tolerate Alex's presence. I'm sorry, sweetheart. I didn't mean that to sound so harsh."

I took the offered segment of orange and smiled at the concern in his beautiful eyes. "I understand, and I agree. They would see me as a threat, a thorn in Lord Sherringham's side that he couldn't possibly tolerate."

"But why did they need to kidnap you?" Helena asked. "I'm so confused."

"It's a confusing situation. And I'm not absolutely certain your brother is guilty of that crime. I suspect that debt is behind my cousin's repeated proposals of marriage." I interrupted myself and turned to Griffin. "What or who is Roget's?"

"Hmm? Roget's? Moneylenders."

"That would make sense," I mused, accepting a second segment of orange. "If Freddie were being pressed to make good his debts, he would be desperate to find an easy way out. We've always had an amicable relationship, and he knew how my father had affected me, so I assume he counted on my timidity as a guarantee of his acceptance. Once we were married, he would have access to my money and be able to pay off his debts."

Griffin choked on a bit of orange at the word "timidity," but sputtered out he was fine when I asked if he needed assistance.

He wiped his eyes, then said in a rough voice, "That means both your cousin and Sherry have employed the same men—a situation that's far too unlikely to be coincidental. There must be a connection between Merlin and Sherry."

Everyone looked at me expectantly. I hated to disappoint them, but had to admit I didn't have the slightest idea of an answer. "I agree, there has to be something there, something the two have in common, but what it is… well, your guess is as good as mine."

"We just need to reason it out." Griffin rubbed his eyes. "You overheard your cousin talking to the two men who attacked us—twice if you count the assault on me at home—"

"Possibly a third and fourth time," I interrupted. "If you include the attacks on Helena and me."

"All right, so now we have four attacks, assuming the two of you were the same men. It doesn't make sense. Either that or they hit harder me than I thought."

"No." I agreed, thinking it out. "I think it's clear now that there were two distinct campaigns of violence against us, one targeting you with a very serious intent, and one focused on Helena and me that is really nothing more than a mild annoyance. But who is behind the latter? Surely Freddie has nothing to gain by frightening us…" The words froze on my lips as my eyes met Griffin's. He nodded. "He didn't!"

"It looks like he did," Griffin countered.

"Did what?" Helena asked.

My lips thinned. "He tried to scare me into marrying him. No doubt he felt that was easier than having me committed and assumedly taking over control of my estate. That rotter! Well, that explains a great deal."

"But not the connection between him and Sherry," Griffin said wearily.

He was looking decidedly tired, so after making him promise he would, under no circumstances, confront his brother or otherwise endanger his life, the St. Johns went home—Helena to fret and Griffin to do a covert search of his brother's papers for proof of his nefarious activities.

I decided I should spend my time in a productive manner.

I sat in the library and worried.

"Alex, for heaven's sake, you are making me nervous! Sit down," Mabel complained the following morning, clicking her tongue when I paced by her for the tenth time.

I sat down and watched her work on her embroidery.

"And don't stare at me. That makes me even more nervous." She looked up from the pinafore she was adorning. "What's wrong with you? You're not normally restless like this."

I stood, too fretful to sit any longer, and went to the window to look out at the overcast morning. "I feel like something is hanging over my head, like I am waiting for something to happen. I feel... unsettled."

She went back to her work. "Go pay a call. Or read a book."

I stared out the window, uneasy.

"Perhaps you could invite Mr. St. John for lunch?" she suggested.

"He's busy today, writing an article for the Royal Geographic Society." I made a face at my faint reflection in the glass. "I plan on visiting Helena later, but she is gone this morning."

Mabel glanced over, the hint of an arch smile about her lips. "With Robert?"

"Yes." I made another face at myself. "They've gone riding."

"That will soon end in a match unless I am wrong, and you know I seldom am," she said, stabbing through the cloth of the pinafore with a smugness that prickled down my skin.

With nothing else to do, and to shake myself free from my sour mood, I spent a few hours at the headquarters of a charity devoted to providing convict's wives with employment.

Much to my regret, Robert was still out when I returned home. Uneasy ennui settled over me again, leaving me almost desperate to be out and doing something. I walked the dogs, played with the twins, wrote letters to distant friends, and sat in the library until Joshua asked if I would kindly take myself elsewhere as my restless lurking made him nervous.

I had just decided to go upstairs and weed through my wardrobe again with an eye to giving away the outcasts, when Robert returned.

"There you are," I cried, happy to see him. "I wondered where you had been. Did you enjoy your morning?"

He looked at me with something akin to grief. "I did, but I shouldn't have wasted Helena's time."

"Don't be such an idiot. She's clearly as smitten with you as you are with her. In fact…" I thought for a moment. "If she's home, I believe I will go see her. You may come with me if you like."

He sighed the sigh of the martyred even though he helped me on with my coat and followed me out onto the street where I caught a cabby's attention. "I have no means," he reminded me once we were settled inside the cab. "I have nothing to offer her but my undying devotion and love. How can I tell her my feelings? I cannot hope to marry her."

"We've been through this before," I pointed out, wanting to lecture him within an inch of his life, but knowing this was a decision he'd have to come to himself. "If you refuse to believe me when I tell you it won't matter to Helena, ask the lady herself. It may surprise you to find out what she considers being important in a suitor."

He looked so doubtful and miserable that I bit back the rest of the lecture that boiled inside me and instead contemplated a visit with Griffin.

The footman showed us into a small, dark, evidently seldom used parlor while he found out the whereabouts of

Griffin and Helena. I looked around with pleasure until I noticed Robert seemed to be in the grip of some nervous complaint: his leg twitched, and he was perspiring freely about the forehead. When the door opened, I was going to ask him if he was sick, but instead I turned with a smile on my lips to greet Griffin, only to come face to face with Lord Sherringham. My smiled faded when the little man puffed up indignantly as he transferred his glare from Robert to me.

"You!" he bellowed at me in an excellent imitation of Griffin at his loudest. "How dare you step foot in this house? How dare you show your face here? You will leave at once! That goes for you, sir, as well!"

Panic clutched at me for a few seconds, but I shook off its barbs, and reminded myself I had faced this monster before, and I could do so again. I swallowed hard, but said in a fairly calm tone, "I am here to see your brother, Lord Sherringham, not you."

"You will not see him, madam. You will see *no one* in this house. Don't think I am not aware of your insidious plans—I am!"

"What plan would that be?" I asked, thinking of the Union plans detailed in my notebook.

Robert, to the left of me, gripped the chair. I was pleased to see he showed no signs of intimidation and instead looked as if he would welcome a battle himself.

"Your plans to ingratiate yourself with my brother. You will find that I am not oblivious as to the reason you have attempted to ensnare him. Can you deny you are guilty of trying to get hold of his fortune?"

I found it curious that the only reason Lord Sherringham could imagine a woman wanting to marry his brother was for money and had that on the tip of my tongue when the door opened and Griffin strolled in.

He had a smear of ink on the bridge of his nose and a corresponding blotch on his hand. He looked so adorable I was hard put to refrain from kissing him in front of Robert and Lord Sherringham.

I looked back at the earl. "I don't deny that I am guilty of an attachment to your brother, Lord Sherringham. But my motives in desiring him do not include greed."

I looked pointedly past him as I spoke, hoping he would take the hint, and would have said more had Helena not entered the room. She looked cool and lovely in a pale pink morning dress, her cheeks bright with matching color. "Is anything the matter? Why is Harold shouting? Robert?"

Griffin stepped forward, lifted my chin, and kissed me gently, his lips lingering on mine, starting a slow burn inside of me. I sighed into his mouth as he pulled away.

"Nothing is the matter, Helena," he said, his eyes smoldering with desire. I smoldered back at him. Lord Sherringham sputtered, but Griffin turned on him. "Sherry, you will apologize to Miss Whitney for your rude behavior."

"I will do no such thing."

Griffin took a step towards him. Although he made no move to threaten his brother, his anger was almost palpable, his voice as hard as marble. "Apologize to her."

Helena and I glanced at one another. We both recognized that tone. Lord Sherringham, still sputtering, looked at his younger brother hesitantly. Evidently he recognized it too, for he turned an even darker shade of red, then choked out, "I apologize for my comments."

"Consider them forgotten," I said softly.

Griffin held the door for his brother. Lord Sherringham glared at each one of us muttering what sounded like a string of oaths, stomped out of the room. I heaved a sigh of relief and turned to Helena with a feeble smile.

"I'm so sorry for whatever Harold said to you." Her eyes wandered to Robert, quickly clouding with worry. I was astonished to see Robert looking pale and wan, as if he would be sick.

"Robert? Are you ill? Sit down and put your head between your knees," I suggested.

He swayed slightly, cleared his throat, and looked even worse, if that were possible. Griffin, standing next to me, was clearly amused, his lips curling into a slight smile. I frowned at him, ashamed that he should be so insensitive to Robert's illness.

"Helena," I said, starting toward Robert in order to help him to a chair. "Would you get him some water?"

Griffin grabbed my arm as I moved past him, spinning me around towards the door and shooed me out of it. "Helena, go show Alex—oh, show her the conservatory."

"Griffin!" I was puzzled by his behavior. "I believe I can do more good here with Robert."

"I doubt that," he said, closing the door in our faces.

"Well!" I said, looking at Helena in amazement. "What was that about?"

She looked as puzzled as I felt as we walked down the hall to the conservatory. "I don't know. Did Harold say anything to Robert?"

"No. He confined his anger to me. But I'm glad to have this chance to speak to you." I sat down on a rattan chair next to a hideous molting macaw in a large iron cage. "I wanted to talk to you about a problem in the Union... er... what does it have?"

She glanced at the cage. "Oh, that's his book. Raphael likes to chew on the paper."

I watched the bird for a moment as he carefully peeled a sheet of paper out of the book, gnawed on it for a moment, then dropped it.

"I want to tell you about something unpleasant. I am sure you won't like to hear it, but I believe it will do you good to know just what is going on."

"Oh!" She grasped the ruffles at her throat. "What is it? Tell me quickly!"

"It's about Maggie Greene," I began, watching the bird out of the corner of my eye. "I very much fear she will get the support she needs to form her own group, and I'm equally sure you would be a feather in her cap. I have every confidence that she will use you in every way possible."

"Use me? How can they use me?" Helena asked.

"Having the sister of the peer leading the act against suffrage has to be valuable to them," I explained, then paused, fascinated as the bird peeled off another page. "What is he reading?"

"Dante's *Inferno*."

"Ah. Suitable."

Helena was silent for a minute before saying, "I see what you mean. It's clear Maggie wants me to join her group just so she can parade me around, rather than for my support. Well, I will know what to say the next time she telephones."

"Has she been telephoning you?"

"Sometimes." She hesitated, then said, "I know how you feel about the militants, but even you must agree that no price is too much to pay to further the cause. Other than Maggie's group, that is."

"I certainly don't feel that way," I said, eager to correct that impression. "I am as devoted to women's rights as any other Union member, but I believe there is a line we must draw. Arson, attacking police, breaking windows—they are all examples of actions that have gone too far. Why, I read in *The Times* that there are women in the east who have made it a policy to ram their hatpins into the flanks of police horses!"

She gasped in horror.

"Can you possibly condone such atrocious acts of cruelty?" I asked.

"No, of course I can't." She wiped at a misty eye. "But you are so devoted to the cause. Was it not you who said to compromise on any part of suffrage was to lose the battle?"

I moved in my chair uncomfortably. "Well, yes. I want to talk to you about that as well. I have decided—you know that Griffin and I—"

She smiled gently. "I know about you and Griffin."

"No, not that. Or yes, that. After our talk yesterday, I've decided that I can't have both Griffin and active involvement in protests. I know it seems cowardly to retrench, but I was thinking about what he said, and how I would feel if he was putting himself in physical danger."

"Are we in physical danger just by marching?" Helena asked, dismay dimming her soft eyes.

I hesitated, absently watching as the bird sat on the bottom of the cage, wadding up the paper into little balls. "Unfortunately, I think we would be. I'm no oracle or sooth-sayer, but it's undeniable that violence against suffragettes is increasing, and with the militant group encouraging repre-hensible acts against innocents—no, I don't think we would be safe. Since I promised Mrs. Haywood that I would attend the meeting tomorrow, I'll do so, but it will be my last such engagement."

Helena patted my hand, giving my fingers a little squeeze. "I shall miss you in the fight for our rights, dearest sister. Without your charming spirit, your sunny counte-nance—"

"Spare me the flattery, Helena," I said abruptly. "I had hoped you would join me in the decision to end our protest careers."

"I will no longer support Maggie Greene, of course," she said, her hand fluttering in vague gestures. "But that doesn't mean I shall leave the cause as you will."

"I have no intention of leaving the Union," I said firmly. "Griffin can have no objection to my supporting the issue in a less active manner. I shall continue to do my part in every way except the actual demonstrations and protests."

She said slowly, "I suppose there are many ways we could make ourselves useful and still make our—" Her gaze dropped.

"Husbands happy?" I finished with a smile.

"Perhaps. Certainly *your* husband will be happy with our decision," she murmured, her gaze on her hands, a delight-ful blush on her cheeks. "I believe...yes, I will stand by your side for the candidate's meeting, and will make it my last demonstration as well."

I was pleased that she would heed my advice, well aware that both Griffin and Robert would not be happy with her continuing in a riskier role. "I know you enjoyed the idea of demonstrating, but I honestly believe this is a solution that will allow us to live in harmony while still empowering our goal to see justice done. Mrs. Heywood herself has said that not every woman is required to go into battle. Warriors can be found in many guises."

She blushed at my frank speech and picked at the embroidering on her sleeve. "You may speak for yourself, of course. You're so happy with Griffin, but I don't believe I shall ever marry."

Another lovesick sweetheart. I sighed as I watched the bird assemble a collection of small paper pellets. "Helena, not twenty minutes ago, I had a conversation with Robert about you."

She looked up, her eyes thick with tears. "What did he say?"

"I can assure you that he feels towards you as you feel about him."

She blushed even harder, a delicate shade that was completely out of my ability. "Oh. I...oh."

"I have a feeling you will soon be as happy as I am." A thought struck me. "In fact, unless I am mistaken, your happiness is the very reason Robert wished to speak with Griffin."

"Oh," Helena said again, this time with a smile that lit the entire conservatory with happiness.

My eyes were drawn to the bird. "What does he do with the paper pellets?"

She looked at me blankly for a minute, then frowned at the macaw. "He ejects them at the servants. He's Letitia's bird."

"That would explain a great deal."

"Alex, why is Robert speaking with Griffin? Why isn't he speaking with Harold? It is Harold who has control over my fortune."

"He *has* spoken with Lord Sherringham."

"He has?" The color faded from her face as she put a hand to her mouth. I expected her to swoon, but she surprised me. "It doesn't matter. I am old enough to marry whom I please. I will have control over my fortune in four years, and then it won't matter what Harold thinks."

If only Griffin has done his job, I thought to myself, *and given Robert the help he needs.* We didn't have a long wait to see if he had; the door opened and both men walked in.

Robert was flushed, but looked cheerful. Griffin no longer looked amused, although I detected a certain twitching about the corners of his mouth that filled me with my own sense of happiness. He held out his hand for me. I glanced at Helena. She looked as if she would faint.

"Helena?" I asked, rising to go to her, concerned about her waxen appearance.

Griffin grabbed my hand and pulled me toward him. "Come. I want to talk to you."

I tried to pull my hand free of his. "Griffin, now Helena is ill."

"No, she's not. Come with me." He pulled me out the door and led me to a small room off the hall. It was filled from floor to ceiling with books. I turned to face him.

"What can you be thinking? First Robert and now Helena—" I stopped. It occurred to me that Helena might not really be suffering.

Griffin nodded.

"Thank heavens," I said, heaving a sigh that had me slumping in a manner my mother would have disliked. "Now I can stop being a confidante of the lovelorn. I can't tell you how annoying that's been."

He frowned for a moment, then spun around and left the room. "Stay here. I'll be back in a minute."

Griffin's study gave an interesting insight into the man. It was untidy, but fascinating. I had just settled down with a book containing engrossing descriptions and illustrations of the natives of Borneo when he returned.

"I wanted to make sure Sherry didn't interrupt them, but I couldn't find him." He frowned at the Borneo book. "That's not suitable reading for a lady."

"Oh, don't be such an old maid. I am a New Woman. I have a lover. Penis sheaths and virgin sacrifices are nothing to me." I looked up to where he stood. "Were you aware that there is a tribe in Borneo that has a ritual of manhood comprising three young men and one nubile—"

He snatched the book from my hands and put it in a drawer, leaning against it. I smiled and stood on tip-toes to kiss him. "The book also had some interesting things to say about mating rites. I believe I would like you to explain them in greater detail."

He wrapped his arms around me and nuzzled my neck. I twined my fingers through his curls and kissed a line along his jaw. "I will be happy to do so at a later date."

"Mmm. I'll hold you to that. Did you give Robert the push he needed?"

"I gave him a whiskey and the benefit of my advice," he murmured as he sucked my earlobe into his mouth. "The rest he'll have to do himself."

"I should ask how you are feeling today," I breathed out, running my hands over his hard-muscled torso. As much as I enjoyed touching him, I couldn't help but wish it was his bare flesh my fingers were skimming over. "The doctor would expect me to check you over."

"Perhaps a physical examination is in order," he answered, his hands tugging and pulling at my clothing until they slipped under my shirtwaist, the warm heat of his palms cupping breasts that had been clamoring for just that very touch.

"I don't believe we have time for that," I pointed out, unable to keep from wriggling against him. He was aroused and would, I believe, have settled for a quick examination if I hadn't remembered something I needed to do. I slid out from his embrace, circling behind a tall armchair. "I have something to say to you."

Griffin put a hand on the chair and took a step forward. "What would that be?"

"It is about us."

"I'm always happy to discuss that subject." He took another step forward, and I found myself in the circle of his arms again.

I put my hands on his chest and pushed out of the embrace. "No, none of that."

"Why not?"

"I need to talk to you, and it is impossible for me to talk any sense when you... you know."

"When I do what?" he asked, moving closer. His lovely amber eyes mesmerized me, deep, endless pools of amber I could gaze into for an eternity. He pulled me tighter. "Perhaps you mean this?"

With a quick, heated kiss, he picked me up and set me down on the desk, spreading my legs and pushing my skirt and petticoat up over my thighs.

"Griffin, we don't have time—"

"We have time for this. I've wanted to do this since that first night when you gave yourself to me," he answered, tugging at the ribbon to release my drawers. A moment later, that garment went flying as Griffin pulled me forward to the edge of his desk, my legs resting on his shoulders as he knelt before me.

"Griffin?" I asked as the dark curls brushed my thighs. "*Griffin?*"

His mouth was warm on my flesh as he kissed a path up my thighs to that spot that had recently been making strident demands regarding him. "*GRIFFIN!*"

His lips and fingers were a brand burning into my tender flesh as his tongue did things I had no idea a tongue could do. He kissed. He sucked. He licked and nibbled and caressed, touching me in ways that made my heart pound and my breath stop in my throat.

I tensed as he eased a finger into me, the familiar tightness of the winding coil inside me promising bliss. A second finger joined the first and suddenly I was there, blazing a trail into the heavens like a fiery comet. I clutched his head to me and cried out his name, almost sobbing with the pleasure of his selfless homage to our love.

He held me until I recovered myself enough to speak.

"Was that, by any chance, in the book of the Borneo natives?"

He chuckled and kissed me. "No."

I licked my lips. "Hmm. That's… different. Is it…? Can I…? Do men enjoy reciprocal treatment?"

He kissed me again. "Very much so."

"Hmm. I will make a note of that, but before I can explore the idea further, I want you to go back around to the desk. There's a subject upon which I need to speak, and I can't do it when you do that."

He withdrew his hand, grinned, then handed me my drawers and leaned against the desk, watching as I put them on. "You have my undivided attention."

I shook out my skirts and took a deep breath. "About the next suffrage protest—"

His expression was as dark as a storm. "Damnation, woman! I know you feel the need to belong to this group, but—"

"I do," I interrupted. "But I spent a good deal of time thinking about you. About us. No matter how strongly I feel about assisting the cause of women's emancipation, I feel more strongly about you."

He started toward me. I held my hands out to keep him back. "Let me finish, please. I can't imagine life without you. For that reason I have decided that—after the meeting tomorrow, which I am committed to attending—I will give up my active involvement in women's suffrage. I will still work to support them, just not in a way that will end up with me imprisoned again."

Griffin set down the pipe he'd picked up, taking my face in his hands. "I have never known a woman like you. You have been through a hell I can't imagine, and yet you have the most generous, loving heart."

"Emma says life with my father tempered me," I murmured against his lips, tugging on his hair until he gave me what I wanted.

"She is correct. You have the strength of the finest sword, yet still twist me around until I don't know what side is up. Sweetheart, I don't expect you to give up your work. I know what it means to you, and although I never thought I'd be saying this, I can't help but admire your dedication to the fight."

"That sounds like a man who has seen the light regarding women's suffrage," I said, my spirits soaring.

He made a face. "I've never been against equality, per se, just how it was being sought. But now I can see that you and the other women have little other choice. I'll support your fight so long as you don't get hurt."

Love for this wonderful man flooded me. It was what I had been hoping for all my adult years—a man who could respect me as well as love me. I placed my hand on his cheek. "As long as I have you, nothing can hurt me. And before you ask, yes, Helena has agreed to follow my example."

He started unbuttoning my shirtwaist, kissing each bit of exposed flesh. "An excellent solution," he agreed, and slipped a few more buttons through the holes.

A sudden loud noise from outside the room disrupted him. We both turned toward the door as it was flung open. Griffin's spun around, using his body to block me from the sight of his brother, red with fury and sputtering incoherently. I quickly redid my buttons, peering over Griffin's shoulder at the earl.

"Griffin," Lord Sherringham roared, "What have you done? How dare you tell that… that…" He glared at me, evidently for inspiration. "…that young scoundrel that he may marry Helena? I found him now, in the conservatory, proposing to her. He had the audacity to say you had given him permission."

I sank into the chair behind me, watching Griffin closely. He didn't look bothered by his brother's dramatics. "I have given my permission, since you will not."

"I forbid this marriage. I cannot forbid you your own mistake." He waved a hand toward me. "But, by God, I can halt another disaster in this family."

"You can't stop Helena from marrying, and I would hope that you have the decency to give her an ample allowance until she is in control of her own fortune," Griffin said, his hands fisted.

"I will do no such thing!" Lord Sherringham seemed to calm down, but I didn't care for the look in his eye. "Very well. As you point out, she is free to marry whomever she chooses. But I am free to dispense her money as I see fit, and I will not see her wasting any of it on that fortune hunter."

I expected Griffin to argue the point, although I knew it would do no good. He didn't, however. He simply jammed his hands in his pockets and said mildly, "It doesn't matter how tight you hold on, Sherry. She will have her money in four years and until then—" He shrugged.

Another wave of love swept over me as I watched him. I knew then he would help Robert back onto his feet in a manner that even the sensitive Robert would accept. Helena would have Robert, Griffin and I would have each other, and everyone would be happy.

"I'm sure you will turn us out now, so that you might welcome *that woman*. I will tell Letitia. Mark my words, Griffin," Lord Sherringham spat out, "you will regret the day you made this decision."

He spun around and slammed the door behind him as he left.

Griffin scowled at the door until I placed a hand on his arm. The muscles beneath my fingers were tense and taut.

"I shouldn't have come today. I'm sorry I've caused so much trouble." I looked into his eyes, dark now with anger, marveling that I felt nothing but love. "Did you know your nostrils are flaring?"

He stared at me for a minute, then threw back his head and laughed. Grasping me in another bone-crushing embrace, he said, "My darling Alex. What man could resist such lover's talk?"

Shortly after that, we went in search of Helena and Robert. We found them where we had left them, although not in the same state. Helena was weeping on Robert's shoulder, and he was flushed and red with anger.

"Ah. I see the traces of a visit from Sherry," Griffin said dryly. He handed his sister a handkerchief. "Helena, stop crying."

Helena took the offered item and attempted to wipe her tears. "But, Griffin! Harold said we could not marry, and he was *rude* to Robert!"

Griffin pulled Robert to one side and spoke with him in a low voice. I went to Helena and put my arm around her. "Don't worry, Griffin will see to everything. He has already dealt with Lord Sherringham, and"—I sighed with happiness—"he was magnificent."

Griffin took us home a short while later in his motorcar. I had a few minutes to ask him if he'd had any luck finding incriminating evidence against Lord Sherringham, but he hadn't found anything.

"You forbade me to confront him," he reminded me. "If I could just get him alone, I could make him tell me what he's been up to."

"Be patient, my darling. He will reveal his hand in some way or another." I started into the house, then stopped. "And for heaven's sake, be careful!"

The following day I was out with Mabel paying calls to her mother's side of the family, but made my escape as soon as I could. I decided to walk home, my spirits high despite the gray clouds.

Passing a nearby church, I watched a wedding procession. In the midst of the bridal couple was a clergyman in traditional black garb.

The sight of the man in profile flooded me with memories of three men cowering in the corner of a small room as Annie yelled and threw crockery. Mr. Hope Freddie had called him. Chills ran down my spine as I remembered Helena's faltering voice saying that, along with her brother, Oliver Hope was her trustee.

"Mr. Hope!" If it were the same man, it would be a tangible connection between Merlin, Percy, Freddie, and Lord Sherringham, the very proof we sought. With these thoughts chasing around my mind, I immediately hailed a cab.

An overturned dray near Griffin's house had me setting off on foot for the last block. As I approached the house, a cab arrived from the other direction and a figure alighted. Thinking it was Helena, I raised my hand in greeting. Thankfully, the woman who walked up to the door didn't see me, because it was clear from her short stature that she was not Helena. She wore a hooded coat and dark dress, and something about her sent a chill of premonition down my spine.

Griffin's butler opened the door and accepted a letter from the woman, who then turned and, without looking to either side, stepped back into the cab. A brief gust of wind blew back her hood as she entered the cab.

There was no mistaking the features of Maggie Greene.

Lost in thought as I watched the cab pull away, I stood next to the stone steps leading up to the front door. Had Maggie left off a note for Helena...or Lord Sherringham? If it was for the latter, why? What would they have in common? Certainly they didn't share the same political beliefs, yet the suffrage movement was the one tie that bound them.

The butler didn't even raise an eyebrow at my request to speak with his master, but informed me he was out. At that news I wrung my hands.

"Lady Helena is in, miss, if you would like to speak with her."

"Helena! Yes! She would know if her Mr. Hope is a clergyman or not. At least I could get that point cleared up. I will see her, please."

The butler showed me into the dark parlor to await her. As I passed a half-moon marble table that stood next to the front door, I noticed the silver salver waiting with a stack of letters for their recipients to claim them. I paced the floor of the parlor anxiously, trying to piece my terrible thoughts together. The sight of the letter in Maggie's hand tormented me. I had to know if it was addressed to Lord Sherringham or to Helena.

With exquisite care, I opened the parlor door and looked out. The hall was empty. I tiptoed to the marble table and stared with a growing sense of horror at the letter on top.

It was addressed to Lord Sherringham and marked urgent.

There is no excuse for my action except one: I was trying to prevent further attacks on the man I loved. I snatched the letter off the stack and raced back to the parlor. The letter was sealed with wax and bore no clue as to the sender. I could not in all conscience open the letter myself, but I hoped Griffin wouldn't feel bound by similar morals.

"Dearest Alex," Helena cried as she entered the parlor and hugged me.

I held the letter behind my back, embarrassed by the theft. "Griffin—do you know where he is?"

Her smile faded at the urgent note in my voice. "Why, yes, he has gone to consult his solicitor. He told Harold he was having a will drawn up. He should be home soon, if you would like to wait for him. Robert went with him to see about some other matter."

"He told—" Fear struck me with an almost palpable blow. I had a hard time swallowing the lump that suddenly appeared in my throat. "And what did Lord Sherringham say to that?"

"He smiled. It… it wasn't a very pleasant smile, but he said nothing…" Her voice trailed off.

I felt almost lightheaded with fear as I brought out the letter and held it wordlessly before Helena.

"I don't understand. Why do you have a letter addressed to Harold?"

"It was delivered by hand. That is, I saw it delivered just a few minutes ago… by Maggie Greene."

Helena's eyes opened wide in disbelief. "Maggie? What would Maggie have to say to Harold?"

I paced the length of the room, barely able to get the words out. "Helena, I must see Griffin. I can't open this letter, but he could. We have to know what Maggie is communicating with your brother. We have to know if he… if he is planning—"

"We will ask Harold," she said, her expression changing from horror to determination. "He's in the library, speaking with a business acquaintance, but as soon as Mr. Jones leaves, I will—"

"Mr. Jones?" I all but shrieked, horrified at the name. "Mr. William—or Merlin—Jones?"

She stared at me as if I had a llama dancing on my head. "I believe his name was William. Do you know him?"

I crumpled into a chair, my knees no longer able to hold me. "Helena, you must tell me, did Mr. Jones have a gold tooth?"

"Why, yes, he did. Alex, are you ill? Shall I fetch someone?" She ran to me as I moaned, my hands clutching my head.

"Everything revolves around Lord Sherringham. Everything comes back to him. Maggie, Freddie, Merlin—it all comes back to one person. You said you just left them—your brother and Mr. Jones. Are they still there? Helena, I must hear what they are saying. That would be the proof we need."

"Yes, I'm sure they're still in the library, but proof of what? What is it you suspect?"

I thought furiously. The library. I hadn't been in Griffin's library, only in his study. "Is there another door to the library other than the one to the hall? Somewhere we can listen to their conversation?"

She shook her head. "No, only the one door. Although there is the alcove."

"The alcove? Could one hear a discussion in the library from the alcove?"

"Yes, it's a small opening on the first floor that overlooks the library. But Alex, you haven't answered—"

And I didn't answer her questions. Instead, I leaped up and grasped her hand, dragging her with me as I ran out into the hallway and up the stairs. "Where is it? Where is the alcove?"

She showed me. We hurried down a narrow hall to a small round room with windows on one side and a curved bench following a dark wooden railing. I peered over the edge and looked down into the library. The room was long and shaped like an L, with the alcove on the wrong side of the short end. To the left, a paneled wall of some five feet blocked my view of the rest of the library. I held my breath and heard the soft murmur of voices.

"Is there no other way to hear?" I whispered.

"No."

"Then I shall just have to lean out and do my best. Hold on to my skirt."

I stepped onto the couch and stretched forward, bracing one hand against the paneling, the other holding tight to the railing. Helena clutched at my belt to keep me from falling.

It wasn't enough. I still couldn't understand what the men were saying. "Let go of my belt," I whispered back at Helena. "Hold on to the hem of my skirt."

I stretched farther forward as she released her hold and was gratified when a man's arm came into view. The words were louder and almost intelligible. With both hands flat against the paneling and my feet wrapped around the bench railing, I stretched a last few inches.

"—will do it tonight, if you can make sure he's unconscious."

The pleasantly bland voice was that of Mr. Jones.

"It shall be done," Lord Sherringham replied.

I see now that my mistake was in trusting the strength of my feet and ankles. Helena held on for dear life when I suddenly slipped down the paneling as my feet cramped and lost their grip on the railing, but she couldn't hold me up as I tumbled down onto the (thankfully) carpeted floor of the library below.

I lay stunned for a moment, unsure of what happened. Then, slowly, my vision returned. I looked up. Mr. Jones smiled down at me, his hands tucked into his waistcoat. Lord Sherringham stood behind him, sputtering and turning a bilious shade of red. His eyes held a glazed, thoroughly unstable look.

"You!" the earl snarled, the unhealthy gleam in his eye growing stronger. Spittle collected in the corners of his mouth. "You are the cause of all my misery! You are to thank for being turned out of my home. You are to thank for the engagement of my sister to a fortune hunter! You are to thank for the alienation of my brother!"

I glanced up to where Helena stood clutching at her throat, staring down at the incredible scene. Lord Sherringham followed my look and gave a great roar of madness, for mad he clearly was. The look in his eye and his incoherent comments made it clear that his anger had pushed him over the edge.

"Helena," he screamed, rattling the windows.

Helena stood frozen with horror, unable to move.

"Run, Helena, run out of the house! Find Griffin—find Robert—*run now!*" The panic in my voice must have reached her, for she suddenly spun around and was gone. Merlin glanced at Lord Sherringham, then dashed out of the room. I hoped Helena would have enough sense to not run straight down the stairs into Merlin's waiting arms.

Lord Sherringham, his hands clenched into fists, his eyes ablaze, walked forward toward me. I rose hastily to my feet and looked for escape. There was none.

"Is there any reason I should not place my hands around your neck and squeeze the life out of you?" he asked in a high-pitched voice.

I took a step backwards, fighting panic.

"A great many reasons," I said, admittedly with a false bravado, my heart beating wildly. I was no stranger to facing down a madman; I just never thought I'd have to do it again. "For one thing, I am not the true cause of your troubles. It just appears that way. Your sister was bound to fall in love at some point, just as some day she will take possession of her inheritance and then your abuse of her funds will be known."

A look of fury spasmed across his face. He took another step toward me, snarling, "It was you who introduced her to Hunter. If she hadn't have met you, she would still be under my control."

I didn't see the blow coming. I would have thought that years of living with my father would have honed my senses to anticipate a blow, but the earl's hand whipped out and struck my face with enough force to send me reeling back into a chair. My cheek throbbed and stung as tears sprang to my eyes. I turned back to face Lord Sherringham, determined to make him admit his crimes.

"And then there's your brother's alienation," I said, my voice raw and rough. "Don't you think your many attempts on his life might have something to do with that?"

The look in his eye was definitely not one of a sane man. "You don't know what you're talking about. You told him to throw us out. It's because of you we will be shamed, disgraced, and dishonored before everyone. His doting mama gave him everything! All they gave me were debts!"

He slapped me again. This time I saw it coming and ducked as he lashed out, but he caught the edge of my jaw painfully. I calculated my chances of either launching an attack or escaping the room, but neither was good. Although he wasn't a large man, his was the strength of madness, and I wasn't feeling my best after having fallen from the alcove.

"I could see why you hired Merlin and Percy to do the dirty work for you, but what about the accidents Griffin had in the house? Was it you who loosened the stair rod and poisoned his food, or was it Lady Sherringham?"

A high-pitched giggled escaped his lips. "My dear Letitia is the most helpful of wives."

"And as for your being turned out of your home, perhaps it wasn't the best idea to burn down Rosewood." That last was a guess based on Griffin's comments, but it hit home.

"Rosewood!" His voice was almost a scream. "He made me do it. The old man wouldn't let me have it to myself. *He* was to have it as well."

I was slightly confused by his use of pronouns, but gathered that he was referring to the fact that the old earl had wanted Rosewood to be a home for Helena and Griffin.

"And now this," I said, pulling out the envelope I had filched from the hall table. "It seems your cohort has something to tell you. Perhaps Maggie Greene wants to tell you about the latest suffrage protest." I spoke louder as the door behind him opened. "Or maybe she has a question about your role ensuring the suffragettes are arrested."

Lord Sherringham was directly in front of me, his hands outstretched and almost touching my throat. I looked over his shoulder and delivered the coup de grâce. "Or could it be that Maggie wants to talk about how much money you promised to give her when she arranges for Helena to be sent to prison?"

He screamed and lunged at me, digging his thumbs into my throat, sending me sliding toward a long, inky pool.

SIXTEEN

"Many people have saved my life, but it never ceases to be a strange feeling." I allowed myself to melt against Griffin, smiling into his hair with utter happiness.

"I might have saved you, but it was only by the slimmest of margins," Griffin said, nuzzling my throat.

"Regardless, you are the brave knight I needed." I sighed with regret when his hands, which had been stroking my back, now shifted around to my front, and added in a whisper, "My love, we are not alone."

The hands retreated, and Griffin allowed me to sit without his support on a brocade sofa. "I didn't know what to think when we came in to see that bastard Merlin dragging Helena toward the library. It took us a few minutes to get her free, and him disabled, and then she wasn't in a state to do anything but say the word 'library' repeatedly."

"It was horrible," Helena said, handing me a cup of tea. "I thought Harold would kill you."

"He might have if Griffin hadn't broken his jaw," Robert said, sitting next to Helena on a loveseat.

"You broke his jaw?" I asked, looking at the love of my life.

"It was the only way I could get him to release you," he answered, his own jaw flexing a couple of times.

We contemplated the recent events in silence for a few minutes. The silence was made all that more stark by the memory of the recent insane screams as Lord Sherringham was taken away, struggling and feral, to the local asylum in a straight-waistcoat.

As a woman's voice sounded in the hall, Griffin rose and excused himself.

"I still can't believe Harold did that to you," Helena said, moving over to sit next to me. "It all seems like a nightmare."

Our heads turned in unison as a horrible scream rent the air.

"That would be your sister-in-law hearing the news," I said in answer to her shocked face.

Helena was on the verge of tears, and I was about to ask Robert to take her elsewhere when Lady Sherringham appeared in the doorway, her eyes burning and hands outstretched like talons.

"You have ruined everything," she screeched, flying at me. Spitting curses, she tried to claw my face. Robert leaped forward and pulled her off before she reached me. The countess struggled briefly, then suddenly went limp, sobbing hysterically.

Griffin arrived, mopping blood from his face where she had clearly attacked him. Waving me back to the couch from which I had risen, he took the countess firmly by the arm and escorted her from the room.

Helena sat with her face in her hands, weeping. Realizing that perhaps Robert could comfort her better than I could, I slipped out of the room and waited in the hall for Griffin.

Later, when a pale and furious Lady Sherringham had left for the comfort of a sister's home, we gathered in the sitting room and I recounted the disturbing conversation with the earl.

"Harold truly did plan to have me imprisoned simply in order to steal my fortune," Helena said, as if speaking the words out loud would make them less painful.

"I'm sorry, Helena," I said miserably from where I was curled up next to Griffin, cuddled into his side, my fingers twined through his. "I believe it would be kindest to think that the madness had taken over, leaving his mind unbalanced and not at all that of a brother you loved."

"Yes, that is true." She leaned into Robert for comfort. "And the madness would explain his attacks on Griffin as well."

"He all but admitted the two accidents you experienced at home were the work of your sister-in-law," I told Griffin. "I assume they were done at the earl's behest."

"I thought Sherry was acting a little odd when I came home after this last trip," he answered, rubbing his chin. "He seemed to be angry all the time."

"To think he would go so far as to kill you." Helena glanced at the bruises blossoming on my neck. "Both of you!"

"I don't understand why he wanted to have Helena arrested," Robert complained, shifting so that Helena was at his side.

I sipped my tea and let Griffin explain it to him.

"I don't know for sure, but I'll wager an examination of Helena's inheritance will show that she was being systematically robbed by Sherry. When you appeared on the scene, Sherry saw at once that Helena was—ahem—fond of you. He knew that even though she couldn't touch the money held in trust until she was twenty-five, a husband might take more of an interest in her fortune and would demand an accounting."

"Lord Sherringham would never have been able to carry off the embezzlement of Helena's inheritance if it weren't for his partner in crime, Mr. Hope," I added. "And speaking of Mr. Hope, is he in the church?"

"Yes," Helena leaned heavily against Robert's shoulder. "He was the vicar in the parish at Rosewood for years. Then he left his post."

I turned to back to Griffin.

"You wouldn't remember because they drugged you, but it was Mr. Hope that Freddie intended to marry us. Freddie and me, that is," I added. "I didn't see much of his face, but I have little doubt that the Mr. Hope, clergyman, who was so obliging to Freddie is the same Mr. Hope, clergyman, who was Lord Sherringham's friend and co-trustee to Helena. I assume the earl helped Freddie in his underhanded scheme after Griffin made known his intentions towards me. I suppose we'll never know until we talk to him."

"But how did your cousin know Lord Sherringham?" Robert asked.

"I believe Merlin Jones was the link between the two men. Freddie obviously tried to play on my fears by hiring Mr. Jones to conduct worrisome, but not really frightening, attacks upon me. It just so happened that each time one was arranged, Helena was with me."

"Helena saw him talking to Sherry, which means he probably passed on Jones's name as a thug willing to be hired for any number of plans," Griffin said.

I nodded. "Plans such as kidnapping you from the masquerade ball, attacking you in your study, and so forth. Yes, I'm quite certain you are right."

"And Maggie Greene—how did she meet Lord Sherringham? And why would she want to have Helena jailed?" Robert's voice was distinctly puzzled.

"I'm sure she met the earl indirectly through Helena. According to the note she left, which Griffin so obligingly opened, she was passing along information about upcoming Union events to him."

Helena looked as puzzled as Robert. "But why would she want to sabotage the Union, Alex? I know you don't support the militants, but surely you can't believe they want the Union to fail?"

"I think in a way they do. Maggie probably realized there were just too many moderate suffragettes and she can never take over the Union. I think her plan is to divide and conquer—bring the Union down by giving sensitive information to the police, thereby insuring that the leaders and most active members would be arrested and jailed. Later, when the opposition was silenced, she would pick up the dregs and form a new organization with herself at the helm and a militant policy in force. She may still do it, too," I mused.

"Well, at least Helena's safe," Robert said, gazing at Helena with a silly grin of bliss. She smiled giddily back at him.

"Yes, I think everything has turned out rather well, all in all," I said, watching Griffin with concern. He had been quiet too long, and I was worried that he was overly tired by the recent days' events.

His lovely eyes met mine and I'm afraid that, for a time, we all looked silly.

Helena and Griffin came to dinner that night, and we explained to my family what had happened earlier, as well as what we had pieced together. Mabel was shocked, Joshua concerned, and Mullin was delighted with the exciting goings-on of the family.

After dinner, I reminded Griffin of the decision I had come to, and that we had one last meeting we were committed to attend.

The argument that followed went round and round until finally Griffin held up his hand and roared for silence.

"This arguing is useless," he said in a conversational tone of voice, his eyes meeting mine. "They will go to the meeting."

I had my mouth opened to make a retort to a particularly unkind remark from Mabel, but shut it in surprise at Griffin's statement.

"They will?" Robert asked him in disbelief.

"Yes. Alex has agreed that this will be her last demonstration, and said Helena has made a similar promise."

"Then it is settled. They will make this last demonstration understanding that they will *in no way endanger themselves*." He glared at me to make sure I noted the emphasis.

"But is it safe?" Mabel asked him.

Griffin's left shoulder twitched, but his voice was even when he answered, "With Sherry put away, I think it is. Even if Miss Greene found out about the demonstration, and Alex tells me no one but the five women who are to attend are being told about it, she has no one to give the information to. I can't see her going to the police. That information would become public too quickly. I think they will be safe."

He placed a hand on my shoulder and looked down at me, his amber eyes warm and fathomless. I beamed at him, ecstatically happy that, at last, our future looked bright. We spent a little time discussing the plan and decided we were to meet the following day outside of the labor hall hosting the meeting. Griffin and Robert agreed to escort us there and back, but would not interfere.

"Unless we see you in danger of being attacked," Griffin growled. I considered protesting his arrogant attitude, but decided the protective urge in a male can have its charms. I smiled at him instead.

Robert and I were early the next day and stood talking outside the hall while we waited for Griffin to bring Helena. Robert told me about a job managing a coffee farm in East Africa. His eyes shined with happiness as he detailed the life he hoped to make with Helena, and how much he would enjoy being in Africa again.

"And what of you? What of the fair Alex?" he asked, turning suddenly to me.

"That will depend a great deal on Griffin. We might travel. I have always longed to travel, and Griffin has mentioned several exciting places he wants to visit—he wants *us* to visit," I said happily.

We fell silent, thinking about our promising futures. Small groups of people arrived, chatting and calling to one another merrily. The audience comprised mostly low to middle-class citizens, a fact I kept in mind when dressing for the event. Rather than wear an afternoon dress or even a suit, I had dressed in a conservative gray skirt and pale blue shirtwaist with a simple straw boater and matching blue ribbon. Recent news stories had hinted that suffragettes were made up of women from the idle class who had nothing better to do with their time, hence my particular pains to appear in a neat but simple costume. I hoped Helena had a similar insight.

Mrs. Knox arrived looking calm.

I moved to her, and said quietly, "Helena St. John and I have made the decision that this will be our last demonstration."

She raised her eyebrows.

"Neither of us wishes to leave the Union," I hastened to explain. "We both would like to support the cause in a less… *physical* manner."

"I quite understand. We have many members who support our efforts without stepping foot in a march or holding a single banner. You need not risk imprisonment in order to be of benefit to the cause." She glanced meaningfully at Robert, standing nearby. "I can understand your decision."

I was going to correct the false impression when she continued. "I also wished to tell you that the Union does not hold it against members if they choose to not serve their sentence in prison. I was happy that you and Miss St. John were released early."

"Helena's brother had us released," I blurted out. "We were prepared to serve our time, but he had us freed instead."

"There is no shame in obtaining a release, my dear." Dark circles under her eyes emphasized her fatigue. I was sure Maggie's destructive plans were the primary cause for her weariness. "No woman is meant for every role."

I spotted familiar figures strolling towards us so thanked her and turned to watch Griffin and Helena approach. My heart performed its usual contractions and physical jerks when I saw Griffin. I wondered idly how long it would take before I no longer received a thrill upon seeing him.

"A very long time, I hope," I said out loud as Griffin greeted Robert, then sighed when I took a closer look at Helena. Rather than dressing down to fit in the crowd, she had outdone herself with a rich plum-colored afternoon dress with pink silk inserts. Her hat was large and extravagant, bristling with ostrich feathers. I dragged my eyes from the horror of her hat to her brother. Griffin was taller than most men around him and presented an impressive picture of physical strength. I believe he would have embraced me if I hadn't stopped him.

"Can it be you no longer enjoy those kisses I thought pleased you so much?" he teased as I held him back with a firm hand.

"On the contrary, I enjoy them too much. Besides which, I know you, Griffin. You wouldn't be content with a polite greeting."

His delicious lips curled into a knowing smile. "There can be no embarrassment in two engaged persons showing their mutual affection."

"There is when that affection is displayed in a public place. And as we are on the subject, I don't believe we *are* engaged."

"We are!" he rumbled, trying to draw me closer.

I eluded his grasp. "No, I think not. For an engagement to take place, there must first be a proposal, and I do not recall having received one."

"Whether you remember it, you did." His jaw took on a familiar stubborn appearance. "I asked you that day at your sister's house."

I blushed at the memory of our activities on that day. "As I recall, you suggested marriage as a solution to a problem. I hardly think that can be classified as a proposal."

"Hrmph." He frowned, eyeing me speculatively. "But you agreed that a marriage would solve the problem of your cousin, so that qualifies as an engagement."

"I'm not sure if I could say an abstract supposition is the same as a statement of fact," I teased.

Griffin glared at me while I smiled sweetly at him. That was how Robert and Helena found us, Helena pointing out that the other suffragettes had gathered and we were wanted.

I glanced at the gathering and a spike of fear gripped me as I saw a face I recognized—one of Maggie Greene's captains was included in the entourage. She stood with the other three women, waiting expectantly for the word to go in. I turned back to Griffin as Helena went to join the group. I wanted to tell him, but one look at his calm, unconcerned face made me bite back the urge. I resolved instead to keep a firm grip on Helena and make sure she was not anywhere near the militant woman.

Griffin took my hand, instantly easing my worry. "You remember your promise?"

"Yes, I've already told you I will stay behind the speakers and not interfere. Helena will be behind me. We will not obstruct or attack the audience or other speakers. We will not take part in any… What was your phrase?"

"Scrummage."

"Scrummages. We will not chant slogans or wave signs lest we should inadvertently strike someone. Do you mind terribly if we breathe?"

"Only if you have to."

His lovely amber eyes were full of trust, love, and even—I might have been mistaken—pride. I grabbed him by the sleeve and pulled him towards me, kissing him quickly, then turned and ran after Helena.

Mrs. Knox handed out the *Votes For Women* sashes. As she did so, she reminded us that our duty was to stand quietly and make ourselves visible, but not vocal or physical. I watched the militant from the corner of my eye, and fretted.

The meeting was typical of its type: working-class men and a few women who came to hear their favorite candidates offering promises that would never be kept, derision against a faulty government that would be corrected under the candidate's office, benefits and good times ahead. In the middle of the speeches, a sudden movement to the right caught my eye. I glanced down the row and saw to my horror that Maggie Greene and two other militants were seated on the other side.

"Damnation," I murmured, worry filling me at the sight of her. I knew the militants were present solely to cause trouble, and I was at a loss how to prevent it since Mrs. Knox was clearly out of her element. Although she leaned sideways and held a brief conversation with Maggie, it was with an unhappy and concerned face she sat back.

Question time came, and several members of the audience rose and asked the standard questions. We sat for thirty minutes before the designated speaker from our party rose and made her way to the questioner's podium; Maggie was among the group, and although I tried, I could not keep Helena at a distance from her. Eight of us stood behind Mrs. Knox, on the surface a solid supportive line, but below, a group divided. I was desperately worried and shot several meaningful glances at Maggie.

"Mr. Chester," Mrs. Knox called out in a loud, clear voice, "if you are elected, will you do your best to make Women's Suffrage a government measure?"

A roar went up from the crowd, and several stewards moved in towards Mrs. Knox. They spoke to her in a low tone. She shook her head and repeated her question, louder than before.

I watched the stewards nervously, aware of the four militants standing directly behind them. The candidate consulted with a short man in an appallingly loud checked suit and derby hat.

"Answer the question, please, Mr. Chester," Mrs. Knox said.

"I am afraid," Chester said finally, "that I am unable to answer that question at this time. It is a matter for some thought, and not one which I have had sufficient time—"

"You are afraid to answer the question!" Maggie shoved Mrs. Knox aside and took over the questioner's spot. "You are the same as every other man here, afraid to let women have any power! You would do well to be afraid!"

I missed the initial assault on the candidate because I was simultaneously pulling Helena away from where she stood near the militants and watching Mrs. Knox in hurried consultation with the other moderate member. I heard the horrified gasp from the crowd, however, and saw the results.

Mr. Chester lay on his back, blood streaming from his head. As I stared in shock, the four militants removed large rocks from their skirts and threw them at the remaining candidates. Two of the stewards grabbed for the women, starting a brawl that seemed to spread instantly to everyone in the area.

Helena struggled against me, trying to reach the women. "Alex, no, we must stop them!"

"Believe me, if I could, I would," I answered, grunting as I tried to drag her backward, away from the brawl. "But I have witnessed that sort of madness, and we wouldn't have any effect."

Suddenly, the room was full of police constables, seeming to stream in from everywhere, racing down the aisles and up from the speaker's platform. The audience, in a panic, pushed their way toward the doors. I was rudely shoved aside by a large man making a hasty exit and lost my grip on Helena. Stewards and policemen dragged the militants through the crowds, towards the back of the hall. I struggled to work my way to Helena, who was now pushed into the far aisle. The number of people attempting to rush down the narrow aisles caused a dense backup of bodies, all fighting frantically to reach the two exits.

As I slipped out of the hold of a constable, I saw Griffin to my left, trying to move through the crowd and make his way down the aisle. He was being pushed backwards by the sheer volume of people, and although I saw him bodily lift people out of his path, I lost sight of him when I was suddenly snatched from behind by a constable. Helena was ahead of me, struggling to help Mrs. Knox. In front of me, one woman was knocked down and trampled by the crowd. I tried to avoid stepping on her as the constable dragged me towards the back of the hall.

Unlike my prior arrest, this time I fought, fought as I had wanted to my entire life, but had always been too frightened to do so. My thumb was bent backwards until I thought it would break. My arms were wrenched behind me and, blinded with pain, I was dragged down the aisle toward the back entrance. I was stepped on and kicked in the process. The policeman ripped the front of my shirtwaist, almost exposing my undergarments.

As I was being dragged down the aisle, I saw a policeman beating one suffragette on the breasts. I kicked out toward him and had the satisfaction of contacting an extremely vulnerable spot. I couldn't see Helena anywhere, leaving me with the hope she had made an escape. Our *Votes For Women* sashes had served as a target for the police who were obviously lying in wait, for only members of our group were being attacked.

The thought crossed my mind that the militants had wanted this result, and I felt certain it was Maggie and her group who had tipped off the police to our presence. Just how Maggie had finagled one of her captains into the delegation was a matter of later conjecture.

They dragged me out to an alley and tossed into a waiting Black Maria. My head hit the side of the van and I saw stars for a few minutes. Shaking my head to clear them, I could feel someone's leg underneath me. I tried to rise and was knocked down as another woman was flung into the van.

The ride to the police station was unthinkably miserable. Not only were we all nursing injuries, I had lost Helena and had no way of knowing what happened to her. Worse, I was sure the militants had sealed our fates—we would be arrested and charged according to their plan. Griffin would have a hard time obtaining a release for Helena and me once the police had convicted us of assault for a second time.

In a repeat of the earlier scene in the police station, we were herded into a small, bare room, then interviewed briefly. When asked whom I would like to notify, I declined to offer any name. I would not have Mabel and Joshua involved, or even my aunt and uncle, because I knew Griffin would find me somehow.

We spent the night in cells alone, a torment made worse because I had no knowledge of Helena's fate. I had inquired of the police, but they either didn't know or refused to tell me. I asked the two other Union members, but no one had remembered seeing Helena after the police had swarmed.

I spent the night alternately weeping and pacing the cell in desperation. By morning, I was near frantic with worry.

"Come along, it's time for you to go before the magistrate," the wardress told me.

"How many members of the Union were arrested, can you tell me?" I asked her on the way there.

"Couldn't say, but there were several people arrested last night because of the riot."

That gave me a minuscule ray of hope that public opinion was turning in our favor, but it didn't answer my question of what had happened to Helena.

I made a pitiful picture for the magistrate with my skirt and shirtwaist torn and dirty. I had lost my hat, had a bruise on my jaw besides the ones Lord Sherringham had left on my neck. My hand was swollen and stiff, and I walked with a pronounced limp. I was, however, defiant and refused to admit my guilt. This time I wasn't given the option of paying a fine. Instead, I was charged with assault upon a policeman and several other individuals and sentenced to nine months in prison.

"Nine... *months?*" I gasped, stunned at the sentence.

I had assumed I would be asked to pay a fine and released upon the payment. Instead, in a nightmarish scene that I will remember for many years, I was driven immediately to Strangways prison with Mrs. Knox and one other member.

My brain seemed to cease working. I couldn't think, couldn't process what happened. The nightmare scene just circled around and around in my head, in between fresh ones. Our clothes were taken from us, and they gave us horrible prison dresses made of coarse material, a flannel singlet and calico chemise, stockings but no garters or drawers, and shoes of different sizes. Both of mine were too small.

A wardress led me to a dark cell that contained only a chamber pot and a bed. The bed was merely a wooden plank with a raised object at the head, presumably a pillow. I was afraid to get near it, since it looked as if it crawled with vermin, and ended up kicking it into a corner of the cell. I was cold, my knee and hand hurt, and I was numb with shock and fear as I sat in the near dark on the hard wooden plank.

The prison doctor came later to my cell to evaluate my wounds. After a superficial exam, he dismissed them. "Nothing serious. The swelling will go down in time. I assume you are on a hunger strike?"

"I am," I answered with as much dignity as I could muster. I knew it was a badge of pride amongst imprisoned suffragettes not to take any food until they were released.

He made a notation on a chart. "You have three days to change your mind. After that, we'll be forced to give you hospital treatment."

I had no idea what he meant, but I was so depressed that I didn't give it much attention. I refused the evening meal and lay on my bed, cold, hungry, and sick with worry.

"You have only yourself to blame," I told myself. "Only this time you've involved Helena."

Guilt over her mingled with my misery, both weighing heavily on me as I sat on the hard wooden cot, heart-sore and sick of myself, until I fell into an uneasy sleep.

The next morning, the prison matron, a short, gray-haired woman with a long face, visited me. "Would you take some fruit?" she asked.

I stood awkwardly before her, my mind still numb, still caught up in the cycle of my own nightmares. It took a few seconds before I was able to answer. "Thank you, no. I will continue the hunger strike."

"Do you have any questions?" she asked, giving me a pitcher of water, which I gratefully accepted. Her kindness lit one corner of my mental hell.

I blinked at her, almost so overcome that I broke down in tears. I had expected the prison matron to be a cold and harsh woman and was surprised by her warmth. "I have two, if you would be so kind as to answer them. Can you tell me if a friend of mine who is also a suffragette? Her name is St. John. Lady Helena St. John."

She thought for a moment and said, "Yes, she is three doors down. She was injured in the arrest, but is doing better."

My heart fell into my stomach. I had promised Griffin I wouldn't allow harm to come to Helena, and I had failed him. I struggled to speak, the lump in my throat aching. "How many women were arrested, do you know?"

"I know that seven were charged, including you. Was that your second question, my dear?"

"No, my second question was about something the doctor said. He called it *hospital treatment* and said I would undergo it in three days. What is this treatment?"

The look she gave me was one my father's housekeeper used to give me when he went into one of his rages. "I hate to tell you, but you should know. If you will not eat in three days, the doctor will subject you to forcible feedings."

"Forcible feedings?" Fear had me swallowing back bile. I had heard whispers of force feedings, but had always assumed the horror of them was greatly exaggerated. "How can he make me eat if I don't wish to?"

She told me in detail how the feedings were done. The description made me heave into the pot. "Think hard about this," she said before leaving. "If you consent to eating, your time here will not be pleasant, but it will at least be bearable."

I sat hunched on my bed, my feet tucked under me to warm them outside of the painful shoes, and considered my new life. It was as if the nightmare of my past had come back to haunt me, this time with the torment of knowing I'd pulled Helena into it. The thought of her lying injured just a few doors down was maddening, and added to the guilt that wound around me like Jacob Marley's chains.

The day passed slowly, with no interruptions except the wardresses coming at each meal to ask me if I would eat. I refused all food.

I thought I had reached the depths of my depression, but I was wrong.

"You have a visitor," a wardress announced the following morning.

I scrambled to my cold, numb feet, my heart singing Griffin's name, but it was Mrs. Prince, one of the Union's head officers, who stood outside my door and talked to me through the grill. "Is there anything I can do for you? Anyone you would like contacted?"

"Yes, I would like to see Lady Helena St. John, who has also been imprisoned. She is in the cell a few doors down and is injured. She is very delicate and should be released for medical reasons. Can you arrange that I might see her? Or can you contact her brother, Griffin St. John, and alert him to her condition?"

Mrs. Prince consulted a small notebook. "I have spoken with Lady Helena's sister-in-law, Lady Sherringham. Regrettably, she has washed her hands of the affair and will do nothing to assist her."

I clutched at the grill in the door, my heart heavy. "But her brother—Mr. St. John—will he not help?"

"I am not aware of a brother."

The room swam. I sat down on the bed abruptly and putting my head between my knees until I could think straight. Why was Helena's sister-in-law contacted instead of Griffin?

Of course she wouldn't lift a finger to help Helena. No doubt her sense of revenge was strong. But where was Griffin? Why was he not moving heaven and earth to get Helena and me out? The despair must have shown on my face as I turned back to the door.

Mrs. Price said as she left, "I will try to have your status raised to that of a political prisoner, rather than a criminal one. I don't hold out much hope for that either, but I will try."

I looked up and croaked out a thank you before giving in to my self-pity.

My father's ghost taunted me.

You have failed everyone you care about. Griffin. Helena. Robert. Mabel.

It is entirely because of your obstinacy and heedless ways that innocent Helena is to suffer.

You could have removed her from the meeting, but your insufferable pride in yourself kept you mute.

I put my hands over my ears to block out the taunting voice, knowing that it spoke lies, but too depressed to ignore it as I should.

An hour later, voices could be heard outside my cell. I went to the door in time to see the prison doctor and four wardresses march down the hall. They stopped at the door opposite mine where a suffragette had been transferred from another cell. I was shaking with fear, although I didn't know why the sight of them should fill me with such loathing.

I soon understood the matron's plea with me to eat some fruit. The hospital treatment was being inflicted upon the poor woman across from me. No matter how long I live, I will never forget the sounds of that horrible torture. When they left the cell, a voice from another cell banged on the door and yelled, "No surrender!"

A weak but defiant, "No surrender!" answered from the victim's cell. The governors had ordered this inhumane treatment so the prisoners would not die martyrs. I sank to the floor, faint with terror, and wondered how I was to survive it. I had lived through all the torments my father hurled at me, and yet this abuse stripped from me every ounce of confidence I had struggled so hard to find.

The following day was the third and final day of my hunger strike. I had not heard from Mrs. Prince, but the prison matron had stopped by briefly. "Lady Helena is recovering, although I am very sorry indeed to tell you she is also on a hunger strike," the matron told me.

I wanted to weep, but there were no tears left to be shed. "Could she not share my cell?" I begged.

"We do not allow that. Not with the suffragettes," she said, giving me another pitying look. "I will keep you informed as best I can about Lady Helena's state. That is all I can do."

I thanked her, too caught in the hellish imagining of what was to come to converse longer.

The days had settled into a routine: I awoke from a nightmare into a waking hell. I wasn't allowed to leave the cell, nor had I any visitors other than the officials and Mrs. Prince. What my family must have thought I could only imagine. Griffin had warned me he could not secure our release again, and despite my conviction that he would do everything humanly possible to free us, I feared we were beyond his help.

"No surrender!" rang out down the hallway in tormented voices as the doctor made his rounds. The screams of anguish, sounds of retching, and other torturous noises brought me nightmares of my past, but slowly, hour by hour, it also served to stiffen my resolve.

"I wanted to be part of this," I told myself the morning of the fourth day. "I have survived worse. I can survive this, too. I am tempered. I am strong. Father tried to break me, and could not. Freddie tried to scare me, and could not. They will try to force me to leave the cause, but I will not."

I was weak with lack of food and sleep when they came for me. The old familiar dread and terror knotted up my stomach until I thought I would fall into an oblivion of darkness, but I dug deep into my psyche, and found an ounce of strength.

I would not break.

The doctor and four wardresses entered the room. "Will you take food?" the doctor asked, sounding almost bored.

Unable to speak or even swallow, I shook my head.

Two wardresses moved into position by taking hold of my arms. I shrank back into the pallet as one held my head, the other my feet. "No!" I tried to scream, despite knowing it would do no good.

It never did.

"You brought this upon yourself," one wardress told me, her voice as rough as her hands as she held me painfully down onto the plank of the bed.

The doctor sat on my knees and leaned across my chest to get at my mouth. I gritted my teeth together to keep my mouth closed, but he had some sort of a steel tool that he used to pry into my mouth.

I held my mouth closed as long as I could, but at last I could no longer bear the pain. As soon as my mouth opened, he stuffed a gap in it, turning the screw and widening it until the gap held my jaws wide open. I thought they would break, but the worst was yet to come.

With a brutal move, he shoved a thick tube down my throat. It was too wide and very long, and I gagged the second it hit my throat. He poured the food into the tube quickly and yanked the tube out. As soon as it was out, I retched the food up all over him.

"Bitch!" He slapped me and shoved the tube down again, pouring more food in it. This time I held it down until he had the gag out.

"Think about that for tomorrow," the doctor said as he and the wardresses left.

I rolled onto my side, tears burning my eyes and cheeks even as I retched all over the floor.

Exhausted and stunned with pain, I sobbed wordlessly with the knowledge that I would not survive nine months of such treatment.

"No surrender!" The cell door across mine clanged.

I looked up, wiping the mingled tears and bile from my

mouth. My throat burned, my jaws ached, and my mouth felt as if I'd been kicked in it. But I survived.

I was tempered.

As loudly and defiantly as I could, I croaked, "No surrender!"

What came next made me crazed almost to the point of insanity. I heard the doctor working his way down the cells and knew Helena must face him soon. I wept for her then, great racking sobs of impotence and fury. Desperately, I tried to find a way to save her from my fate.

I found no answers.

The matron came to see me that evening. I was lying on my bed, shaking with cold and shock, my mouth still bleeding from the metal implement the doctor had used to pry open my jaws, my throat shredded by the large tube. She handed me a jug of water and I sat down.

"I won't ask you how you are, because I can see that for myself," she said. "I promised to tell you about Miss St. John, as I knew you must be worried about her. She is as well as can be expected, but I am worried that she has a fever. I have asked the doctor to see her. He said he will do so in the morning."

I stared at her dully, not comprehending what she said. It was hard for me to concentrate, but I made an effort and focused on each word she spoke.

"Please, please have him release her." My voice came out cracked and hoarse. "She is too fragile to withstand this treatment."

"I will do what I can. Try to get some sleep now."

Not even Inner Alex could think about Griffin. I knew he wouldn't abandon Helena and me, but obviously, he could not gain our release. Thinking of him hurt too much. I pushed away thoughts of him, and of our once-glowing future, feeling I was paying enough penance without destroying what remained of my heart.

Time ceased to exist for me. I know it must have been the following day when I heard the doctor making his rounds again, but I had no feeling of time passing. There was no distinction between what was real and what I imagined. I could hear the screams, the sounds of the struggle, and the defiant, "No surrender!" follow the doctor as he came down the corridor. A rattle at my door indicated he had arrived. I gritted my teeth and looked up to see a wardress beckoning at me.

"Get up and come with me. The governor wants to see you."

She had to repeat the message before I could comprehend it. My legs were so weak, I stumbled into the door as I left my cell. Taking a deep breath, I fought to stand up straight, and walked slowly and deliberately after her. I had to concentrate on taking one step after another, but at last I made it to the governor's offices. The wardress left me sitting in an outer chamber, the door locked behind me. I sat with my head between my knees to keep from swooning, sure they had brought me in to tell me Helena had died. I wondered how long I could stand the treatment, certain now that I wouldn't be released, and equally certain I would not last the entire sentence.

I would never see Griffin again.

There were no tears left for me to shed as I waited endless, grievous hours, dreading every passing footstep in case it should bring me news of Helena's demise. Unused by the lights and relatively fresh air, I stood up and walked around the room to regain the use of my legs. The door opened behind me, but when I tried to turn quickly, I stumbled and would have fallen had powerful arms not caught me.

"Alex, my beautiful, brave Alex," a voice murmured in my ears, a familiar voice that accompanied kisses pressed to my forehead. "Tell me you're all right, sweetheart. Tell me you haven't been hurt."

I lifted my head and Griffin's beloved face swam before me. Reaching a hand up to touch it, I asked, "Where on Earth did you get a black eye?" just before I fainted.

SEVENTEEN

"Helena!"

I wept tears of sheer joy when, five minutes after Griffin and the wardress brought me around, Helena staggered into the room.

"Alex? Griffin?" She collapsed into Griffin's arms, weeping hoarsely. I made my way over to them, hugging them both, feeling my own happy tears mingle with hers.

"You look much better than I imagined," I told her, although I noted her eyes had a feverish brightness to them.

"I am just so happy to see you both," she said, letting Griffin ease her into a chair.

"I have brought you some tea," the wardress said as I took the seat next to Helena.

We looked at each other, then at the wardress. She made an annoyed sound and added, "You can drink it. You've been officially released. They dropped the charges against you."

I have had many beverages in my life, but none that tasted of such ambrosia as did that hot, sweet tea.

As we were sipping it gratefully, Robert raced into the room and flung himself at Helena's feet. Griffin had been hovering between Helena and me, but with the arrival of Robert, he sat next to me, pulling me to his side with a protective arm.

"Robert? Oh, my dear, darling Robert!" Helena murmured, stroking his head. When he looked up, his face shocked me. He had a torn lip, an oddly shaped nose, and two discolored eyes.

I turned to Griffin, who was scowling at the wardress as she fussed with the tea things. "What happened to Robert? Did he break his nose? And why do you both have black eyes?"

He pulled me closer. "I'll tell you once we're out of this damned place."

Much to my relief, we were allowed the opportunity to have a quick wash, and given our clothing to wear, although Helena had to be carried out of the prison. I made it on my own feet to a waiting carriage, and collapsed into his embrace on the way home. I was a little puzzled why we were taking Joshua's carriage home, but leaning against Griffin with his arm around me, I didn't feel like inquiring. I did ask how he had secured our release.

"I saw some people," he said grimly. "Letitia helped."

"Letitia?" Tucked as I was against him, I couldn't see his face, but watched his Adam's apple as he spoke. "I thought she refused to help Helena?"

"She did until it became worth her while to change her mind."

I wanted to ask him how he did that, but a suspicion took hold and was confirmed when we stopped in front of my sister's house.

Mabel and Joshua were on the doorstep to greet us, as was Doctor Melrose. Robert carried Helena up the stairs to the guest room, the doctor following closely behind.

"Shall I take you to bed as well?" Griffin asked.

I tried to summon up a smile. "Is that an improper suggestion, Mr. St. John, or do you just wish to be rid of me?"

Griffin kissed me gently in response and after I had a more extended washing session, and donned cleaned clothes, helped me into the library. I sat on the leather couch with my feet up, wrapped in a rug, and sipped the brandy Griffin ordered me to drink. He sat on the floor next to me, close enough so I could twine my fingers through his hair in between sips.

"All right," I said, putting the brandy snifter down, pulling free the hand he kissed. "Enough, my head is swimming. Please tell me what has been happening? How did you get us out?"

"Letitia put me in touch with some of Sherry's friends. I showed them a few letters she gave me, which detailed his plan to destroy the suffrage movement, you, Helena, me… and incidentally, several members of the House of Lords who did not see eye-to-eye with Sherry. They agreed to help me in order to cover up what would be an otherwise ugly scandal involving a peer and the House. When the police were presented with the testimony of two impeccable witnesses who stated that you and Helena were unjustly arrested, the charges were dropped and they freed you."

I ran my finger lightly along his jaw. He took my hand again and kissed my fingers. Little sparks of fire ran down my arms to start a thrumming deep inside me I thought I'd never feel again. "What did you have to do to make Lady Sherringham help you?"

"I gave her something she had wanted for a long time." He glanced away, his jaw tight.

"Your house?"

He didn't answer until I put a hand on his cheek and turned his face toward mine. "Yes. How did you know?"

I traced my finger down his nose, so overwhelmed with love for him I had to swallow twice before I could speak. "A guess. They always seemed to be lord and lady of the manor there. I assumed they felt the house was rightfully theirs even though your brother lost it. With her husband locked away, what else does she have?"

Mabel accompanied a maid laden with a tea tray. "You will be happy to know that Doctor Melrose says Helena isn't suffering from any illness, just exhaustion and malnutrition."

"Thank God," I murmured gratefully.

She poured me a large cup of tea and loaded a plate with food. "You drink that tea first, then eat."

I looked askance at the food. "Mabel, there is no way I could eat half of that."

Griffin took the plate and said quietly to my sister, "I'll see that she eats."

Mabel beamed at him, looked at me fondly, and bustled out. I took a few sips of the tea and sighed as it slid down my sore throat. "Oh, that is heaven."

Griffin sat next to me on the couch, kissing my throat in a most distracting way.

"What have you done with Mabel?" I asked, having gathered enough wits together to remember how to speak. "I expected to receive a tongue-lashing like none I have received before."

"And I'm sure you will receive one," he said with amusement, transferring his kisses to my jaw. "I think she's simply grateful you are back."

I turned my head until he gave me what I wanted. His mouth was warm and caressing, not demanding and aggressive as it usually was, but soft and teasing, gently stroking away the horror of the last few days and replacing the pain with pleasure.

I pulled away from the hot lure of his mouth and touched his bruised eye. "Now, tell me about that."

He sighed and made himself comfortable, which meant I was made extremely comfortable half-draped across his chest. "Hunter and I were on the balcony of that blasted hall, watching over you."

I made a sound of protest, but he stopped it with his mouth.

"I won't tell you unless you drink that tea," he said, pulling away and nodding toward the cup. "And no interruptions."

I hurriedly picked up the tea. "Continue."

"We had a feeling there was going to be trouble, so we watched over you two from the balcony. When the police sprang out from their hiding places, we knew you were in a dangerous situation. We tried to get down to you, but the entire crowd panicked, and we were caught on the stairs, pinned and unable to go anywhere. By the time we made it downstairs and onto the main floor, the police had most of the women rounded up. We went to free you and ended up fighting the police." He touched his eye gingerly. "I got this as a souvenir. We were charged with assaulting a policeman and thrown into jail for three days. I tried to reach everyone I knew who had some pull, but had no luck."

I put down my tea, touched that he had risked his own life for ours.

"When we were released, I went home and found that Letitia had refused to help Helena. I knew your family didn't have the contacts to help you, so I persuaded Letitia to give me Sherry's journal and the letters that detailed his plans."

I thought for a few moments. "And now you are homeless?"

"Yes," he grimaced. "Your brother-in-law has kindly offered to shelter Helena until I can set up a new house."

"And Robert? Have you promised to help Robert so he can marry Helena?"

"Ah, Robert. Oddly enough, I have an acquaintance in East Africa who is looking for someone to manage his sizable coffee farm while he is away."

"Really?" I asked, unsure if he really had such a friend or if he was simply taking the best means to the end.

He gave me an enigmatic smile. "Hunter thinks it will be ideal for him. I have a feeling that in time, my friend will sell him the farm. I think Helena will like Africa."

"There's Freddie to be taken care of yet," I said slowly, relaxing into the pull of his warmth. "I dislike the thought of him being allowed to escape without repercussion for his part in everything."

"Your cousin will be taken care of," Griffin said with a grim note of promise in his voice that I decided I would not chastise. Freddie had made his bed; I wished him joy lying in it.

"And what about us?" I asked, trying for a light tone, but my throat was still too sore to be successful. "Do you think I would marry a man who doesn't even have a home?"

His amber eyes glowed with an incandescent light that lit up all the darkness within me, filling me with warmth, and love, and hope.

The corners of his mouth lifted. "Won't you?" he asked, pulling me onto his lap, his hand sliding under my skirt and up the length of my bare leg.

"Well," I said softly as I nibbled his ear, "as you are asking properly this time, I suppose I will."

EPILOGUE

11 July 1900

My dear Emma,

I pen this letter in haste and regret—haste because we (Griffin and I)—leave in the hour for a trip to East Africa. The regret comes in the form of not waiting for you to return from Paris before we were married, but I'm sure you will understand when I tell you we were married in haste not because of any impending natal event, but because I simply could not stand Mabel's outdated ideas of proper behavior toward a man about whom one has a biblical level of knowledge.

Griffin thought it would be best for us to be married quickly, lest I do bodily harm to my sister in my attempt to seduce him. Those are, as I'm sure you know, his words, not mine.

Helena and Robert married at the same time, although not for the same reasons. Helena feared that somehow Lord Sherringham might be released from the asylum, and she felt it was better to be safely married should that unlikely event occur.

Presently, we are taking Helena and Robert to a coffee plantation in East Africa before we continue south, to the Transvaal, where Griffin has friends he promised to visit.

We plan to return within the next six or seven months, so I hope to see you then.

Oh, if you see my cousin Freddie when you return home, feel free to pretend you do not know him. His credit with society is about to take a substantial dive. I had a long talk with my aunt yesterday at our wedding, and she assured me that now I was safely married (her words), they would remove Freddie from their home. She said Freddie had told them his fears I might not be entirely sane, which is why they kept him under their roof, where they could make sure he did nothing to harm me.

I wish they had told me this, but Aunt Caroline says she did not want to distress me when I was so newly freed from my father's control. Uncle Henry is going do what he can to spread news of Freddie's insolvency, and desperate attempts to illegally gain himself a rich bride. There's nothing society loves less than a fortune hunter, so I imagine he will find himself without many friends.

With haste and much love,

Alex

NOTE TO READERS

My lovely one! I hope you enjoyed reading this book, which I handcrafted from the finest artisanal words just for you. If you are one of the folks who likes to review books, I'd love it if you posted a review for it on your favorite book spot (be sure to tell me if you do, so that I can lavish praise all over you).

If you're looking for some fun behind-the-scenes tidbits, exclusive shorts, etc. feel free to join my newsletter. Signup is at my website at www.katiemacalister.com

Speaking of the website, first chapters of all of my books are available there for your perusal, as well as updates, a printable book list, and more.

www.ingramcontent.com/pod-product-compliance
Lightning Source LLC
Chambersburg PA
CBHW050824190726
48286CB00007B/1980